The end . . .

Parents were trying to get their children back to sleep, the baby was crying as its mother fumbled about in a bag looking for a bottle. Some people were holding on to each other, their eyes wide with fear. Though the aircraft was stable everyone was feeling that sickening pull at the pit of their stomach as their body sought equilibrium against the forces of gravity and inertia.

For some reason, some unknown force, Roger Tores glanced out of the window. The cloud had lifted and was now floating above them. His face tightened in terror as he realised blackness he saw was not the empty night sky but the deeper darkness of a mountain . . .

D0974359

About the author

Bill Murphy started off as a screenwriter by trade – winning an award at the prestigious Houston Worldfest for one of his early works. He lives and works in County Cork, Ireland. This is his first novel.

Tin Kickers

Bill Murphy

CORONET BOOKS

Hodder & Stoughton

Typeset by Palimpsest Book Production Limited,
Polmont, Stirlingshire
Printed and bound in Great Britain by
Clays Ltd, St Ives plc

Hodder and Stoughton
A division of Hodder Headline
338 Euston Road
London NW1 3BH

FLIGHT ACL248, 35,000 FEET, ON THE 112 RADIAL, HERMOSILLO VOR-DME, 717 NM FROM MEXICO CITY

The peaks of the Sierra Madre rose above the thick carpet of cloud like black islands on a white sea. The moon shone like an arc light across the cold sky lighting the way south. Thousands of feet below in the rocky canyons of the Tarahumara a carved headstone, its eyes hooded in supplication beneath the dark heavens, implored God's wife, the veiled moon, for the fortune of good winds.

The cockpit was quiet, its myriad of instruments silently maintaining vigil over the plane's vital systems. The two engines whined low and constant, thrusting the plane across the sky, the ATIS weather bulletins warbling like bird chatter in the background.

'It was only three days back from the garage . . . three days,' Hunter protested as he noted the fuel readings on the routine cruise-checklist.

He was a young pilot, very able, very sure of himself, very likeable . . . except when he went on about his '68 Mustang.

'Only three days and it crapped out, right there in the middle of the friggin' freeway,' he continued. 'I bought it from a buddy a mine for fifteen grand – a genuine piece of American automotive history he told me.' He looked up for a moment as if suddenly having to remind himself of something. 'I think he's flying seven-forty-sevens with Northwest now . . . You used to fly the big boys, didn't you, Skipper?'

Captain Luis Juarez stared out through the inch of laminated glass and plastic that separated them from the freezing air outside. He closed his eyes for a moment, feeling the aircraft quietly trembling under him.

'. . . Skipper?'

'Yeah!' Juarez grunted, annoyed with his young co-pilot's incessant talk. But he softened his tone. He was letting things get to him too easily these days.

'Yeah . . . yeah, I did. Great aircraft, light as a feather to fly. Light as a feather.'

'What made you sign on for these old crates?'

'Supposedly to spend more time at home – no more long hauls, no more over-nights,' said Juarez.

'How long were you . . . together?' Hunter asked.

'Twenty-five years,' Juarez sighed. 'Now we're fighting over who gets the dog.'

A monotonous little voice in their ears rattled out the weather update for the area. Light variable winds from the east and heavy cloud at 10,000 feet.

In the forward galley chief flight attendant Rosa Valasquez prodded the water heater into action. After twenty years in the air she was well used to these slight malfunctions and privately considered herself more technically able than some of the pilots she flew with. The three other flight attendants were scattered throughout the plane taking care of the passengers. Rosa paused for a moment, staring into the shiny chrome plating of the ovens, and ran her finger over a soft pocket of skin under her eye. She smiled to herself. All old birds of the air must suffer fatigue eventually.

'I'm glad that's done,' Gina sighed as she entered the galley, plonking a tray of plastic glasses on the worktop.

'Don't worry, you'll get used to it,' Rosa reassured her latest recruit.

Gina took off one of her shoes and began massaging her aching foot.

'How do they expect us to work in these heels?'

'They expect us to look our best at all times.' Rosa smiled. 'But with legs like yours, honey, I guess you'd look good in clogs.'

Gina had been with the airline four weeks and had quickly become the target of every male in the company who fancied his chances. But they were all too late.

'At least the delay at LAX has tired them out.' She meant the one hundred and forty-two passengers behind them who had endured a four-hour delay due to mechanical problems at Los Angeles International Airport. 'How much time have we?' she asked.

Rosa looked at her watch.

'Just gone 11.45. We've another hour or so before we wake 'em up. Time for a quick coffee, I'd say.'

'Are the delays usually this bad?' asked Gina, now massaging the other foot.

'They can get a lot worse in the summer.'

'Do you think we'll have to over-night?'

''Fraid so.' Rosa punched the water heater. 'The hotel isn't bad, though, a lot of the charter crews use it.'

'I was supposed to meet Tony in the morning. We were going to pick out the flowers for the church.' Gina smiled, excited by the thought of her wedding preparations.

A light blinked on a panel above the ovens.

'It's 7D again,' Rosa observed wearily.

Every flight has one. A businessman returning home from a long and tedious convention, a marine on leave, a minor actor playing out the cliched role of the drunk or just your ordinary run-of-the-mill pain in the ass.

Gina battened the last trolley into its compartment. 'I'll go.'

'You sure?' Rosa smiled, proud that her latest recruit was willing to brave the beast that is the drunken passenger.

'How many has he had?' Gina asked, wondering what she was letting herself in for.

'Too many.'

Roger Tores could hang on no longer. He nudged his

sleeping girlfriend, who awoke in a groggy expectation of arrival.

'Are we landing?' she asked, squinting out of the dark oval of the window.

'Not yet, honey,' said Roger. 'I just need to go to the little boys' room.'

'Jesus, when are we going to get there?' she wondered, pulling a blanket around her shoulders and closing her eyes again.

Roger looked at his watch. It was coming up to midnight, almost a full eighteen hours since they'd left their little apartment in New York's lower east side. He squeezed himself out of the seats and headed aft to the lavatory.

The cabin lights of the aircraft were dimmed and most of the passengers were asleep, or trying to sleep, or somewhere in between. Like zombies they slouched in their seats. Somewhere a baby was whining, its mother wearily rocking back and forth, humming a comforting tune. Older children slumped in their seats, passed out from excitement or exhaustion. Some still wore Hallowe'en masks about their necks, their parents too tired to remove them. A devil's bright red face leered from the body of a little girl, her brother a bony-white ghoul next to her.

Captain Juarez leant both hands on top of his instrument panel and gazed at the thick banks of cloud below.

'Pretty dense. Hope it clears before we make descent.'

Hunter continued the routine instrument inspection and didn't even glance outside the windshield.

'Have you moved out?' he asked.

'Yeah, my brother's got a place in Marina del Rey. It's small but the view's nice.'

Juarez was about to get up to stretch his legs when a red light flashed on the light shield.

The two men immediately tensed in readiness; any light that is red and flashing is always cause for immediate concern.

'What is it?' Juarez asked.

'We've got a "Fire-Warn",' Hunter announced.

'What system?' Juarez scanned the instruments for any other signs of malfunction.

Hunter looked up at the overhead panel to find out which area of the plane wanted attention. Three fat little squares of light were flashing brightly.

He smiled and shook his head.

'Auxiliary Power Unit.'

'Jesus!' Juarez breathed angrily. 'That's the fourth time this month. I'm gonna kill those guys in maintenance.'

Hunter reached up and was about to extinguish the lights.

'Should we ignore it?' He hesitated before punching out the switches.

Juarez again stared out at the night and the dots of starlight winking far in the blackness of the sky.

'No . . . let's go by the book. Shut it down,' he groaned. This had indeed been the fourth flight in as many weeks on which the Auxiliary Power Unit, the back-up power generator at the rear of the plane, had proclaimed itself faulty. The three previous times had proved to be false alarms. However Juarez had been trained to trust his instruments and if they said something was wrong, it was not his place to question but instead to take immediate corrective action. There would be time later when they were safely on the ground to challenge the integrity of the warning systems.

'Okay, fuel valve shut-off.' Hunter moved his finger to the APU valve switch, a thin, silver button, like a light switch, and flicked it back. This opened the circuit breakers on the APU and effectively cut off the fuel line to prevent possible spread of fire.

'Check!' he announced triumphantly, the simple operation complete.

Juarez turned his eyes to the light shield again.

'Roger. Re-set the "Fire-Warn".'

'Re-set the "Fire-Warn",' Hunter sang, and moved his finger over the button that was still blinking. He pressed it in, then pressed again so that it popped out into its normal position. If there was a fire, it would flash.

Juarez nodded his head. No fire. Nothing wrong except perhaps a faulty wire, somewhere among the miles of cabling which ran like arteries and veins throughout the body of the airplane, feeding power to over 15,000 electronic devices, everything from a passenger reading lamp to the computer navigation system.

'I'm gonna roast those guys at GenAir,' he promised himself, 'I mean . . . Jesus!'

'Red's out, no fire. The APU's cryin' wolf again!' Hunter chorused as if he'd known it all along.

Juarez felt like slapping him.

Gina stood patiently waiting for the man in 7D to drain the last drops of vodka from his plastic glass.

'Another one where that came from, *por favor*,' he said, relishing the prospect of more drink.

Gina held out the tray with another glass, a half-moon of lemon perched on the rim. She smiled dutifully. 'Here you are, sir.' There was a faint tinge of contempt in her voice.

But all he noticed was her white teeth, her tumble of raven black hair.

'You sure are pretty.' He gave a leering smile, as cheap as his crumpled cream suit.

'Er . . . yes, sir.' Gina smiled again, trying desperately not to squirm.

'What's your name?' he asked just as she was about to turn away. 'I bet you have a real pretty name . . .'

In the cramped plastic confines of the washroom Roger Tores splashed some water against his face and imagined for a moment it was the white surf crashing on the sands of Puerto Escondido, a golden splinter of land which jutted into the azure blue waters of the Pacific. When he opened his eyes he found himself momentarily in darkness. Then the lights flickered back on and he could see his own tired face looking back at him from the little vanity mirror over the sink.

He wiped his eyes and flushed the toilet.

In the cockpit Hunter was telling his inattentive captain a joke about a pilot flying a Fokker when suddenly he went quiet.

'Hey! What the—'

'What?' Juarez asked vacantly, half thinking this might be part of the joke.

'Some of the instruments . . . I don't know.'

'Mine are okay,' Juarez observed.

Hunter strained his eyes, running a check-read over the instrument panels.

'No, flight instruments are fine . . . it's the engine monitors.' Another light was flashing.

'AC electric system has tripped,' he said calmly.

As Roger Tores made his way back from the rear of the plane he pondered for a moment the miracle of flight: one hundred and forty people sitting in a silver tube, asleep, shooting through the freezing black sky, miles above the earth. He stopped for a moment and looked out at the glinting edge of the left wing that held them aloft. He wondered what it would be like to be out on that wing, to stand against that wall of rushing wind, so powerful it could punch the lungs out of your chest.

Reminded of an old episode of *The Twilight Zone* where a passenger kept seeing a monster creeping across the wing, tearing at the metal, he smiled to himself and decided he'd better move on before he began seeing things and was carted off the plane in a strait-jacket.

As he turned his eye caught a brief flash of light reflected from the wing. He paused to look again, wondering if it was the navigation lights he had seen. He was curious as the light did not appear to be red. He didn't know much about aviation but he knew aircraft shared the same indicators of left and right as ships at sea. He was about to turn away again when his eye caught a blue flash as a shower of sparks rocketed out from beneath the wing from the metallic cone of the engine. Roger jerked back his head in surprise.

Instinctively he looked around the cabin to see if anyone else had witnessed the fireworks. But the interior of the plane remained still and calm, the rows of passengers slumped beneath the dim lights. Further down he could see a flight attendant, standing with a tray, talking to a passenger. He looked at the engine again but everything appeared normal. No more flashes, no change in the steady purring vibration under his feet. Probably nothing to be worried about, he convinced himself, and moved forward once again towards his seat. But he couldn't quite shake the feeling of unease from his mind.

'You know, you look a lot like my wife.' The drunk reached out to grab Gina by the arm. 'When she was younger and thinner, of course.' He winked.

Gina instinctively moved back from him. Their instructors had taught them to remain polite at all times but not to let a passenger touch them.

She managed one last smile and had turned to leave when she heard another man call to her.

'Excuse me, miss!'

Oh, God, what now? she thought to herself.

She put on her best smile again and walked some rows down from the drunk, ignoring his entreaties for her to talk to him. She found Roger Tores sitting in his middle seat on the port side of the plane.

He whispered so as not to wake his girlfriend whose head rested against the window, shaking slightly with the vibration of the plane.

'Excuse me, miss, I'm sorry to disturb you . . .'

Thank God, a polite one.

'Yes, sir. Can I help you?'

Roger looked at his girlfriend for a moment and lowered his voice even further.

'I'm sure it's nothing,' he said, hesitating, 'but I saw some sparks.'

The drunk piped up again. 'Come here, darlin'!' he shouted hoarsely back at Gina.

'I'm sorry, sir?' She looked at Roger blankly.

'Sparks – I think I saw some sparks coming from the engine.'

Roger's girlfriend stirred, woken by the drunk's noise. 'Are we nearly there yet, Roger?' she asked, trying to focus with bleary eyes. 'It's getting cold.' She shivered.

'Not too long now,' he assured her as he put his arm around her and she nestled against his chest like a child. 'Go back to sleep.'

Gina looked out at the wing, its sharp outline cutting through the night sky. Everything seemed fine.

'I'm sure there's no problem, sir. But I'll tell the captain,' she whispered.

The drunk was now hollering loudly for another drink. She turned swiftly around to him, barely able to contain her anger. 'Please, sir! There are people trying to sleep!' she rasped.

He just smiled back at her, the class clown trying to push a new teacher to the brink.

'Just another little drinkie, eh? How about it?' He waggled his empty glass.

Gina rolled her eyes. Anything for a bit of peace and quiet. As she took the glass from him the plane lurched forward and down, slamming her sideways against a seat. Some of the passengers awoke with the sudden movement and seemed to gasp collectively with surprise.

Picking herself up, Gina rushed to the forward galley where Rosa was picking up some bottles which had rolled out onto the floor.

'Are we descending?' Gina asked.

'Feels like it,' Rosa said calmly.

The plane rocked again and sent some trays careening across the galley worktops and on to the floor.

'What is it?' Gina shouted.

'Just turbulence,' Rosa snapped back, her voice strained. She calmed herself. 'Just turbulence.'

The panel above the ovens lit up like a Christmas tree.

'That's woken 'em,' Rosa said with a marked lack of surprise.

Gina remembered the polite young man.

'Some guy said he saw some sparks coming from one of the engines.'

'Sparks?'

'Yeah. Should we tell the Captain?'

Rosa thought about it for a moment. She looked at the lights flashing; could sense the growing disquiet among the passengers in the cabin.

'You go and see to the passengers, I'll go and tell the Skipper.' Rosa caught Gina by the hand, sensing the young woman's unease. 'You'll be fine, you're a natural,' she reassured her.

Gina smiled and readied herself to face the passengers, whose reactions could range from annoyance to near panic. Before she went through the curtain Rosa stopped her.

'Which engine?' she asked. 'What side did he see the sparks on?' Gina could see Roger Tores, halfway from the cabin to her right. 'Oh . . . on the right,' she said and hurried to the passengers.

In the cockpit of flight ACL248 several little red lights were flashing on the instrument panels, like worried passengers each demanding attention. The autopilot was disengaged and Hunter held the control stick with both hands, his muscles tight with the effort of keeping the plane level. He watched the slowly turning needle of the altimeter and the numbers tumbling on the spindle like the drums of a one-arm bandit.

'Altitude three-one-five-0!' he announced and glanced at the airspeed indicator. 'And 350 knots.'

Juarez spoke calmly into his head-set radio while checking his map.

'Center, this is Aero Centrale 248. We have a single engine shutdown. Request descent to one-four-0 and divert to nearest suitable field.'

The communications radio hissed as a Mexican controller acknowledged his request.

'Roger Aero Centrale 248. Mazatlan closed for runway repair. Be advised Torreon International open approximately 300 nautical miles south-east of your position. Make left on to heading one-two-zero and descend and maintain minimum one-four-0. High terrain at 10,000 . . .'

'Roger, turning left on to heading one-two-zero, descend and maintain minimum flight level one-four-0 . . .'

Juarez paused for a moment, then nodded.

'Aware high terrain at 10,000 feet.'

Hunter continued to call out their altitude and rate of descent. 'Altitude passing through two-seven-five. Vertical speed – minus 2,900 feet per minute!'

Rosa tapped on the cockpit door and entered the flight deck. 'Excuse me, Captain.'

'What is it, Rosa?' Juarez asked without taking his eyes off the instruments.

'A passenger reported seeing sparks coming from one of the engines . . . I don't know if it's important but I thought it best to tell you.'

He turned around. 'Which side?'

'Er . . . the right.'

Juarez nodded, relieved. 'Yeah, we've just shut it down. We're changing course and diverting to Torreon.'

As the plane descended into the cloud bank fleecy, cotton-like wisps floated over the windshield.

'We're getting into cloud,' Hunter rattled like a warning bell.

Juarez noticed the concerned look on his senior stew's face. 'Don't worry, the other engine will get us there just fine,' he assured her.

'What should I tell the passengers?' she asked.

Juarez thought about it for a moment, his attention distracted as Hunter called out their altitude. 'Passing 23,000 feet.'

He turned back to Rosa. 'For now just tell them we have to divert for purely precautionary reasons.'

'They're not going to like it.' She shook her head, remembering the delay at LAX.

'None of us likes it,' Juarez muttered as he grabbed hold of the control stick.

Rosa closed the door of the cockpit behind her and left the pilots to their business. She had one hundred and forty-two very tired and anxious passengers to face.

Juarez flexed his fingers.

'All right, Phil, I have control.' He firmly gripped the control stick and took over command of the plane.

Hunter released his hands from the stick and relaxed his arm. 'You have control, Skipper.'

'We gotta level off and maintain height.' Juarez' voice was strained from the sudden effort of controlling nearly 60 tonnes of aircraft.

'Can't see a damn' thing in this shit,' Hunter cursed as the windshield was now covered in thick sheets of cloud.

Rosa entered the galley to find Gina barely coping with a tray crammed with drinks, pills and sick bags.

'They're getting a bit restless out there. Are we landing soon?' Gina struggled to keep the tray level.

'We're diverting,' Rosa confided quietly, wondering how she was going to tell the passengers.

'Diverting!' Gina cried.

'Engine problem, routine procedure.' Rosa had gone through this sort of thing before and knew it was never worth getting into too much of a fuss over. Machines sometimes malfunction. The pilots had everything under control and were doing the right thing by diverting. But she wasn't sure her passengers would be so understanding.

'What are you going to tell them?' Gina asked, piling extra bags on the tray.

'We'll just have to cope as best we can,' Rosa said as she picked up the intercom mike.

'Good luck!' Gina managed a smile as she went through the curtains.

Roger held his girlfriend tight and looked about the cabin. Parents were trying to get their children back to sleep; the baby was wailing as its mother fumbled about in a bag looking for a bottle. Some passengers were holding on to each other, their eyes wide with fear. Though the aircraft was stable everyone was feeling that sickening lightness in the pit of the stomach as their body experienced the negative g-force of rapid descent. The intercom gave a polite bing and Rosa's calm voice became the focus of attention of everyone in the cabin.

'Ladies and gentlemen, may I have your attention please . . .'

For some reason, at some unknown prompting, Roger Tores glanced out of the window. The cloud had lifted and was now floating above them. His face tightened with terror as he realised the blackness he saw was not the empty night sky but the deeper darkness of a mountain looming above the airplane.

APARTMENT 304, 29th STREET, WASHINGTON DC

On a bedside table the luminous green digits of a clock shimmered 04.47. A shrill beep seared through the air, pulsing. A figure buried beneath the bed-clothes stirred and a hand reached out to stamp out the sound of the alarm. But still it persisted, beating away like a little bug. Ron Carter was just awake enough to realise what the noise was. He reached for the lamp and switched it on with such awkward force that he nearly knocked it to the ground. Blinking, he scrambled around the table and picked up his pager. He squinted at the message like a myopic jeweller, grabbed the phone and pressed a quickdial number. The line hummed for about five seconds before a voice answered. 'McKenzie,' was all it said.

'Hi, Bill, it's Carter. What's up?'

He was already out of bed and getting dressed as McKenzie gave him the briefing.

'Ron, we got a bird down. Passenger jet.'

'Where is she?' Ron asked, holding the phone between cheek and shoulder as he struggled into his jeans.

'Somewhere in the Sierra Madre.'

Ron stopped.

'Mexico?' he asked.

'Yes. We've got a long-range Lear rolling at National. Be there in thirty minutes.'

'I'll be there in twenty.' Ron slammed down the phone and opened the wardrobe. He pushed aside the stiff black jacket of a pilot's uniform and dug out a bag from behind. He opened the zip and checked its contents of measuring tapes, checklists, dictaphone and camera. All the tools of his trade. At thirty-six he was one of the younger aircrash investigators in the NTSB and it always amused him when people wore a slight look of surprise on first meeting him, expecting a much older man. It was due in part, he thought, to his name, Ron – an old man's name his sister always lamented. But it was the name he shared with his father from whom he also inherited his fine dark features and cyanic blue eyes. From his mother he took his tallish, lean physique and a broad smile that crinkled the skin on his temples. But there was no family precedent for his love of flying and after 10 years as a pilot with Delta he'd applied for a position at the Office of Aviation Safety when a close friend died in an air accident. No one was more surprised than Ron Carter when he received a call from Bill McKenzie telling him he'd got the job.

REAGAN NATIONAL AIRPORT, WASHINGTON DC

Ron pinned his car to a halt at the security check-point. In the distance he could see the white FAA LearJet waiting on the apron outside one of the hangars, its engines idling in a low whine.

'Morning, Mr Carter.' The security man touched his cap in salute. It was still dark, an hour to sunrise.

'Morning, John. They all here?' Ron nodded in the direction of the plane.

'All here,' said the man as he raised the barrier at the push of a button.

Al Martinez and Bob Tunamachier made their way across the apron to the plane, arms wrapped about themselves against the freezing wind.

'Blue Christ, it's cold!' said Al, rubbing his hands. A small and usually dishevelled imp of a man, he prefixed most of his sentences with a colourful profanity.

'Any idea where we're heading?' Bob wondered aloud. At six foot three, he towered above his friend.

Al shook his head. 'No idea. I just got word to get my butt here ASAP.'

Bill McKenzie stood at the top of the steps of the plane, waiting like a teacher for his pupils to board the bus. He was a Senior Air Crash Investigator at the Office of Aviation Safety and had worked with the National Transportation Safety Board for over twenty-five years. The NTSB was set up in 1967 as an independent safety agency to investigate major accidents in all modes of transport. McKenzie joined up at the time when Nixon had tried to bring it under direct government control. However the Board held on to its autonomy and was proud to be answerable only to the elected members of Congress. Though political appointees, the incumbent five members of the Board endeavoured to maintain that rare commodity in Washington: independence from the federal administration.

'Come on, you guys,' barked McKenzie, a cigar butt stuck to his lower lip.

'Any chance of letting us know where we're goin', Bill?' asked Al.

'Mexico, Al, sunny Mexico. Now get inside and I'll give you the low down once we're in the air. Where's Carter?'

McKenzie scanned the compound.

'Here he comes,' he breathed around his cigar as he saw a figure running for the plane.

'Come on, Ron, let's get movin'!' he shouted.

Ron clambered on board as the jet wound up its engines and started to roll.

Inside the plane the rest of the men were already settled and strapped into their seats. Pete Cooper, an ex-pilot from Kansas with an electrical engineering degree, was rhythmically running his hand up and down a day's growth of beard, barely able to keep his eyes open.

Beside him, the burly figure of Jerry Wojowski bent over an aircraft manual. Looking like a grizzled tight-end with a thick frizz of blond hair Jerry was the most studious of the men and always poring over a manual of some kind.

Harv Tiefson, ex-air traffic controller, took off his glasses, held them at arm's length and gave them a wipe with his sleeve before replacing them on his long sharp nose.

Next to him sat Greg Mates, one of the industry's most eminent metallurgists, a metal-fatigue special-ist. He was fast asleep, lightly snoring.

All these men were on call twenty-four hours a day, 365 days a year, to go anywhere in the world when a major air accident occurred involving an American plane.

This was the Go-Team.

Ron stumbled into his seat as the plane rolled down the runway for take-off.

He was surprised to see the man sitting next to him.

'Willard?'

Bob, who'd sat down opposite, was even more startled.

'What the hell are you doing here, Willard? I didn't know you were on the Go-Team.'

'Hi, guys, nice to see you too!' he said wearily, by

now accustomed to the suspicion, and sometimes downright hostility, with which the investigators regarded him.

Grant Willard was a Fed, a Public Affairs officer from the Department of Transportation and recently transferred from the Federal Aviation Administration, the government's aviation authority and the people who implement or disregard the recommendations of the NTSB.

The only black man from Kerowlie, Louisiana, to graduate from Harvard Law School, Willard was used to being considered an outsider. However the affirmative action policy in career advancement had found him climbing the high ladder of the Department of Transportation management structure in record time. But nothing had prepared him for his new job. Due to some high-profile accidents in recent times and reports in the media of conflicts between the NTSB, the FAA and the airlines, it was felt that major accident investigations should adopt new procedures in reporting their findings. Previously the investigation team had relied heavily on the co-operation of the interested parties to the accident, such as the aircraft manufacturer, the engine maker and the airline. However, the new procedures proposed to downgrade the interested parties' participation in the NTSB investigation.

Already nicknamed the 'Sunshade Exclusion', the new procedures also meant that investigation findings could, under special circumstances, be discussed in closed sittings. In previous times all Safety Board hearings were conducted in public under the so-called 'Sunshine Act'. Grant Willard was the man tasked with introducing the new procedures into the Office of Aviation Safety – an NTSB department full of men and women who rarely welcomed government interference. But for the moment Willard could pull rank on every man on the plane, even McKenzie.

Still he felt obligated at least to state his reason for being there.

'The Board thought it would be a good idea for me to go along, see for myself what it's like,' he explained.

'You ever been at a crash site before?' asked Bob.

Willard thought about it for a moment.

'I was in the Railroad Office for a few months, saw a lot of wreckage there.'

'It's not the same,' Al uttered dismissively.

'Why? What's so different?' Willard asked.

The rest of the investigators remained silent. Willard looked around, a raw recruit among the battle hardened.

'Wreckage is wreckage, right?' he said, voice rising an octave.

Ron turned to him.

'The smell . . . you'll never forget the smell,' he said quietly.

Willard smiled incredulously but the other men did not stir and he could not be sure if they were again playing their favourite game of the weeks since his arrival: that being a constant and childish round of pranks and jokes at his expense.

His smile suddenly dropped off his face as the LearJet gunned down the runway and fired itself into the air. Willard gripped the arm rests and shut his eyes tight. He hated flying.

As the LearJet cut through the sky a thin line of sunlight bled across the eastern horizon. Each of the men took out their notepad for McKenzie's in-flight briefing. Grasping a wad of faxes and papers from his satchel, he laid them on his knee. 'All right, gentlemen,' he began, putting on his thick reading glasses, 'we haven't got much information yet but I can tell you we have a Drayton BD-12 of Aero Centrale, a small charter airline based at LAX. Its flight number was ACL248 and it left Los Angeles last night four hours late at 22.05 hours Pacific.' He turned the page. 'It disappeared off radar sometime between midnight and one in the morning.'

'Do we know the reason for the delay?' asked Pete.

McKenzie shook his head. 'Not at this time, but you know the charters, always something – their slot, fuel problem, maintenance. Could be a million things.' He shrugged.

Pulling out another sheet of paper he looked up and down it. 'In command was a Captain Luis Juarez, forty-six-year-old senior skipper, lot of experience. Co-pilot was a Philip Hunter, twenty-six. Both men had exemplary records.'

'Is this a call-in or do we have the lead?' Ron asked.

'We have the lead on this one,' McKenzie replied. 'The airline is American based and the aircraft US registered.'

Sometimes the NTSB were called in by another country's aviation authority when an air accident occurred even when the airline or the airplane were not American. The NTSB teams were widely regarded as the most experienced and effective of the world's small community of air crash detectives.

'How many on board? Have we any numbers yet?' asked Bob.

McKenzie shuffled through his jumble of papers. Information was always sketchy in the hours immediately after a crash, especially for charter flights. He fished out a small scrap of fax paper.

'There were a hundred and forty-eight souls on board. American tourists and returning Mexican workers. Initial word is . . . no survivors.'

They all remained silent for a moment. Though the job of a crash investigator is to examine the wreckage and try to find the cause of the accident there is always at the back of the mind an awareness of the human tragedy involved.

McKenzie took off his glasses.

'Okay, guys, assignments will be as usual. Pete – structures, Jerry – powerplants, Bob – systems, Harv – operations and ATC, Ron – flight recorder recovery,

Greg – witnesses, if any. Al, after initial site inspect you go on maintenance.'

'Do we have anything on the maintenance company?' Al asked hopefully.

McKenzie glanced at his papers again.

'Not much.' He shook his head. 'General AirFactors, an LA-based multi-contractor. Mostly charters and cargo lines. A lot of central American stuff.'

'Any previous entries on them?' asked Jerry.

McKenzie gave a little smile. 'Come on, Jerry, you know the boys at the FAA are still tucked up in bed. It will be a couple of days before we get any background information. For now the crash site's our main concern . . . our only concern.'

Willard coughed as if to announce himself.

'Er, Bill . . . perhaps we should say something about new procedures,' he said.

'Oh, right,' McKenzie acknowledged, not without a hint of reluctance in his voice. 'The DOT and FAA, with the Board's co-operation, have decided to initiate some new standard reporting procedures on any new investigations.'

The men groaned.

'Shit, more procedures,' Bob cursed.

'They will make things run a lot smoother, especially when it comes to the media,' Willard tried to assure them.

Al muttered under his breath, 'Smoother for who, I wonder?'

'What exactly do you mean by new procedures,

Willard?' asked Ron. New procedures usually meant more paperwork. The offices in the NTSB head-quarters on Independence Avenue were already awash with reams of paper – reports, tests, manuals, you name it they had it on paper.

'All findings should be immediately reported to the PO representative for correct dissemination to the media,' Willard stated.

Air crash investigators did not particularly like reporting anything until they were quite sure of their information. The media's usual tendency towards sensationalism had on many occasions distorted an investigator's casual remark into a shocking banner headline.

'You mean, we have to report to you,' Ron said, unable to keep a knowing smile from his lips.

Williard was stumped for a moment. He hadn't thought about it in such basic terms, but that was it: the investigators would now be required to give him all their findings as soon as they got them.

McKenzie moved in to defuse the tension.

'Look, guys, Willard's here to try and help us out in handling the media and liaising with the FAA and the DOT, so just let him do his job. For now we've got more important things to worry about.'

He looked out at the thickening orange band of sunlight on the horizon. 'I suggest we all try and get a few hours' shut-eye, it's gonna be a long day.'

GENAIR MAINTENANCE HANGAR 2, EL SEGUNDO, CA

Paul Edmunsen was wiping a screwdriver against his smudged white overalls as he watched two men at the other end of the hangar, their bodies silhouetted against the slab of white light between the huge doors. He knew who they were but their animated discussion made him wonder what they were talking about.

Dressed in an immaculate grey suit, Jacob Roseman rarely ventured into the huge corrugated shed. A tall man with finely carved features covered by thin, pale skin he preferred the plush, carpeted offices in the main building to the oily concrete of the hangar floor. He was after all the Director of Operations of General AirFactors and left the 'ground' work, as he called it, to his Director of Engineering, Jack Taylor. But today Roseman had news that every maintenance company dreads. His first call was to the company lawyers, his second to Taylor. One of their planes – one of the fleet they took care of, serviced, repaired, nurtured – had crashed.

Edmunsen could see Taylor looking at the ground and rubbing his neck, a sure sign he was stressed out. All the junior mechanics had learned to steer clear of him when he did this. He was, however, a very good teacher and what he did not know about the workings of an aircraft, any aircraft, wasn't worth knowing. He wore the company cap and jacket. An Air Force mechanic in Korea, he had always worn a uniform of some sort, was proud to, it made him feel part of a team.

Roseman left Taylor and disappeared into the bright sunlight that shone onto the concrete outside the hangar. Edmunsen made himself look busy as Taylor headed towards him, walking quickly between the lines of aircraft that crowded the building like giant toys in various stages of disrepair.

Edmunsen hurried to a bench where Chief Mechanic John Marx was signing off some work for the morning shift.

'Hey, Marx, Taylor's comin' – looks pissed,' Edmunsen warned, his Georgia drawl dragging over the words.

'Taylor's always pissed,' Marx growled, still writing on the log sheet.

Marx had recently been promoted to the position of chief mechanic, an appointment he'd been trying to get for fifteen years, many times seeing younger and newer men passing him over. He was plump with a red blotchy face which seemed to flare brightly whenever he dropped a spanner into the compression chamber of an engine or, more frequently, when he polished off a bottle of bourbon with a clique of other older mechanics at the local watering hole.

He put down his paperwork for a moment and

rubbed his eyes. He had been on shift since three o'clock the previous afternoon and it was now eight in the morning.

As Taylor walked by Edmunsen turned and pretended to be working on a fuel pipe that was lying conveniently on the bench.

'Morning, Jack,' Marx said wearily, finishing the sentence with a yawn.

Taylor stopped, his gaze fixed on the ground.

'Er . . . guys,' he began, not really knowing what to say. Edmunsen continued his fake examination of the pipe.

'What is it, Jack?' Marx asked, sensing something was up. At this time of the morning Taylor was usually barking out orders or spouting some tirade against decreasing standards within the aviation maintenance industry or indeed the country as a whole.

'That . . . er . . . Aero Centrale BD-12 we had in yesterday.' Taylor stumbled on the words.

Even Edmunsen now turned around.

'Come on, Jack, what is it?' Marx frowned, bracing himself. They'd spent a lot of time on that plane.

Taylor looked at the two mechanics. His head began shaking slowly, unable to believe what he was about to tell them.

'She went down.'

Marx leant against the bench as his knees buckled. As if a heavy stone had dropped to the bottom of his stomach, his whole body suddenly felt leaden and he wanted to vomit. His plane had crashed.

Edmunsen's mouth dropped open slowly with shock. 'Sweet Jesus Christ!'

As if to fill the silence Taylor began to talk in a dead autonomic tone.

'She crashed into a mountain in the Sierra Madre. No survivors. No idea what happened . . . nothing.' He swallowed hard.

After the initial shock of hearing the news, the realisation of their possible role in the disaster began seeping into Edmunsen's mind. He looked back and forth between the other two as if they hadn't realised what he just had.

'Jesus Christ . . . we worked on that plane just last night,' he stuttered, almost weeping, his throat tight with panic.

But the two older men knew exactly what was going to happen. They would be investigated and possibly implicated in the deaths of one hundred and forty-eight people. That is if they had fucked up.

HIDALGO DEL PIERO AIR FORCE BASE, SINALOA, MEXICO

The LearJet gently taxied to a stop near a line of army-green huts. As Ron got off the plane he immediately noticed at the side of one of the camouflaged hangars a line of stretchers bearing the shapes of human remains under white sheets. As a relay of choppers landed and took off the blizzard beneath their rotors caused the disembarking men to shield their eyes from the dust.

'Must be just bringing them in,' Al shouted against the clatter of the blades.

'Surely there must be more?' Willard remarked, estimating only forty or fifty stretchers on the tarmac.

'Sometimes there isn't even that much left,' Ron said sadly.

An Air Force officer ran up to McKenzie, shook hands and motioned for the others to follow as they headed for one of the hangars that fringed the airfield.

Inside they rested against the wooden tables which lined the briefing room.

McKenzie introduced the officer. 'Guys, this is Colonel Pinchon of the Secretaria de la Defensa Nacional, our liaison with the Mexican Government.'

Pinchon smiled warmly at the men. 'Good morning,

34

gentlemen. On behalf of the Government, I welcome you to Mexico. I am only sorry that it is such tragic circumstances that have brought you here.'

His expression became suitably grave.

'We have made available two helicopters to take you to the crash site.'

'Is it very high up?' Ron asked.

Pinchon moved to a map sellotaped to a blackboard.

'Yes, senõr,' he said, pointing to a spot on the map coloured in purple which denoted the high mountains which ran like a thick spine through the northern half of the country. 'The plane came down here. It is one of the higher points in the Sierra Madre, reaching over 10,000 feet.'

'How far is the wreckage spread?' McKenzie asked, putting on his glasses again.

'It is hard to tell yet, but we do not think it is too far, perhaps over a square mile or two,' Pinchon answered.

Bob nodded his head. 'Yeah, that would be consistent with a straight-on impact with elevated terrain.'

'We are still recovering the bodies,' Pinchon said, 'a temporary morgue is being set up in one of the hangars.'

'What's the terrain like?' Pete asked. 'I mean, do we need climbing gear?'

'No, it's possible to walk, signor, but the ground is very rocky with harsh vegetation, some mountain streams and pools.'

Al shook his head. 'It ain't gonna be easy.'

'Can't be much worse than Valujet, I suppose,' said Bob, remembering the hot summer of '96 spent wading through the Florida swamps, ever fearful of alligator attacks, after a DC-9 crashed there and sank beneath the thick mud, taking those on board with it.

'I have arranged for some equipment.' Pinchon led them to a table covered with hiking boots, anoraks and backpacks of essential supplies.

Willard saw a row of hand guns laid out next to the provisions.

'What do we need these for?' he asked, shocked.

'This area is a favourite with drug smugglers, it is best that you are armed.'

Ron picked up one of the guns and opened the cylinder.

'A single-action .38. Very nice.' He smiled, running his finger over the cold steel. His father had taught him how to handle a gun when he was eleven years old, and though it had become increasingly unpopular and almost illegal in some states, he still liked to spend a couple of hours a month at the range.

Pinchon handed one of the guns to Willard who was shaking his head.

'No, thank you, can't abide them,' he stated firmly.

McKenzie looked at his watch.

'Only seven hours' daylight, gentlemen, let's get ready,' he urged.

*   *   *

As the helicopter rose higher over the barren, crust-like façades of rock, Ron could see the mountain tops of the Sierra Madre stretching into the distance, their volcanic peaks jutting into a blue sky made pale by the bright sun. He wondered what visibility was like here last night. Could the pilots see these giant faces of rock? McKenzie tapped him on the shoulder and pointed to a mountain about a mile to the east – unremarkable and indistinguishable from the rest, except that it had a charred black scar cut on its face.

Ron nodded. This was where she'd come down.

The ground beneath was hard and jagged, easy to break an ankle on. Sharp tree limbs seemed to reach out and pull at their jackets, tear at their skin. Pinchon led the way with some of his men. A dull green UH-60 helicopter hovered overhead, another stretcher with a body twirling beneath it. Soon the trees thinned and spread open, uprooted and slashed like match sticks. The soil was black, scorched and still steaming. Shards of metal and melted plastic fused with the burnt earth.

'Where is it?' Willard asked, looking around for the wreckage of the plane.

'This is it,' said Ron.

'But where is she?' Willard asked again in desperation.

'All around you.' Ron waved his hand to encompass the site. When a 60-tonne plane and nearly

10,000 litres of fuel hit a mountain at over 300 miles an hour, very little is left, and most of that is usually consumed by fire.

The investigators spread out and mingled with the military search parties, picking tiny pieces of wreckage from the ground. The helicopter had moved away taking more remains back to the Air Force Base and suddenly the crash site became very quiet. No one talked, just wandered amid the devastation. The trees were draped with rags and bits of paper like some tawdry decoration. Half a man's body hung from one of the branches. The soldiers were trying to lower it as gently as they could.

The wind changed slightly and the trees rustled with the sudden gust. Willard's nose twitched and he had to pinch it with his fingers to keep from getting sick. It almost choked him. It was the smell of a crash site: the sting of burnt fuel and the stench of smouldering flesh.

Ron walked along under the trees at the edge of the impact site and picked up a child's Hallowe'en mask. One side was blackened and melted by the fire. He looked up and saw a soldier placing a woman's high-heel shoe in a plastic refuse bag.

Further up Bob fell to his knees next to a cigar-shaped hunk of metal, badly scorched but still recognisable as a jet engine. Taking out his torch, he peered inside the three-foot aperture at the fan disk, a carousel of titanium blades emanating from a central shaft. During flight these blades would be revolving several thousand times per minute, sucking oxygen into the engine.

'Which one is it?' Ron asked as he came nearer.

Bob mumbled, his torch wedged between his teeth as he gave the blades a close inspection.

'What?' Ron asked.

Bob extracted the torch from his mouth. 'The starboard engine. At least, I think it's the starboard – No. 2 engine judging by the pylon.'

'Anything?' Ron asked a little prematurely. It would be hard to say at this point if the engine had any clue to offer.

'All I can say is that it might not have been running when they hit the ground, just windmilling,' Bob replied.

Ron leant closer and looked in as Bob pointed to a thick soup of leaves and wood chips on the blades.

'If she was running the tree material would have been melted and charred by the engine temperature,' he said.

Al had found the other engine, the port-side engine, about seventy yards away, now just a cylindrical lump of dull silver. He peered inside the front section and was surprised to see that the fan disk was missing. He stood up and looked around the area for a moment but couldn't see any sign of it. He leant down again and reached inside the engine to pull out a syrupy grout of ingested tree bark – still he could not see any trace of the fan disk.

They all heard a voice calling in the distance. It was

Willard. He had climbed down a small ravine that had a pool at the bottom fed by a cascading stream of water. Jutting from the water was the tail fin, the Aero Centrale insignia of a sombrero perched on a golden sun, scratched and torn but still recognisable. Submerged below was a ten-foot section of the rear fuselage which had been severed from the rest of the plane. This was by far the largest piece still intact. It was also the area in which the Flight Data and Cockpit Voice Recorders were stowed.

'Down here, down here!' Willard shouted as the other investigators ran to the edge of the ravine. The vegetation around the gorge seemed different from the rest of the crash site. Due to the abundance of water and the shelter afforded by the ravine the vegetation here flourished to tropical proportions with thick vines of hardbush crowding down to the pool.

Willard stood on top of the small piece of fuselage that still stood above the water, steadying himself by holding on to a tree branch.

'This is it, isn't it? The black box should be down there, shouldn't it?' he cried, barely keeping his footing on the smooth wet metal. Ron and Al made their way down the face of the ravine.

Willard went quiet, suddenly aware of a slow movement over his shoulder. He turned to see what it was. McKenzie and the other investigators wondered why he had suddenly become so silent.

'What is it, Willard?' McKenzie's voice echoed

about the ravine. But he did not answer. Only Ron and Al who had reached the pool could see what was drawing Willard's attention, freezing him to the spot.

'What the fuck!' uttered Al, mouth agape.

About a foot above Willard's head a snake coiled its long body about the branch he was holding on to. Afraid to move, Willard nearly shat himself.

The snake curled its head, streaked with bright yellow, its two black marble eyes fixed on Willard.

'Don't move!' Al shouted.

I can't fucking move, Willard thought to himself.

Ron slowly made his way towards the tail fin, stepping carefully along the rocks that edged the pool. Willard turned his head slowly away from the snake which began to hiss and reared as if about to strike. Should he make a dive for it? he thought to himself, but his feet felt as if cased in concrete, pinning him to the spot.

Ron slowly took out the .38 and moved closer. Willard was directly in front of the snake which coiled menacingly behind his head.

Seeing the gun, he gasped, 'Jesus, Carter! What are you doing?'

'Okay, Willard, relax,' said Ron in the calmest voice he could muster at that moment.

He slowly raised the gun and pointed it straight at Willard. 'Oh, fuck . . . fuck . . . fuck,' he repeated like a mantra as he heard the snake hissing behind him. He was strangely aware of the absurdity of a gun being pointed at one side of his head while a deadly snake aimed its fangs on the other.

'On the count of three move your head to the right,' Ron directed Willard, holding him firmly in his sights.

Willard began trembling. 'Christ, you're gonna kill me . . . Oh, fuck . . . Oh, fuck . . .'

Ron moved a little closer. He knew the snake was about to strike.

'Hold it together,' he urged Willard. 'On three move to the right.'

'To the right? Whose fuckin' right? Mine or yours?' Willard's voice cracked with desperation.

'Your right, Willard, *your right*! Got it?' Ron replied quickly. He would only have one shot. Before Willard could say any more Ron began counting as he opened the safety catch.

One . . . two . . . he cocked the hammer . . .

Willard wanted to shut his eyes. All he could hear was the snake behind him. Then the hissing stopped as the animal drew back its head.

. . . THREE!

Willard swung his head to the right and Ron pulled the trigger. The snake was pulling back to strike when a bullet blew its head to pieces and its body fell limp on the tree. Slowly it unwrapped itself from the branch and flopped on the ground like a severed piece of rubber hosing.

Willard looked at Ron as if to ask if it was all over but hadn't the breath to utter even one word.

As the rest of the men lowered themselves down the ravine Pinchon examined the body of the dead snake.

'Ah, just a common boa,' he declared, 'rare up this high . . . but not poisonous.'

'Oh, fucking great,' Willard said, still shivering from shock.

'He would have strangled you, though, if he'd caught you,' Pinchon added cheerfully.

'Hear that?' McKenzie clapped Willard on the back. 'Looks like you owe Ron a drink.'

The sun was sinking again over the peaks as a Mexican Air Force diver rose to the surface of the pool. He held in his arms the bright orange box that contained the flight recorders and possibly the answer to what led ACL248 to its death.

DEPARTURES HALL, LOS ANGELES INTERNATIONAL AIRPORT

A man slowly walked through the busy hall. Strongly built, he carried a small bag slung over his shoulder. Beside him strode a woman, much younger than he, also carrying a bag. It seemed quite light and empty. She wore a bright floral print dress which hung loosely on her petite body. They didn't seem like a couple. They headed to the washrooms. The man turned and smiled at the woman before he went into the men's room while she leant against the wall outside and began running her fingers through her long strawberry blonde hair, glancing about her at the passing parade of travellers and airport staff.

The man found a vacant cubicle and went in, snapping the lock shut behind him. Placing his shoulder bag on the toilet seat, he slowly unzipped it and took out a small radio which he stood on top of the cistern. Underneath some folded clothes was a paper-wrapped object. He fished it out, holding it carefully like a precious cache of jewels. He gently opened the paper and gazed for a moment at the putty-like substance in his hands. He laid it to rest next to the radio and stopped for a moment as two young men entered the washroom, laughing about some incident in the bar. Delving his hands once more into the bag he took out what seemed like a heavier object, wrapped in a sheath of light paper. It had the shape of a whiskey bottle. He placed it in a sturdy plastic bag which he retrieved from his coat pocket and laid them on the ground next to the wall. Next he turned to the radio once more and flicked open the battery compartment.

There were no batteries inside. He slowly unwrapped the putty and neatly squeezed it into the battery compartment. Closing it again, he placed the radio back inside the shoulder bag and grabbed it by the handle. He lowered himself like a weight-lifter and very gently picked up the bag with the bottle. Smiling to himself, he wondered why he was being so cautious.

Outside, the woman was watching the ongoing opera of the departures hall around her. A little boy was spilling candy over the floor, to the annoyance of his mother who ran about the place picking it up. A couple were making out on a seat, oblivious to the businessman who sat next to them hiding himself from the spectacle behind the opened sheets of his *LA Times*. A whole troop of boy scouts were excitedly talking and laughing with each other, the leader counting heads to make sure he had everyone.

A man in a bright Hawaiian shirt and shorts made his way slowly through the concourse, a black camcorder held to his eye.

When her partner at last emerged the blonde smiled nervously at him. He nodded and handed her the plastic holder with the bottle and she in turn put it in her own shoulder bag. They turned and joined a tide of passengers heading for the security check point at the end of the hall.

The queue was moving slowly as each person had to put their baggage on the conveyor which would take it under the machine to have its contents X-rayed. There were three security personnel in attendance. One of them directed people through the detection door, which picked up any metal object concealed in their clothes or even their bodies. Many a time they would be perplexed when a passenger had to go through the door several times even though they had removed all watches and jewellery and emptied their pockets of coins and keys, only for the passenger at last to reveal he had a metal plate in his head.

The blonde woman placed her bag on the conveyor and watched it disappear under a curtain of small flaps into the darkness of the X-ray machine.

The security man motioned for her to walk through the metal detector arch. On the other side, behind the X-ray detector, the operator watched as the outline of a bag and its contents of clothing, make-up, a purse and a book moved slowly across the screen. In the middle of the group, lying on its side, was the long shape of a bottle. The liquid inside appeared as a plasma-like substance on the monitor. Jack Daniel's, the operator guessed to himself, judging by the shape of the bottle. He always tried to guess the contents of baggage. Not only was it his job, it was the only way to make the long day seem shorter.

The woman glanced back as her partner was placing his bag on the conveyor, about to go through the detector arch.

In the queue behind, not far down the line, the man in the Hawaiian shirt was still filming with his camcorder. Through the viewfinder he watched the woman and her partner head off towards the departure gates, their bags once again hanging on their shoulders.

'Excuse me, sir!' He could see the security man pointing to him through the lens. 'You'll have to put that through.'

'It won't damage it, will it?' the tourist asked. 'I don't want to lose all my vacation stuff.'

'It'll be fine, sir, everything has to go through the machine,' the security man insisted.

The man turned off his camera and placed it on the conveyor and walked through.

The machine operator watched the X-ray image of the camera gliding across his screen – a neat box of wires and circuits. A three-chip digital, he thought to himself, pretty expensive piece for a tourist.

As the man emerged on the other side of the checkpoint he picked up his camera and turned it on again.

The security men smiled at each other as the tourist walked quickly down to the departure gates, the camera again placed to his eye.

'First time in LA,' they laughed.

At gate 119 the man and the woman stopped and turned around as the tourist with the camcorder came walking up behind them. He could see their digitised images watching him as he approached.

As if readying herself for confrontation the woman swept back her hair with a swift movement of the head. Her companion seemed unsure what to do and just stood there holding tightly to his bag.

The man stopped, lowered his camera and smiled vacantly at them. The woman beamed back, a flash of perfect teeth.

'Get it?' she asked him.

He nodded, almost laughing with excitement.

'You wanna do the piece here?' he asked, looking around at the lighting.

'Good a place as any.' She nodded and turned to her companion. 'That was easier than I thought,' she said, relieved.

'Told you,' he said.

The other man checked his camera and flicked a switch at the side. 'Okay, Mary, ready when you are, give me a level.'

She cleared her throat and stared into the lens.

'This is Mary Shaw, reporting for American Network News . . .'

NATIONAL SIGINT OPS CENTRE, FANX 5 BUILDING, FORT MEADE, MARYLAND

The National Security Agency is tasked to provide for the Signals Intelligence (SIGINT) mission of the United States – to secure the communications systems for all arms of the American Government
—We Protect the Protectors

Airman Dalton Truchs sat in the long corridor just opposite the doorway marked *M-Group – Admin. (Transit Records) Room 509*. The door opened and an Air Force officer swiftly strode out, carrying a black briefcase.

Truchs jumped to his feet and saluted. The officer gave a brief acknowledgement and continued down the corridor to the elevator. Another man appeared in the open door. Dressed in civilian clothes of tan trousers and a red shirt, he smiled at Truchs and held up his index finger.

'Just one minute,' he said and closed the door behind him.

Truchs sat down again. He felt a little nervous. Twenty-two years old, with a wife and three-week-old baby, he had been granted a transfer from the Clerks Department of the Air Intelligence Agency at

Kelly AFB, Texas to Meade with the promise of a $50 a week pay rise and an apartment with two bedrooms.

He opened up the welcome pack that the NSA personnel office had given him on arrival. There were vouchers for the cinema, a shopping points card, membership to the servicemen's club and an invitation to join the golf club. He read through the colourful information leaflet on the NSA again.

Established by a Presidential Directive in 1952 by President Truman

- SIGINT covers all media of communications; electronic, telemetric, written or otherwise, foreign and domestic
- in 1986 the NSA appointed a combat support agency of the Department of Defence
- though not a military agency the NSA provides intelligence for the Navy, Air Force and Army.
- premier training ground for the country's codemakers and codebreakers
- Fort Meade Facility classified as world's second most powerful computing site
- one of the highest concentration of top mathematicians
- largest employer in Anne Arundel County

- recycling program of over 250 tons of paper annually
- headquartered at Fort Meade, named after Maj Gen George Gordon Meade, whose defensive strategy at Gettysburg turned the war in favour of the Union – home to nearly 35,000 military and civilian employees
- 93 miles of road, 1,670 buildings, banks, credit union, post office, hospitals, chapels – a little city

He closed the information pack, almost dizzy with all the facts and figures, the sheer immensity of the place. He looked down the corridor, fifteen or so closed doors on each side, not a sound coming from behind any of them.

'Airman Truchs?'

He turned around to see the same man standing directly opposite him with the door open.

'Sorry to keep you waiting . . . please, come in.'

Truchs stood up and followed him into a large square room with a high ceiling and rows of shelving reaching to the top on three sides. On the other wall a stack of trays covered the entire wall. They were labelled alphabetically from A–Z and filled with variously coloured files.

'Welcome to the "Paper House"!' the man said brightly. 'I'm Marcus Gayley, by the way.'

He reached out his hand.

'Good to meet you, sir,' said Truchs smartly, almost standing to attention as he gripped Gayley's hand.

'Please sit down.' Gayley gestured to a stool in front of a large desk which dominated the centre of the room. He glanced over the stacks of paperwork that lined the walls, stood in piles on the floor and spilt in waves across the desk.

'Where shall we begin?' he wondered.

Truchs looked at him, staring vacantly, unable to give any suggestion at all.

'I know,' said Gayley, brightly, 'how 'bout a coffee? You have to have a coffee to start the morning off, right?'

'Yes, sir,' Truchs smiled obligingly, 'that would be nice.'

'Have personnel gone over your duties with you?' Gayley asked as he walked over to the coffee maker.

'Yes, sir. They said it'd be mostly filing, collating and cataloguing,' answered Truchs.

He glanced at the NSA insignia on the wall by the window, beneath it the words: *Protect the Protectors – Watch the Watchers*.

'At first it might seem a little daunting,' Gayley continued as he poured out two mugs of boiling coffee, 'but it's basically our job to sort the files that are coming in from the field, from the other groups and agencies, and either archive them or ready them for dispatch out again to whoever . . . it's not the most exciting job in the world but utmost discretion is assumed. I mean . . .' he turned around, a spoon in his hand '. . . you have been briefed on security, haven't you?'

'Fully, sir,' Truchs assured him. 'Got my security pass cleared this morning – Class 2.'

'Good.' Gayley smiled again. 'Sugar?'

'No, thank you, sir.'

Truchs looked around the room. There was something missing.

Gayley brought the two cups over to the desk. 'I know what you're looking for,' he said, setting one in front of his new assistant. 'A computer, right?'

'Yeah, I was kinda wondering,' admitted Truchs. 'I thought everything would be computerised.'

'Oh, a lot of it is,' said Gayley, 'but people still mistrust the electronic storage of sensitive material; they still like to keep their secrets on paper,' he mused, relishing the taste of his coffee. 'Well, that's basically it,' he said, like a man cheerfully resigned to a life of boredom. 'We're the intelligence community's paper pushers. Welcome to M-group.'

'Thank you, sir.' Truchs took a drink, pretending to like the thick black gunk.

'Oh, please don't call me sir all the time,' Gayley insisted, 'I'm not your commanding officer, just your boss,' he added playfully.

'Yes.' Truchs smiled and forced himself to drink another slug.

NTSB OFFICES, INDEPENDENCE AVENUE, WASHINGTON DC

The corridors of the old grey building seemed cold and quiet as Ron made his way down to the basement. While the members of the Safety Board and some of the Office of Aviation top brass enjoyed relatively luxurious offices over in L'Enfant Plaza, the investigators on the Go-Team made do with crammed rooms in the large austere building where the FAA were also headquartered. It seemed ironic at times that the organisation with which the investigators had most disputes shared the same building.

Ron opened one of the large green exit doors and walked along the narrow passage until he came to a thick pine door marked SOUND LAB 1 (Vehicle Recorder Analysis). Low rumbling sounds were emanating from inside.

He found Gordon Pruett bent over a table lined with level faders and indicator needles. Thirty-nine years old, Gordie was thin and looked as if he didn't get too much sunlight – or human contact for that matter. He was one of the quietest members in the Engineering Services Division but knew more about flight recorders than pretty much anyone else in the world including the manufacturers, who were always trying to tempt him from his lair beneath the busy traffic which flowed like a river of metal along Independence Avenue.

The room rumbled with the sound of some fearsome unknown monster.

'What's this . . . *Jurassic Park 3*?' Ron asked.

Gordie looked up and turned down the volume.

'Hi, Ron.'

He glanced at the console that Gordie was working at, a bank of dials and knobs and a computer screen blinking with a wave form running across it like a skipping rope.

'This a new addition to your collection of toys?' asked Ron.

Gordie smiled and ran his fingers along the black panels of the desk, his voice almost purring with pride. 'This little baby is a Mark IV, 32-track, multi-phase isolator.'

'Come again?' Ron asked, looking at the dizzying array of buttons.

'An egg-scrambler,' said Gordie. 'Picks out individual sounds by signature frequency against an ambient wall.'

'No shit,' said Ron, not bothering to ask any more questions. So long as it worked he left the technicalities to Gordie.

'What's the status on the 248 tapes? They ready yet?' he asked.

Gordie got up and led him to the sound room, a small sealed area with some seats facing a wall of audio equipment.

'The FDR is still being dried out in the lab, we have to take it real slow,' he said, 'there was a small amount of water contamination.'

Ron had noticed a tiny hole in the steel casing of the black box when they took it out of the pool at the crash site. Built to withstand three and a half thousand times the force of gravity, the casing was still susceptible to damage and was vulnerable when submerged. It is impossible to build a piece of delicate equipment that can protect itself completely from the ravages of an air crash.

'We will get something, though?' he asked, worried that without the FDR the investigation would have to fight an uphill battle. For the Flight Data Recorder logged all the basic flight conditions on board an aircraft for a period of twenty-five hours before starting over again. The digital data on its memory card would show the investigators how all the vital systems of the plane were functioning before she crashed.

'Like I say, we'll have to take it very slow, leave it to dry out completely,' warned Gordie. 'It's an old model DFDR, though, not all that many parameters covered. A small carrier?' he asked.

'Yeah,' Ron nodded, 'Aero Centrale, a charter company based in LA.'

'Can't say I've heard of them. Thank God for deregulation – cheap spares an' cheap fares!' Gordie sang.

'Thank Carter,' Ron lamented.

In 1978 Ron's namesake President Jimmy Carter signed the Airline Deregulation Act and thus heralded an era of unprecedented fare reduction and price wars as the airlines fought for the 'open' air routes. The small regional charters flourished but had to survive on a shoestring and the general drive for cost cutting led many in the industry to believe that standards of safety were being sacrificed at the sacred altar of the cheaper airfare.

'CVR looks okay,' Gordie said as he led Ron to a table upon which the voice-recording storage memory module extracted from the black box was attached to a computer via a cable for transfer.

Gordie checked the levels on the computer screen. 'She's fine, no contamination on the tape. The quality ain't that great, but all channels have recorded.'

The CVR recorded four channels from two 'hot' mikes, one on each pilot, one cockpit 'area' mike and one radio jump-seat microphone.

'When'll it be ready?' Ron asked.

'I'm making a master copy right now through the spectrum analyser for time coding and sound ID. But I reckon this afternoon should be okay.'

Ron watched the sound logs on the monitor.

On it the silent voices of Captain Luis Juarez and First Officer Philip Hunter made the levels jump and quiver.

Ron took the stairs again and entered the Go-Team offices. At the other end of the corridor Ron could see Al going into his room. He was just back from LA. Ron followed him in.

Al plonked a load of files on his desk, sighing with relief at unburdening himself.

'So did you talk to the guys at GenAir?' Ron asked.

'Yeah,' was all Al would say as he went to the coffee machine and poured some black tar-like substance into a cup with the word 'Alan' on it. 'Patient and ever happy' read the little quote underneath, a present from his wife.

Ron followed him over. 'And?' he pressed.

'They were okay, seemed pretty co-operative.'

'So what did you get?' Ron persisted.

Al looked contemptuously at the mound of files on his desk.

'Paperwork, lots of paperwork. We seem to spend most of our days going through damned paper-work.' He was always complaining about something – paperwork, the coffee, travelling, late nights at the office – all the stock in trade of a crash investigator's life.

'And then we got that prick Willard giving us more procedures,' he went on.

'Well, he's still down in Mexico getting in the way, at least he's not breathing down your neck here.'

Al shook his head and smiled.

'What?' Ron asked.

'He's here.'

'Willard?'

'Yeah, came back with McKenzie and me through LA.'

'Shit. Nobody told me they were coming back already,'

Al emptied his cup. 'Nearly a week and no real clues on site. I hope the recorders have something. How're they doin' anyway?'

'FDR's gonna' take a bit of time, but the CVR should be ready today.'

'Good,' said Al, 'McKenzie was hoping it would be ready when he got back.'

'Where is he?'

'In his office. Watch it, though, he's not in the best of moods,' Al warned.

Ron knocked on the door of McKenzie's office and pushed it open. McKenzie was sitting at his desk, Willard leaning over him holding a burning lighter to the older man's cigar.

'Ah, good, Ron.' McKenzie leant back, puffing out a blue cloud of smoke. 'Come on in.'

'Heard you just got back,' said Ron as he sat next to Willard. 'Hi, Willard.'

'Hello, Ron,' Willard answered limply, exhausted from his trip.

McKenzie too looked shattered. Six days on a freezing mountain seemed to have taken its toll. He gave a rasping cough. Ron was concerned. He'd never seen his boss look so bad.

'You okay, Bill?'

McKenzie barked back, 'Yes, I'm fine, thank you. I just wish people would stop asking if I'm . . .' He stopped, suddenly hearing the harshness of his own voice.

Ron, a little shocked, looked at Willard who just glanced away and rubbed his eyes.

McKenzie forced a smile. 'Sorry . . . it was a long flight an' I guess I'm gettin' a bit old for this sort of thing.'

Ron nodded.

'Anything on the recorders?' his boss asked.

'Yeah, I just came up from the lab. The FDR's gonna take some time.'

'How long?' McKenzie asked.

Ron shook his head. 'Don't know. We gotta take it slow according to Gordie.'

'And the CVR?'

'Should be able to have a listen this afternoon.'

McKenzie nodded his approval. 'Good, I've got to brief all the interested parties tomorrow.' McKenzie was not looking forward to having to update the so-called interested parties: Aero Centrale, Drayton, the engine builders Juno, and of course the maintenance company, GenAir.

They had a right to know what was going on and would normally be used as consultants to the investigation, lending whatever expertise was required by the investigators. But McKenzie was only too aware that each of the parties had their own agenda of self-protection that would not necessarily be in accord with the interests of the investigation.

Willard shifted in his seat. 'We'll have to give something to the press after the briefing, they'll want to know what's going on as well.'

'It's a bit early yet, isn't it? I mean, we don't really have anything for them,' Ron pointed out.

'The Administration and the Safety Board are anxious that we keep everyone informed,' Willard glanced at McKenzie, 'especially the media.'

The media, he thought. Now they have a monopoly on how to twist the facts. Sometimes when there's nothing at all to twist.

119TH STREET, HAWTHORNE, SOUTH-WEST LOS ANGELES

Paula Balgotti crossed her name out.

Ten years of marriage wasn't easy to let go of; her surname changed, her friends changed, the bank accounts still had to be changed. She glanced over at the answering machine – that would have to be changed, her ex-husband's voice still greeting incoming calls. In fact the easiest part was getting rid of *him*. One Saturday night she just packed his bags and left them outside the door. He never even knocked.

She scribbled in her maiden name, Alvarez. Looked down the application form, her pen poised over the box marked *Previous Work Experience*. What could she put in? A waitress for one year, a housewife for ten, a secretary in a back-street garage for two weeks. She crumpled up the sheet of paper into a neat tight little ball and dropped it into the trash can – which reminded her, that would have to be emptied. He'd also taken care of the trash.

She was already running late for her crummy little job as secretary in Max's Deals on Wheels down on La Cienega – a crummy little second-hand car dealership, run by a crummy little man called Max, surprisingly enough. As she dragged the bulging bin liner out on to the patio she ran a quick mental checklist: don't forget to call the plumber, don't forget to ring her mother to remind her she was picking up Jordan, her four-year old son from school today, don't forget to lock the back door.

The only thing left was Lucy.

She called out her cat's name as she made her way down the garden.

'Lucy! Lucy!'

The grass felt cool and crisp beneath her feet, crunching between her toes as she made her way to the trash cans.

Don't forget to put on your shoes.

She opened one and held her breath against the hot stink of decaying refuse as she lobbed in her own sack and closed the top quickly again.

Walking up the garden, she began looking in the bushes, leaning into the hedges.

'Lucy . . . Lucy!' she called out.

But there was still no sign.

She went inside again and poured out a small saucer of milk.

'Lucy!' she called, going outside. 'Come on, girl . . . where are you, baby?'

She heard a rustling of leaves from the small palm that grew up the side of the apartment building. Saw a white flash of fur as her cat leapt from the tree to the balcony of the apartment above Paula's ground-floor quarters.

'Come on, baby . . . come on . . . want your milk?'

Lucy leapt on to the patio in one graceful movement and rubbed her sleek fur against her mistress's legs.

Paula set down the saucer and caressed the cat's back as it greedily lapped at the milk, throat purring like a little motor.

As Paula stood up again and was about go back inside she sensed movement, somewhere on the balcony on the apartment above her. She shaded her eyes from the sun with her palms and looked up. But there was nobody there. All she could see was the long black barrel of a camera lens.

She hurried inside and locked the door behind her.

THE SWANKY SCOUNDREL BAR, NORTH CAPITOL ST, WASHINGTON DC

Ron and Al took up their usual perch at the end of the bar and ordered lunch.

'You gonna have a beer?' Al asked, taking out a twenty.

'No, thanks, better keep a clear head for this afternoon,' said Ron, looking about him at the usual noisy mixture of Government workers that filled the bar, from Congressmen to filing clerks, from IRS auditors to air crash investigators.

'Trying to make me feel guilty,' Al joked, as he signalled to the waitress for service.

Someone clapped them both on the back.

'What have you to feel guilty about?' Bob shouted. 'Hi ya, guys!' He smiled as they turned around to him.

'Looks like everyone's back,' observed Al.

Bob took a seat next to them and ordered a Scotch. 'Pete, Jerry and the rest of them stayed on,' he said, feeling lucky to have gotten away at last from the crash site.

Ron passed the Scotch from the waitress to Bob. 'Found anything new on the engines?'

Bob thought about it. 'Well, we recovered the port engine, but . . .' he narrowed his eyes as if still struggling with a long-standing puzzle '. . . part of the fan blade section is missing,' he continued, 'and we can't yet tell if it sheared off with the impact or . . .'

'. . . or whether it came off in flight,' interrupted Ron.

Bob nodded gravely. 'It's way too early to tell.'

'Where is that?' Al strained his eyes at the TV over the bar. 'Looks like an airport.'

Ron also craned his head up at the TV. 'Yeah, but which one?'

On the screen was a slightly grainy, jerky picture of a woman and a man standing near a departure gate. The woman had long blonde hair and wore a floral print dress.

Al turned to the waitress. 'Please, turn up the sound . . . that's what's her name, that reporter,' he shouted excitedly. The sound of the TV battled with the cacophonous din of the bar until they could just hear the woman talking into the camera. ANN's award-winning reporter Mary Shaw was holding up a bottle of Jack Daniel's.

'Not only were we able to take liquid explosives, disguised here in this bottle of whiskey, but we were also able to carry in our hand luggage plastic explosives, concealed in the battery compartment of a radio.'

The camera pulled in as the man next to her took out the radio from his bag and opened the battery compartment. The camera focused on the pale substance stuffed inside like a large glob of chewing gum.

It moved up to Shaw again.

'I have here with me retired Army explosives expert, Mr Tony Gurnan.'

She turned to Gurnan, who smiled rather awkwardly for the camera.

'Mr Gurnan, are you surprised at how easy it was for us to smuggle these dangerous explosives past airport security?'

'Sadly, Mary, no, I'm not,' Gurnan stated in best Army yes-sir-no-sir style. 'It is well known that even the most modern security systems are inadequate at detecting the determined terrorist who wishes to get on board aircraft with these lethal substances, and as we have seen with atrocities such as Lockerbie such people exist.'

Bob stared at the TV and shook his head. 'Aw, shit, those damn' reporters scaremongering again.'

'Thing is, though, they're right,' Ron remarked. 'I mean, the public doesn't know how vulnerable they are.'

'Come on, Ron, that's crud an' you know it,' Al said.

'Do I?' he asked, with a quizzical look

Shaw was wrapping up the report, staring into the camera as if looking into the very hearts and minds of her audience.

'In these days of increasing air travel and with the growing sophistication of bomb-making materials, many people in the airline community are beginning to voice a very real and immediate concern for the security of America's airports. This is Mary Shaw reporting for ANN at Los Angeles International Airport.'

'Ah, she's in LAX,' said Al, 'thought so.'

Bob shook his head in disgust.

'I hate that type of reporting, does nobody any good.'

RECORDER ANALYSIS LAB, INDEPENDENCE AVE, WASHINGTON DC

They all sat quietly in the soundproof room as Gordie prepared a playback of flight 248's cockpit voice recording. The tape had been written digitally to a hard disk and was time-coded for convenient retrieval. With the press of a button Gordie could start the recording at whatever point he desired, replay any section and fast forward to any particular moment. McKenzie looked at his watch then glanced at the only vacant seat in the room.

Bob doodled on his notepad as Al chewed his nails.

'Stop, will you?' said Bob, annoyed.

Willard looked around at the rows of dials, switches and knobs that took up half the room.

Ron was reading a thick manila file marked 'Confidential'. It was Captain Juarez' most recent CRM report which Ron had collected over in the FAA offices. Once a year some airlines required their pilots to attend a Cockpit Resource Management programme. Initially set up by some of the larger airlines, this course allowed pilots to talk about their grievances and voice their concerns about the many stresses involved in their job. More directly, however, the programme was designed to encourage pilots to communicate effectively with their colleagues and so foster an atmosphere of co-operation and sense of teamwork within the flight crew. The old tradition of the Captain being God and unwilling to countenance any advice from his junior pilots was deemed archaic and dangerous.

Ron ran his finger through the columns of Juarez' last CRM assessment in September, just under two months prior to the crash. He had scored above average in all areas of communication and response control. His finger stopped at the assessor's final comments which testified to Juarez' continued suit-ability for command. He was by all accounts a fine and able pilot.

The door opened and the tall, spindly figure of Fred Stranksi bounded in.

'Sorry I'm late, Bill.' He smiled and flopped on to his chair.

'Okay, everyone's here,' McKenzie said.

Stranski extended his hand and grasped Willard's with long thin fingers, perfectly white and soft. 'Hello,' he said, a toothy smile on his face.

'How do you do?' Willard responded, wondering who this strange man was.

As if aware of his thoughts, Ron answered, 'Fred's our resident shrink.'

'Head of the Human Factors Study Group at the FAA,' McKenzie gave his official title, 'an expert in flight-crew behaviour.'

Stranski was still smiling at Willard. 'The human element is usually the most crucial part of any mis-hap,' he said, as if reciting an ancient adage. Of course he was right: about 70 percent of air accidents are attributable to human error, a statistic played like a scratched record by those promoting the need for further automation in the business of flying planes.

Get the human out of the control loop and you eliminate the majority of potential mistakes to be made, they believed. Naturally most pilots opposed this view. Certainly Ron did, especially after shocking reports in the early-nineties when the much heralded and highly computerised range of Airbuses were executing uncommanded barrel-rolls over the skies of Europe in consequence of some little glitch in the flight computer's endless line of program code.

'Right, someone close the door and let's get cracking,' said McKenzie, his voice urgent. 'Gordie!'

He duly pressed a key and across the twenty-inch monitor a wave signal pulsed. Two large speakers first hissed with static then rumbled into life. All the men listened intently.

'How long is it?' Willard asked.

Ron whispered, 'The last twenty-five minutes.'

'Actually this one managed about thirty-seven minutes,' Gordie informed them.

On another, smaller monitor a cursor flashed, waiting to convert the audio signal using voice-pattern recognition software into text read-out. Gordie had already sampled each of the pilot's voices and tagged them into the computer so it knew which pilot was talking. Gordie had christened the program HAL, after the computer in Kubrick's *2001 A Space*

Odyssey, his favourite film. Because most CVRs were not of good sound quality the software struggled to produce a more than 60 percent recognition of actual words but it was a useful tool in the initial stages of the CVR analysis.

The wave form hopped.

'Here she comes,' Gordie said.

Over the speakers the men could hear the ambient sounds of a cockpit, the engine hum, the various air vents, the radio chatter.

HAL's cursor jumped to life and began tapping out words in unison with First Officer Philip Hunter's voice. He was talking about his car.

Hunter: . . . from a buddya mine for fifteen grand – a genuine piece of American automotive history he told me . . . I think he's flying seven-forty-sevens with Northwest now . . . you used to fly the big boys, didn't you, Skipper?

SILVERPINE DRIVE, WESTCHESTER, LOS ANGELES

The traffic was quiet enough for the kids to have a game of hockey in the middle of the road. On each side the manicured gardens presented a long line of identical bungalows. At the back of one of the houses, John Marx turned on the light in his shed. Though he had been given time off work he hadn't slept much and had to spend a lot of time in conversation with the GenAir company lawyers, who coached him on what he'd have to say to the NTSB officials. He was totally beat from fatigue and worry. He retreated to his shed and began sanding the wing of one of his model remote-control planes which he was repainting. His wife appeared at the door, a cardigan over her shoulders. The sun was falling and the late-evening air was thinning to the coolness of night.

'Don't you get tired of fixing planes?' she asked.

Her slightly greying hair was held in one sweep behind her ears by a hairband. A member of the Rotary Club, a golfer on ladies' day, hoarder of coupons, she seemed the perfect wife of the Eisenhower years. Marx had not made love to his wife for nearly six months. What was the point? They were now too old for 'that sort of thing', she would say, dismissing his awkward and usually drunken advances.

He remained silent and ran his finger along the smooth edge of the wing.

His wife produced a large brown envelope from behind her back.

'This was dropped through the door for you today,' she said, holding it out to him.

He looked up at her. So what? It's called post, he felt like saying. Probably just a magazine or a new set of plans for a model plane.

But she was a practised mind reader.

'There's no stamp on it, someone just dropped it through the letterbox and drove off before I could see who it was,' she said, annoyed.

'I'll have a look at it later, put it down over there.' He pointed to the side of the bench.

'Who's it from?' she asked. She had been tempted to open it herself.

'How should I know?' he barked.

She shook her head. Since the crash he had been impossible to live with. Placing the envelope on the bench, she tugged the sides of her cardigan around herself and left him to his toy.

Marx continued rhythmically to run the sandpaper up and down the wing but was unable to take his mind off what was in the envelope. There was no stamp, like she said. Perhaps it was something to do with the investigation, some document drafted by the lawyers for him to sign. He had considered getting his own counsel. In his darker moments he wondered would the company try and disassociate itself from him and leave him carrying the can if there was found to be negligence in the maintenance of the aircraft. The whole thing kept turning around in his mind. He shook his head as if to stop it racing to any further ridiculous conclusions and picked up the envelope.

There was no letter, just a 10 × 8″ black and white photograph. At first he just squinted at the hazy image of what looked like two people in an embrace. He looked closer. His eyes widened again.

Jesus! The girl.

His head shot up and he glanced around to see if anyone was watching. A small ridge of sweat lined his forehead. Whoever had taken this must have been following him. The photograph shook in his hand as he turned it over. Scribbled on the back as if by a child's hand were the words: 'I know my redeemer liveth'.

Marx had seen those words before.

BOARD ROOM, NTSB OFFICES, L'ENFANT PLAZA, WASHINGTON DC

One of the the largest in the building, the fifth-floor boardroom seemed quiet and empty with only a handful of people around the huge table in the centre. As if awaiting the reading of a will everyone observed a respectful silence. Far in the distance the white dome of the Capitol rose majestically, piercing the cold blue Washington sky.

Around the dark oak table sat the corporate and legal representatives of the interested parties of flight ACL248. At the top, presiding, was Bill McKenzie with Willard beside him in support. Behind Ron, Al and Bob sat like second stringers, brought along to bolster the side, to field any awkward technical questions. At a desk near the door sat the tiny bird-like figure of Carol Cummings. Though only thirty-eight she seemed older and in many respects was almost like a mother to the boys of the investigating team. She organised their scribbled notes into legible reports, she booked their flights and reminded them of their children's birthdays or sent flowers to their wives when they were away in some God-forsaken place picking through the wreckage of an airplane. Her fingers were poised over the stenograph, her eyes large and round behind her glasses, staring at the keys, waiting.

Willard cleared his throat and offered a welcoming smile. 'Before Bill here begins the preliminary report on the accident findings so far, I would like to thank all of you for being so patient. In accordance with new Safety Board procedures it is our intention regularly to inform all interested parties of any investigation findings as soon as they come to hand so that everyone knows exactly what's going on. This is to avoid any unnecessary, and possibly harmful, speculation.'

Ron, Bob and Al stared at the ground, wishing he'd just get on with it. Carol's fingers danced over the keys, recording every word. McKenzie looked nervous as he fumbled through the notes of the prelim report that lay in front of him. The rest of them just nodded politely as Willard spoke. He looked straight into their eyes. He had learnt this on one of the many management courses the Department had sent him on: engage your audience's attention at all times, show them you mean business and are in control.

'We would, however, appreciate it if you could refrain from speaking with the media until we have issued our own statement at today's press conference,' he said.

McKenzie frowned for a moment, dreading his appointment with the newshounds.

Willard continued, 'So before we begin, can you please state your name, position and the party you represent . . .' he gestured in Carol's direction '. . . for the record.'

They all looked at each other for a moment, not knowing who should begin. An athletic-looking man with a dark pock-marked face started. 'Er . . . Brad Fucelli, Chief Design Director, Juno Airmotive Industries.'

Juno built the engines for the BD-12.

Next was an older man, his belly straining the buttons of his waistcoat. 'George Mahoney, legal counsel for Aero Centrale, Los Angeles.'

He turned to the man next to him who glared around the room and cleared his throat.

'Ed Blair, legal representative of Drayton Industries, Bethlehem, PA. Aircraft builders.'

Though Drayton was a billion-dollar concern, it was one of the smaller players among the aircraft giants such as Boeing and Airbus. Its management had over the years steadfastly held out against acquisition by the majors. The BD-12 was its short-to-medium-haul workhorse with 358 of the type in service all over the world. Despite the fact the design was nearly thirty years old, the plane's rugged dependability had made it perfect for many of the smaller airlines, especially the charters.

Sitting bolt upright at the other end of the table, facing McKenzie, sat a very tall lady, dressed in a black pants suit.

'Emma Klein,' she intoned in a deep voice, 'legal counsellor for General AirFactors, El Segundo, California.' She turned her head slightly to her right and introduced the man sitting next to her. 'With

Mr Jack Taylor, Director of Engineering for GenAir.'

Ron watched as Taylor shifted in his tight grey suit which seemed to be some years out of fashion.

'Captain Geoff Downes,' the next man introduced himself. 'President, Airline Pilots' Association.'

Very good-looking with a crop of silver hair swept back from his tanned forehead, he seemed like an airline PR's dream, perfect for adorning the cover of the company's brochures – the suave, handsome captain. He sneezed suddenly and had to cover his nose with a handkerchief handed to him by the woman sitting in the next chair. Suddenly his image was shattered.

'Thank you,' he squeaked, pinching his nostrils.

'You're welcome.' She smiled.

She had long black hair, tied in a ponytail down her back. With her light golden complexion and bright blue eyes, Ron wasn't sure if she was wearing make-up or not. He couldn't help staring at her. Who was she with? he wondered.

'Nancy Kronziac,' she said, and spelt her surname for the record. A smile hovered on her lips. 'Federal Bureau of Investigation.'

Ron murmured to himself, 'A Fed . . . Jesus!'

'Thank you, ladies and gentlemen,' Willard said, the formalities over with. He turned to McKenzie. 'Bill, you wanna take it from here?'

McKenzie nodded and took out a small, thin manila folder.

'I want you to understand that this is only a

preliminary report and as such can only act as a brief outline of the events of flight 248 up to the point of impact. Nothing is written in stone and there is a long way to go in the investigation. So please bear with us.'

Downes sneezed again. Taylor loosened his tie. The rest of them took out their notepads as McKenzie put on his glasses, opened the folder and began.

BRANCH COPY – EYES ONLY

NATIONAL TRANSPORTATION SAFETY BOARD

OFFICE OF AVIATION SAFETY WASHINGTON, DC 20594

Preliminary investigation Report – DCB – 00 – G – 021 (Aero Centrale ACL248)

Team Leader: William McKenzie

Aircraft Type: BD-12 (B-series) Registration: N379AZ
Manufact: Drayton Industries. Fuselage No.: 311
                                  Stamp date: 3/24/1989
Powerplants: 2 x Juno AirMotive XD104
Capacity: 145 pass / 5 cabin / 2 flight

Tin Kickers

PREAMBLE

On 31 October flight ACL248 en route from Los Angeles International (LAX) to Mexico City (MEX) disappeared off Mexico Approach Radar at 00.27hrs (approx) PDT.

Wreckage of the plane was found on high terrain in the Sierra Madre mountain range at a point 780 miles (approx) north-west of Mexico City.

Most of the structure has been recovered, though is severely damaged by the impact and post-impact fire. Both flight recorders have been retrieved. The Cockpit Voice Recorder (CVR) is in good condition and has been reviewed by the investigation team. The Flight Data Recorder (FDR) is still in preparation at the NTSB Vehicle Performance Lab. Some slight water contamination has been detected and so the unit will be dried out in controlled conditions. It is, as yet, unknown when it will be possible to extrapolate the data streams.

EVENT SUMMARY

At 23.55hrs the commanding officer ordered shut down of the Auxiliary Power Unit (APU) in accordance with standard procedure as a fire warning was indicated on the light shield annunciator section. (The flight crew were not unduly alarmed as this had occurred on previous flights when the fire detection sensors had received several maintenance write-ups in recent weeks)

Bill Murphy

Several minutes later (exact time undetermined) an electrical malfunction interfered with some instrumentation. The cause or path unknown. Primary flight controls and instrumentation were, however, unaffected.

Soon after, the aircraft experienced a power anomaly and lost some airspeed and altitude. This was assumed by the senior officer to be an engine failure and to avoid possible fire damage an engine shut-down procedure was initiated.

However, due to the inital instrument malfunction the errant powerplant could not be readily identified. Commencing on a standard procedure the captain ordered engine No. 2 (starboard) to be closed off. He alerted Mexico ATC and was cleared to divert to Torreon International Airport, 380 miles (approx) south-east of their position. ACL248 was directed to turn left on to new heading and to make descent to 14,000 feet and maintain. However the plane continued to descend past 11,000 feet. Both crew members were unfamiliar with the new flight path but were cognisant of the high mountains in the area. Visibility of the terrain was restricted by a heavy cloud extending down to 10,000 feet. The plane continued to descend despite increasing throttle power and flaps extension. Realising he may have been flying on a damaged engine the captain tried to restart engine No.1 (port) in the hope of restoring altitude.

However at 00.27hrs the CVR ended coinciding with the aircraft's impact on the mountainside.

As he finished, McKenzie took off his glasses again and closed the folder. The room remained silent for a moment until Mahoney shook his head in disbelief. 'He shut off the wrong engine?' His eyes darted between the investigators. 'Juarez shut off the wrong engine?'

Everyone began shuffling in their seats. Downes' face reddened with anger at Mahoney's assumption.

'Now hold on a minute!' he barked.

Mckenzie put up his hand.

'All we are saying at this time is we believe from the inspection of the powerplants that the plane was running on an engine which seemed to be already damaged before impact.'

Downes raised his voice indignantly, compelled to protect the good name of his dead colleague. 'How can you be sure the wrong engine was shut down? Maybe they were both faulty. How can you be sure?'

'We can't.' Al shook his head.

'It's too early yet to be sure about anything,' added Ron.

'But you've had a chance to have a good look at the engines by now, surely?' Blair challenged, staring at Bob.

'Both powerplants have been examined,' he confirmed. 'The starboard engine seems to have been in good working order before point of impact, but the blades do not show signs of rotating at operational speed at the time of crashing.' He looked around the room. 'She was cold.'

'And the other engine?' asked Klein

'The port engine . . . the *damaged* engine,' Bob emphasised, 'was running full-on when they hit the ground suggesting, that they . . .' he hesitated, realising the gravity of what he was about to say '. . . that perhaps they were running on one damaged engine during descent. This might also explain why they couldn't maintain altitude even when they applied the throttle.'

Fucelli, feeling besieged, shook his head. 'But what sort of damage have you found in the port engine?'

'The fan disk and part of the turbine shaft failed sometime prior to impact,' Bob stated.

'Any idea of the cause?' Fucelli wanted to know. 'Bird ingest? Loose seals? Bearings?'

Bob just pursed his lips. 'Can't tell yet.' He shook his head.

Taylor, who had remained quiet throughout, bent forward.

'Has the shaft section been recovered?' he asked, his voice hoarse and gravelly.

'No,' Al replied, 'but there are still a lot of pieces on that mountainside.'

The questioning continued, each representative

concerned with their part of the plane, each fishing for as much information as possible to take back to their bosses to see if they would have to prepare a defence for their equipment or operations against possible allegations of negligence.

Blair wanted to know about the status of the airframe. McKenzie fielded that one.

'The integrity of the fuselage, wings and control surfaces seemed to have been intact prior to the collision,' he said. 'Of course, there isn't much left of anything to speak with any certainty on that.'

Blair continued to probe.

'So engine failure may be the major causal factor in this accident?'

This set the room alight.

'Wait just a goddam minute!' Fucelli shouted. 'It hasn't been proven that the engines were at fault here. Besides no one has said anything yet about maintenance.'

Klein shot a murderous look at Fucelli.

'I think the engine manufacturer is seeking to deflect blame on to others,' she retorted.

'What about the pilots?' Mahoney asked. 'The wrong engine was shut down after all.'

'Jesus, what've you got against the pilots?' Downes shouted at him. 'Have you no respect for the dead?'

They all began to argue, slinging accusations like mud at each other.

McKenzie shook his head.

'This was a bad idea,' he said.

Willard kept quiet, shocked at how the proceedings were degenerating.

Getting to his feet, Ron raised his voice above the rest. 'Please! Please!' he implored them.

Having secured their attention, he lowered his voice.

'Look, you've got to understand that it is too early in the investigation to be pointing the finger of blame at any particular cause or individual. We will be trying to do our best to find out exactly what happened and hopefully to prevent it from happening again. This is just a preliminary report and as such things are very sketchy for the moment.'

'What are you going to tell the press?' Fucelli wanted to know.

Ron looked at Willard. This was his department.

'Exactly what we've told you,' he said calmly. 'Everyone has the right to know. And,' he continued, 'I don't think that we have necessarily singled out anyone in the report.'

'That's bullshit,' snapped Downes, 'an' you know it.' He stared at McKenzie and then at Ron.

'Come on, you know the press are gonna see one thing and one thing only – pilot error, straight an' simple . . . the dead guy holding the stick.'

Ron had no reply. No one had.

Nancy Kronziac's voice broke the uncomfortable silence which had descended on the room.

'May I ask if you are considering any element of sabotage or foul play in the investigation?'

This was something that none of them had considered up until that point. But as special agent in the Domestic Terrorism Unit of the FBI Counterintelligence Group it was Kronziac's job to monitor NTSB Investigations to see if there was any sign of criminal activity which might have played a part in the crash.

'Right now we're treating it as a possible combination of human factors, weather conditions and mechanical difficulties,' McKenzie confirmed.

Kronziac nodded and closed her notepad, glad the Bureau would not be involved. The criminal investigation of air crashes mostly meant chasing the perpetrators through foreign courts, usually of countries hostile to any US intervention.

Willard seized the opportunity to wrap up the meeting.

'All right, ladies and gentlemen, thank you. I think that about does it for now. We will of course be keeping you informed of any new developments as soon as we have them.'

They rose from their seats and gathered up their notes and papers. Some of the lawyers were already tapping at their cell phones, calling their masters.

McKenzie rubbed his face, as if trying to wipe away the memory of the upsetting scene.

He leant close to Willard. 'That was getting ugly.'

Willard was inclined to agree, but said nothing, wondering what the press were going to be like.

THE SWANKY SCOUNDREL BAR, NORTH CAPITOL STREET

Ron and Al had taken up their usual position at the bar which was thronged with Government staffers relaxing after another long day grinding the wheels of the federal services. Bob made his way from the washroom through the crowd and took his seat, which no one else would even dare try to take. Ron called for a Scotch. After the briefing with the interested parties he felt he needed one. Bob and Al needed no such excuse and called two shots for themselves.

'What time's it on?' Al asked, looking at the TV above the bar.

'Pretty soon, I reckon,' said Ron as he glanced at his Rolex, a present from an ex-girlfriend who was a stew with Cathay Pacific and regularly brought him back exotic gadgetry from Hong Kong and Thailand. Fell off the back of a rickshaw, Bob would joke, doubting the watch's authenticity.

'Here it is.' He pointed at the screen.

The waitress dutifully upped the volume before they even asked. They were her most regular customers and they always tipped good, unlike the guys from the IRS who were suitably tight with their money.

On the screen a man appeared on a podium ready

for a live press conference for the local news channel. He looked very pale and drawn. The caption keyed in on the bottom of the screen named him simply as William McKenzie, NTSB. Willard sat in a chair in the background looking out at the assembled press.

As the reporters and photographers settled down McKenzie introduced himself and began reading out the salient points of the preliminary report. When he finished the usual clamour of questions ensued, each reporter vying for his attention. However one reporter screamed higher than the rest. As the camera swung to her Al excitedly pointed at the screen.

'That's her again . . . what's her name . . .'

Bob squinted at the TV.

'Shaw, I think. Yeah, that's it . . . Mary Shaw,' he confirmed.

They listened intently as she posed her question. Al felt like shouting, telling everyone in the bar to shut up.

Shaw held the microphone close to her lips.

'Can you confirm, sir, if the cause of the crash is directly attributable to pilot error?'

McKenzie shook his head, more in annoyance than denial. The newshounds had caught the scent.

'Ah, for Jesus' sake!' Al shouted at the TV.

McKenzie replied to the question in a strained, deliberate manner.

'We have nothing to add at this time other than the facts which I have already given in my statement

. . . and if you were listening,' he continued, 'you would know that nothing was mentioned about pilot error.'

Bob smiled. 'That's it, Bill, don't give the fuckers anything.'

Ron watched McKenzie intently, he'd never seen him so pale before. His boss had done plenty of news conferences in his time but Ron felt he was really straining under this one.

Shaw persisted with her questioning, shouting above the other reporters.

'Mr McKenzie, sir, can you confirm suggestions that the captain of ACL248 shut down the wrong engine?'

Al turned to Ron, his face stiff with shock and anger.

'How the fuck does she know about that?' he cried.

But Ron kept his eyes on the screen as McKenzie was visibly struggling to answer.

Al shook his head. 'How did she find that out? Nobody said anything about it.'

There was suddenly a commotion on screen as the TV camera swung from Shaw to the podium and then zoomed to the ground. McKenzie had collapsed. People rushed to his aid, crowding around his motionless body. Willard was shouting for a doctor.

GEORGE WASHINGTON UNIVERSITY HOSPITAL, 23rd STREET

Ron always hated hospitals, especially the hot smell of disinfectant that permeated the air. He made his way quickly to the ICU. It was even hotter in there. At the end of a row of gurneys he could see McKenzie prone on a bed, tubes up his nose, an IV strapped to his arm. A nurse was gently propping up his pillows. Willard was sitting in a chair nearby flicking distractedly through a magazine. He smiled when he saw Ron.

'Jesus, how is he?' Ron blurted as he stared at McKenzie's ashen face.

'He'll be okay,' said Willard, in a hushed voice. 'They said it was just a mild attack.'

'Attack?' Ron stuttered.

'Yeah, his heart,' said Willard. 'I guess the strain was building up.'

Ron went closer to the bed.

'Shit, he looks like hell,' he whispered.

The nurse turned to him and smiled.

'He can hear you, he's not asleep.'

McKenzie's eyes fluttered open as a weak smile curled his dry lips.

'Whadda ya mean, I look like shit?' he said, his voice brittle.

Ron leant closer.

'Hi, Bill. Took a bit of a tumble, eh?'

'Yeah, right in front of a coupla million people.'

'I always said you were a bit of an exhibitionist,' Ron laughed.

'Please, not too long,' the nurse warned as she checked the IV line. 'He's very weak.'

Willard nodded to her as she left to tend to the other patients in the unit, checking their charts and making them comfortable.

'This is probably a stupid question,' Ron said as he drew up a stool next to the bed, 'but how are you feeling?'

McKenzie closed his eyes momentarily as he struggled to move his legs.

'I'm okay now,' he said weakly. 'I'll live, though I dunno how. They're telling me I'll have to chuck the Cubans.'

Ron smiled. 'Think of the money you'll save on those suckers.'

Strength seemed to return to McKenzie for a moment as he held Ron by the arm. Willard stood up and came closer to the bed, wondering if something was wrong.

McKenzie lowered his voice to a murmur.

'Listen, Ron, I'm gonna be out of action for a bit . . .'

'You'll be back soon,' he interrupted.

'Just listen,' McKenzie blurted out, 'for Christ's sake!'

Ron was about to call the nurse only McKenzie

held him tight. 'I've just been talking with Willard about the case,' he said.

Ron shook his head. 'Forget the damn' case,'

'We can never forget the case, an' you know it. We never stop working the clues. It's in our blood.'

'Yeah, and look what it's done to you,' Ron retorted. 'You've gotta take it easy, Bill. Forget the case. We'll take care of it.'

'The Board wants you to take over,' McKenzie said.

Ron was shocked.

'What?'

'They want you to take over as lead investigator,' McKenzie confirmed.

'But I'm the youngest on the team. What about Bob or Al . . . or any of the others?' he insisted.

'Look, they want you. Willard got the word a few minutes before you came in.'

Ron looked around at Willard who was straining his ears to hear what they were saying.

Noticing what was going on, the nurse walked quickly up the ward to McKenzie's bed.

'Gentlemen, please, you'll have to leave. Mr McKenzie is very weak.'

'Okay, nurse.' Willard smiled. 'Come on, Ron.'

But McKenzie held on to his arm. His voice was weakening again but he had to say it.

'Don't take the job, Ron,' he warned. 'This is a messy one, stay out of it.'

The nurse moved between them, prising McKenzie's

hand away Ron. 'Come on now, please, he must get his rest, you'll have to leave,' she demanded.

McKenzie closed his eyes again, exhausted.

'Come on,' Willard urged as he led Ron out of the ward. He was still unable to comprehend what McKenzie had said to him.

'I gather he told you?' Willard said as they walked down the corridor.

Ron thought about it for a moment.

'Is it true?'

'Yeah, believe or not,' Willard confirmed. 'The Vice Chairman himself suggested you as Investigator-in-Charge and the other Board members went along with it.'

Ron stopped.

'Why?' he asked simply.

'Beats the fuck out of me. Guess they think you're solid material and the other – what do you call yourselves, tin kickers? – they seem to think highly of you, too. Who knows? Maybe you're a regular Columbo.'

'What if I say no?'

'What if you say no?' Willard repeated and laughed at the absurdity of the idea. 'What if you say no?' he said again, then stopped laughing. 'I don't think you have any choice in the matter.'

'Don't I get time to think about it?' Ron asked.

'Jesus, Ron, they ain't gonna put the investigation on hold while you try and get your head outa your ass and around this problem. We're talkin' about the lives of one hundred and forty-eight people here. It's a done deal, you're up.'

'Jesus,' was all Ron could say.

'One thing, though,' Willard warned.

'What now?'

'You gotta keep me informed of how things are going at all times. Any new developments and you sing to me. Everything.'

Ron nodded his head knowingly.

'I suppose the Board's appointed you my guardian angel?'

'Fuck, no.' Willard recoiled, 'I'm not gonna hold your hand through this. You've just gotta report to me, tell me what you're doing.'

'New procedures, right?' Ron smiled.

Willard nodded and smiled back.

'Right. Welcome to the programme.'

Ron shook his head in disgust as they continued down the corridor.

FAA OFFICES, HUMAN FACTORS STUDY GROUP, INDEPENDENCE AVE

Ron found Fred Stranski's door open and walked inside. The psychologist was lying straight as a plank on the floor, his jacket and shoes off, eyes firmly closed.

'Morning, Ron,' he said, not moving.

'Er . . . Hi, Fred, you okay?'

'Oh, don't mind me,' he replied. 'New relaxation technique a colleague suggested I try – supposed to induce a deeper state of rest. Could be good for pilots on long haul.'

Ron looked at him, puzzled.

'What's the secret, no pillow?' he joked.

Stranski tapped his head.

'Up here. You have to think of the most elaborate maze imaginable and find your way out. It's very relaxing actually. Anyway . . .' Stranski jumped to his feet. 'Congratulations,' he said as he put on his shoes. 'Sit down, sit down.'

'You heard,' said Ron, pulling up a chair.

'Sure, everyone's talking about it.'

'Yeah, great news,' Ron intoned flatly.

'Oh, sorry about Bill, by the way. I hear he's gonna be okay, though.'

'He should be fine,' Ron agreed, 'Just a bit strung out for the moment.'

'Well, it's understandable,' Stranski commented as he sat behind his desk.

'He's not the only one in shock.'

'Wanna talk about it?' Stranski asked with a mixture of concern and hope. He loved to analyse everything and everybody. The slightest little remark could set him off.

'Well,' Ron began reluctantly, 'I'm not sure what I can say. Shit, I'm not sure what to even *think*.'

'Come on Ron, you can't tell me you don't want the job, it'd do your career prospects a lot of good, that's for sure.'

'Would it?' asked Ron.

Stranski began to realise Ron's doubts were real.

'But surely McKenzie wouldn't drop you in it if he didn't think you were up to the job?'

'That's just it,' Ron sighed, 'It was the Board who gave me the nod, not Bill . . . he actually advised me against it.'

Stranski leant back on his seat.

'I guess they have more confidence in you than you think,' he suggested.

Ron remained silent, still wrestling with the doubts somewhere in his mind.

'I dunno Ron, it's up to you, I'm don't think I can help you here.'

'I know,' said Ron, setting aside the issue for the moment, 'There's something else you can help me with.'

He took out his little black notepad.

'Captain Luis Ramon Juarez, what can you tell me about him?'

As head of the Civil Aeromedical Institute's newly formed Human Factors and Cockpit Environment Study Group, Fred Stranski had information on every commercial pilot registered with the FAA.

He pulled out a file from a drawer beneath his desk.

'Yeah ... Juarez ... Juarez ... I was looking through his file yesterday.'

Opening it he pulled out a ten-by-eight of Juarez and handed it to Ron.

'Handsome fellow,' remarked Ron, looking at the photo.

Stranski scanned the front page of the file.

'Forty-six years old, recently divorced, two kids.' He ran his eyes further down the page. 'twenty-five years in the air, fifteen of them in command. An unblemished service record, valid first-class airman medical cert passed just five weeks previous with no restrictions. 20/20 distant and near vision without correction. CMR assessments – all favourable.' Putting down the file, he concluded, 'A very able pilot by all accounts.'

'You know, in some quarters he's the chief suspect,' said Ron, scribbling a few notes.

'I watch the news, there's a lot of speculation,' Stranski agreed gravely.

'But you haven't found anything to suggest there were any personal problems interfering with his ability to command the flight?' Ron queried.

Stranski stretched back in his chair.

'Well, it's possible that the divorce was on his mind – but that doesn't necessarily mean it was a major factor or even a contributory one in the events leading to the accident. You were a pilot yourself, Ron, and pilots have problems just like everyone else, right?'

He nodded. 'Yeah, sure.'

'So just because a pilot got out the wrong side of bed that morning,' Stranski continued, 'or didn't get a peck on the cheek from his wife, doesn't mean his plane is going to fall out of the sky. That's not our concern here.'

'What is?' Ron enquired, sensing something else was on Stranski's mind.

Stranski paused for a moment to consider what he was going to say.

'Pilots are what we call positive reactors,' he began. 'In other words they always do something in reaction to an event or crisis. They react immediately. When something goes wrong some people just cannot do anything about it – they are paralysed by their fear, frozen by the shock of the moment. But pilots, they react.'

Ron wasn't quite following.

'But we're trained to react,' he explained, 'it's our job . . . their job.'

Stranski smiled.

'Exactly,' he said, 'but that does not mean it's always right. Sometimes it's better *not* to react.

Sometimes it's better not to do anything at all until you're sure you know what's wrong.'

He could see by Ron's expression that he wasn't really buying this.

'Look, you've seen accidents that were caused by a rash decision, right?'

Ron was reluctant to concede this.

'Maybe,' was all he would say.

Stranski continued, 'Juarez did what his training told him to do.'

Ron nodded.

'I assume so.'

'He reacted swiftly and positively,' Stranski persisted.

'Yes . . . yes,' Ron said impatiently.

Stranski stopped for a moment.

'But he shut down the wrong engine,' he added, as if imparting a terrible truth.

Ron felt he was the sole defender of the dead pilot.

'But maybe he . . .' he struggled for the right defence '. . . just hadn't the luxury of time. Accidents have also been caused because nothing was done in time.'

'Maybe you're right, maybe he didn't have any time,' Stranski agreed, rather annoyingly.

'Maybe he just had no way of knowing which engine was at fault.'

'Maybe,' Stranski said again. 'Maybe.'

Ron felt as if Stranski was playing with him. He liked to do it, was always trying to get people to hang themselves. But there was always a purpose behind it. Stranski could be infuriating with his little games but there was always some reason.

'You think you've got me in a corner, don't you?' Ron asked.

'No,' Stranski replied frankly, 'but at least you're beginning to think.' He tapped the side of his head and then suddenly picked up a piece of paper and wrote something on it.

'Are you a gambling man, Ron?'

He smiled wearily, tired of the mind games.

'What do you mean?'

'Do you ever have a bet?'

Ron shrugged. 'I sometimes put a few bucks on the Redskins.' He looked at his watch. 'Listen, I got a lot of stuff to do today.'

Stranski folded the piece of paper.

'Pick a number from one to four,' he said.

'What's this? *Wheel of Fortune*?'

Stranski persevered. 'Please. Humour me. Pick a number from one to four. Quick, off the top of your head!'

'Jesus . . . three!' Ron snapped back.

Stranski slipped the piece of paper over the desk to Ron, an expectant smile on his face. 'Congratulations.'

Ron picked up the little square of folded paper and opened it. Scribbled on it was the figure three.

'So you're a clairvoyant,' said Ron as he rolled up the paper into a little ball.

'No,' Stranski replied, 'just a keen observer: 65 percent of people asked that question answer three. You see, they hear the numbers 1, 2 and 4 – pick a number one-to-four, and they pick three, the one they didn't hear. Everyone tries to be a smart ass, even in their subconscious.'

'Wow, spooky. But what the hell's it got to do with anything?' Ron wanted to know.

'There are four possibilities, Ron, like the four corners of a square, four corners for the clues to hide in. Don't back yourself into just one. You have to search them all, all the angles. You owe it to the people who died on that plane to ask all the questions, the right questions.'

Ron thought about it for a moment.

'All the angles, right?'

Stranski smiled.

'All the angles.'

The sky was brightening with patches of pallid blue emerging from behind thick ribs of cloud. Ron breathed in the crisp morning air as he walked back to his car outside the FAA building. He took out his cell phone and dialled the office. A familiar voice answered.

'Hi, Carol . . . it's Ron. I'm just coming outa Stranski's. Can you tell the boys to meet me in McKenzie's office . . . yeah, I mean my office in, say . . .' he looked at his watch '. . . forty minutes. I should be there by then, I've gotta go see someone first. Thanks.'

ANN STUDIOS, 13TH STREET AND
NEW YORK AVENUE

WE GET THERE FIRST was emblazoned in sparkling chrome letters above the reception desk. A row of TVs showing several different channels blinked beneath a bigger monitor which showed the well-known face of Ernie Saunders, the station's longest running topical news show host. They were just breaking for a commercial as a flashy ad for Nike swept across the screen.

'Yes, sir, can I help you?' The girl behind the desk displayed a row of white teeth at Ron.

'Mary Shaw, please.' He smiled back.

'And your name, sir?'

'Ron Carter. From the NTSB.'

She smiled again. 'The NTSB?'

He was tempted to say *National Trading Standards Bureau*, which always seemed to freak people out. It was one of Al's favourites.

'She'll know who I am.'

'Yes, sir,' she replied and called Shaw on the switchboard.

Ron waited no more than fifteen seconds before a young man opened a large door to the side of the reception desk. He smiled at Ron and motioned for him to follow.

*   *   *

The studios were a labyrinth of narrow corridors lined with offices, glass booths and editing suites. Studio hands hurried to and fro, carrying video tapes and props. The walls displayed photographs of some of the network's most famous presenters and their even more famous guests. At the end of each corridor, bracketed high on the wall, was a monitor showing commercials.

'You recording at the moment?' Ron asked.

'Yeah, Ernie Saunders, he's going out live right now,' the kid replied, as if it was the coolest thing in the world.

'Really?' Ron tried to sound impressed. He hated Ernie Saunders, who bugged the shit out of him.

'Actually we're going through the viewing booth now,' the young man said as he pushed open a door which led them into a room lined with seats like a tiny movie theatre. Ron instinctively crouched down as he crossed the room, thinking he might be in someone's line of sight. But there was hardly anyone there, just a couple of restless kids with their mother and a man in a dark suit standing near the back, the lights of the studio reflecting in his glasses.

The studio hand stopped. 'Well, there it is,' he said. 'Live TV.'

Ron peered out though the glass panels which looked out over the studio. In the white glare of the lights the set looked pathetically fake and wooden. Ernie Saunders, in the flesh, sat around a table with two others. He turned as a man behind one of the cameras counted down his fingers to signal the live feed.

'Hello and welcome back to the show,' Saunders addressed the camera. 'Today I'm talking with Senator Phillip Mayhew, Republican candidate in the upcoming Illinois Governorship; Miss Lindy Tate, Director of the Workers' Rights Bureau at the King Institute of Human Affairs; and with us in New York, Jim Layton, Deputy Secretary at the Department of Transportation.'

Live by TV link Layton smiled from his little box perched behind the others. Ron had met him once at a party in the DOT. He seemed all right, a bit of a brown nose maybe, but all right.

Saunders turned to Mayhew. A thickly set man, with an angular jaw, he met Saunders' gaze with a look of studied sincerity.

'Can I ask you, Senator,' Saunders began, 'if you believe that your bill on Workers' Protection will gain enough support in the Upper House to carry it through?'

Mayhew cupped his hands like a preacher about to sermonise.

'Well, Ernie, I believe that every representative, from whichever party, is interested in protecting the rights of the American worker.'

He paused for a moment before continuing. 'Contrary to popular belief we have seen a decline in productivity in this country due to varying reasons. But what this bill seeks is to redress the balance by US companies again taking pride in indigenous American workmanship . . .'

'But will the Government back the bill?' Saunders interrupted, turning to the TV screen.

Layton shook his head.

'The administration's position on this is one of mediation. We have to examine the facts as presented to us. It's really our job to ensure that everyone gets a fair deal. We will do everything to protect jobs but we must also protect the basic human rights of foreign workers here.'

'Come on,' the stage hand urged Ron, 'Miss Shaw will be waiting.'

As they opened the door to exit on the other side of the viewing room another man with tight silver hair abruptly came through. He apologised as he brushed past Ron and walked to the back of the room.

The kid led Ron down another corridor to a door marked 'Edit Suite 3A'. After knocking he opened it and introduced Ron to the blonde woman sitting at a mixing desk.

'Hello, Mr Carter,' Mary Shaw said, hardly taking her eyes off the news footage rolling in fast motion across a screen in front of her.

'Good morning.' Ron offered his hand.

'Congratulations are in order, I believe?' She curled the side of her mouth in a sly little smile. 'Heard you been bumped up to lead the 248 case. I thought they'd get a more senior man for the job.'

Ron noticed a faint smirk on the face of the kid who hovered by the door like a bell boy.

'Okay, thanks, Cal,' Shaw dismissed the young man who hurried off down the corridor in search of another errand.

Shaw looked up from her desk at last. She gave Ron a quick once over which he found surprisingly embarrassing. It must have showed.

'Well, what can I do for you?' she smiled, almost purring.

'The news conference yesterday . . .' he began.

'Yeah, how's McKenzie? Hope it wasn't anything to do with my questions,' she said, her smile lingering.

Though attractive, Ron found her features surprisingly soft, almost child-like.

'Well, that's what I wanted to talk to you about,' he began. 'You obviously had a tip off that pilot error was suspected to be the cause of the crash.'

Her smile disappeared.

'Maybe it was just a hunch, reporter's intuition,' she replied.

But Ron wasn't biting.

'Come on,' he laughed, 'who gave you the word?'

Shaw resisted. 'I'm really not at liberty to discuss such things, Mr Carter.'

'Well, it would be very helpful to know if we had a leak in the team or if one of the interested parties gave you the information.'

'And you want me to finger my source?'

Ron decided honesty at this point was his only option.

'Well . . . yes,' he answered, 'I would appreciate it.'

It was Shaw's turn to probe.

'Would your appreciation allow you to – how shall we say? – be more amenable to giving us special insight into the investigation?' she probed, sniffing at a possible lead.

Ron smiled. The game was tied.

'Miss Shaw,' he said, 'it is now our policy to co-operate with the media as closely as possible. New procedure,' he added, sounding like Willard.

Shaw fought to contain herself.

'You are the man to talk to now aren't you? The IIC on the 248 case? Would you give me a personal interview?' He could almost see her nose twitching, sniffing for a possible lead. McKenzie always said the press were like dogs – one dog barks at something and the rest bark at him, and they could make a hell of a lot of noise. Ron had no definite answer to any of her questions.

'Perhaps,' he said.

'Perhaps?'

'Maybe. Who tipped you off?' he shot back.

Shaw remained quiet for a moment.

'I don't know,' she confessed. 'It was an anonymous call made to the station. No name given.'

'And you acted on it, without any confirmation?' he pushed.

'Hey, I was right, wasn't I?' she retorted. 'I mean, pilot error *is* being considered as the cause? Is Juarez the main focus of the investigation? Did he shut down the wrong engine?'

Ron pulled back, the game suddenly over.

'I'm sorry, Miss Shaw, I'm not at liberty to discuss this further.'

'But you are considering it,' she persisted, 'why else would you be here?'

Ron opened the door to leave.

'So what about that interview?' she asked. 'It could make things easier for you to work with us on this!' she shouted after him.

But he was gone.

As Ron made his way through the viewing booth he didn't bother to stop this time to watch the show. Lindy Tate, a mountain of a woman with a booming voice, was holding the floor, taking on the US Government no less.

'What Mr Layton and his people do not realise,' she pointed out, 'is that this bill is a clever piece of legislation aimed at maintaining the power of the large industrial companies in the west and mid-west – Senator Mayhew's back yard, in fact,' she added, eyeing him with disdain, 'and will lead to a further downgrading in the status and rights of the immigrant worker upon whom, it must be said, this country depends . . .'

NTSB OFFICES, INDEPENDENCE AVE

Carol Cummings had just sat down at her desk with a fresh cup of coffee and was about to start on a mound of dictation when Ron swung through the doors.

'Morning, Ron,' she greeted him cheerily, expecting the usual banter about the traffic or the weather that he would engage in with her every morning.

'The others here?' he asked impatiently.

'Yeah . . . all in your office,' she stuttered, surprised at his gruffness. 'Though I haven't seen Mr Willard. Do you want me to page him?'

Ron just shook his head.

'Don't bother,' he said, about to go through to his office. But before he went he stopped and turned around, a thoughtful expression on his face.

'Oh, Carol, can you get me a transcript of the prelim meeting with the interested parties?'

'Er . . . sure.'

Four of the investigating team were sitting around the table which McKenzie used for progress briefings. He would usually sit at the top end, chewing on his cigar, and bark out directions or suggestions as to how the investigation should be carried out. In the moment before the other men realised he was there, Ron took a deep breath, as if to dispel the doubts within himself. He still wasn't sure if he wanted the job. He had made a big mistake by going to see Shaw.

Bob looked up.

'Hey, hey, it's the big chief.' He smiled broadly. 'Late for his own meeting.'

The others clapped. Gordie hummed a pathetically discordant 'Hail to The Chief'.

'What do we call you now? . . . Sir? . . . Mr Carter?' Al joked.

'How about *El Gran Señor*?' Jerry bellowed out as if it was hilarious.

'What the fuck is that – *El Gran Signor*?' asked Al. He always took Jerry up on his bad jokes.

'You know,' he explained, 'this whole Mexican thing.'

Al shook his head. The others laughed again.

Bob stood up and with mock formality led Ron to McKenzie's chair. 'Okay, let's see if your ass's big enough.'

He afforded them a slight smile and tried to hide his embarrassment. It felt so strange having to boss these guys around.

'All right, gentlemen, let's get to business,' he said, as he sat down.

They each settled down and opened their pads and folders. Ron felt like a teacher commencing class.

'Okay, Jerry, you first, what ya got?'

He shuffled through his notes, which were strewn haphazardly across the table.

'We've recovered the engines and they've both been safely transported back to Del Piero Air Force Base,' he began. 'I have given engine No. 1 a thorough inspection and can confirm that there was a fan disk failure which led to the ejection of the disk and part of the turbine shaft section from the engine.'

'Any clue as to how it came off?' Ron queried.

Jerry shrugged.

'No, not yet,' he said. 'Of course metal fatigue is an obvious possibility so I'll be doing a fracture analysis and a thermal image.'

Using highly sophisticated heat-sensitive equipment the tiniest of cracks, smaller than one hundredth of a millimetre, could be identified. A pattern of these would indicate metal fatigue which accounted for most structural failures in an aircraft.

'Do everything on it,' Ron commanded. 'UV, dye tests, the works.'

Jerry gave a slight nod of the head.

'Okay.'

Ron could feel the others looking at him. He wondered for a moment if he was overdoing it. He couldn't forget that each of these men had more experience than he and knew their patience would quickly wear thin if they thought he didn't know what he was doing. Friendship wouldn't enter in to it. There would be too much at stake.

'What about the missing fan disk?' he asked.

'Greg and Pete are still down there,' Jerry answered.

Ron pointed at a map of the crash site which was pasted to the wall.

'Tell them to go back along the flight path if they have to,' he insisted. 'Ten, twenty miles, run it through Windfall.'

Windfall was a special program developed to simulate on a computer the trajectory of a falling object, taking into account wind conditions, height and the weight of the object.

Jerry nodded and made a note. It would be a big undertaking to try and search that area.

Ron turned to Bob.

'What's the news on the APU?'

'Jerry is sending the detector rod up to LA,' Bob answered.

'Maybe we could use a lab in California to run the test,' Ron suggested, 'rather than having to ship everything back here – how about the FBI? They've got a facility out there in LA.'

The other investigators remained silent, not really sure if that was a good idea.

'We've also begun stripping out the electrical system at Hidalgo del Piero . . . or what's left of it,' Bob offered rather ominously.

'All right, good,' said Ron as he scribbled the words 'detector rod' in his notebook.

'Okay, Al! What about the maintenance records?'

Al began picking up heavy black binders from beneath the table. Each had the GenAir logo on the front. He piled them on the table one on top of another until they formed a mini tower block of information charting the maintenance history of the aircraft, right down to its rolling out papers.

'The plane has a good record,' he stated, a little amazed by the fact. 'It was in service with United for a long time so was kept in pretty good condition.'

Each of the men picked up one of the folders and began flicking through.

'It had no serious write-ups and manufacturer's service bulletins were addressed. All FAA applicable ADs were complied with – well, at least to the minimum requirement.'

'Typical,' Gordie said, rolling his eyes.

Some of the smaller airlines, to save money, usually complied with Airworthiness Directives issued by the FAA to the minimum degree only. Even some of the larger airlines had a sometimes worrying policy of 'minimal adherence'.

'There were just a few minor carry-over items, nothing alarming. The workcards for the last round of "C" and "Q" checks were in order,' Al went on.

'"C" checks were carried out on aircraft in four inspections, each after 1,150 hours of service. The more comprehensive "Q" check was carried out after the regulated 11,000 hours or 42 months. There were other checks which varied in detail and frequency.'

'What about the company?'

'Well,' said Al, 'their maintenance programme is approved and certified under FAA regulation 121 and they have a good record too,' he added, almost surprised. 'The engineering staff there seem competent enough. I talked to the two technicians who worked on 248 the day of the crash . . .'

He looked at his report for confirmation of the names.

'. . . a John Marx, the super who signed off the work, and a younger guy, Paul Edmunsen. They seem to think the recurrent problem with the detector was because of a faulty batch from the manufacturer.'

Bob snorted. 'Well, they would say that, wouldn't they?'

Ron wrote down Marx's name and underlined 'detector rod'. 'Did you ask them about the day of the accident?' he asked Al.

'Yeah,' he confirmed. 'They said Juarez was into them three times, said he was anxious, very anxious.'

'Eager to get off the ground, I suppose,' offered Jerry, understanding the pressure on pilots not to miss their slot.

'Maybe too eager,' added Gordie in a half whisper.

'Is that it?' said Ron, ignoring Gordie's comment.

Al nodded slowly, 'Yeah, basically.'

Ron picked up on Al's reticence.

'You don't seem too convinced.'

'I just wanna talk to those guys again, clear something up,' he said.

'Okay, keep me posted,' said Ron, and turned to Gordie, hope in his eyes.

Gordie began his answer before even being asked.

'I've run the CVR through the egg-scrambler and isolated the signals from the ambient wall . . . it's really hard, though,' he began, rubbing his forehead in frustration. 'They were old microphones they had in the cockpit, not very sensitive, more feedback than a Hendrix lick . . .'

'Okay, just tell me what you got,' Ron interrupted.

Al glanced at Bob. They'd never seen Ron so edgy.

Gordie took out a pocket Sony tape-player and pressed the play button. The little speaker buzzed with noise and then the pilots' voices crackled into life.

'I've picked up an unidentified noise approximately twenty-two minutes before the end,' said Gordie, placing the whirring tape-player in the middle of the table. They all leant closer.

'Here it comes,' he said and turned up the volume. Between the distorted voices there was a sudden sharp click.

'There!' Gordie exclaimed and turned the sound down.

Bob look puzzled.

'Sounds like a switch or something.'

Gordie turned the tape-player off and put it back in his pocket again.

'I'll run it through the egg-scrambler again at another frequency and see if I can find a match with any of the circuit breakers,' he said, adding with a sigh, 'it's gonna' take some time, though.'

'Do whatever you can,' urged Ron. 'Now tell me the FDR is ready?' he said hopefully.

Gordie shook his head and apologised.

'Jesus, Gordie!'

The others were shocked at Ron's impatience.

'We're working on it as fast as we can,' Gordie pleaded, 'but we have to be careful drying it out.'

Ron calmed himself down. Getting angry wasn't going to help matters.

'Okay, okay,' he said, 'I'm sorry. Just let me know as soon as it's ready.'

Gordie nodded affirmatively. 'You got it.'

Carol tapped on the door and entered carrying a bundle of read-out paper.

''Scuse me, Ron.' She came in and handed him the read-out, giving her usual obliging smile. 'The transcript of the prelim you wanted.'

He took it eagerly.

'Yeah, thanks, Carol,' he said, already running through the lines of recorded conversation from the meeting with the interested parties.

Sensing the general air of seriousness Carol beat a hasty retreat and closed the door firmly behind her.

Ron remained silent, closely studying the paper before him as if oblivious to the other men in the room.

'Listen, I gotta get going,' said Jerry. 'Gotta see a man about an engine,' he added, trying to lighten the mood.

'Yeah, me too,' said Gordie, seizing his chance. 'I'd better see how the FDR is doing.'

They both gathered their paperwork and exchanged puzzled looks with Al and Bob who were mystified by Ron's behaviour.

'Right, yeah, thanks, guys,' he said as they were just going out of the door. 'We'll talk again soon,' he added, still poring over the transcript.

'Ron, are you okay?' Bob asked, getting worried.

'You know you can talk to us. I mean, we're still buddies, right?' Al said, fearing Ron's new appointment had somehow sent him off the deep end. 'We don't want you ending up like Bill.'

Ron looked up at them.

'I went to see that reporter,' he began, 'about the leak, but she said she didn't know who it came from.'

'Leak?' Al's brow creased. Maybe his friend *was* going mad. 'Leak? In here?' he asked again.

'You don't think it came from one of the boys?' cried Bob, horrified by the idea.

Ron thought about it for a moment.

Al's frown deepened.

'One of us?' he asked. 'No, of course not.' Ron dismissed it from his mind. 'It was probably one of the interested parties at the prelim. At least, that's the only other possibility.'

Al decided they should go with Ron on this. Humour him, at least for a while.

'Well, who has the most to gain from the accident

being blamed on pilot error and was at the meeting?' he wondered.

'There was the airline,' suggested Bob.

Ron shook his head.

'No . . . they wouldn't want to look as if they employ incompetent pilots.'

Al felt a little stupid and hung his head, thinking about the possibilities more deeply.

'And it certainly wasn't Captain Marvel . . . what's his name? The Pilots' Association guy,' said Bob.

'No, probably not,' agreed Ron.

'Nor the FBI honey,' Al added, remembering Agent Kronziac.

'So who've we got?' Ron scanned the transcript, hoping for some clues.

'The manufacturer? The engine maker?' suggested Bob.

Ron spotted something.

'Or the maintenance company,' he uttered excitedly. 'Listen to this . . . Jerry had just said that the port engine showed signs of blade damage. Fucelli then asked what caused the failure, a bird ingestion or a loose seal. Jerry replied that he couldn't say. Then,' Ron emphasised, '*then* Taylor asked had the missing shaft component been recovered?'

He looked up from the transcript, searching the faces of Bob and Al, wondering if the same conclusion had dawned on them.

'"*Has the missing shaft component been recovered?*"' he echoed Taylor's words.

Al and Bob stared blankly at him, unable to get the significance.

'Can't you see?' Ron tried again, like an excited kid. 'Taylor asked had the shaft been found.'

'Yeah . . . and?' Al said, completely lost.

Bob leant forward.

'No one had said anything about it being missing,' he exclaimed, smiling at the realisation.

Ron nodded, smiling also.

'Right,' he said, almost wanting to hug Bob. 'All we said was that there was damage in the compressor. No one ever said that the fan disk or parts of the shaft were actually missing. Hell, we weren't even sure ourselves what damage was done.'

Al stared intently at the transcript in front of Ron.

'Maybe he just assumed it.' He shrugged, 'I dunno . . . it's not that unreasonable. I mean, what you're saying is that he knew about the cause of the engine failure . . . Christ! Even before we did?'

'I'm not saying anything,' Ron replied, realising himself it was all bit shaky, 'but I think we should go and have another talk with Taylor and his people.'

He scribbled in his notebook the word 'GENAIR', and noticed his hand was trembling with excitement.

As they came out of the office Willard was standing by Carol's desk reading some messages. He seemed surprised, even a little suspicious.

'You guys had a meeting without me?' he asked, wounded.

'Where were you?' retorted Ron, figuring attack was the best defence.

'Over with the Chairman,' Willard answered.

The Chairman of the Board had a plush office at the top of the building in L'Enfant Plaza, complete with en suite bathroom with a panoramic view over the city.

'You're supposed to keep me informed at all times,' Willard said.

Ron replied, 'We tried to reach you,' with fake earnestness.

Carol buried her head deep, staying well out of it.

Willard calmed himself, restraining an overpowering urge to bawl Ron out – he knew it wouldn't get him anywhere, just deeper into conflict.

'Look, I suggest we have a sit down, run over the game plan.'

Ron smirked. 'Game plan?'

'Yeah, maybe first thing in the morning?' suggested Willard.

Ron shook his head.

'Sorry, can't.'

'Look, Ron . . .' Willard was rapidly losing his cool.

'I'm moving the investigation to the LA field office in Gardena,' declared Ron matter-of-factly, covering up the fact that he had just decided this.

'You are?' said Bob, disbelieving his ears.

All Al could do was laugh. He liked the idea of moving out of the cold Washington winter to the balmy climes of California. But Willard began smiling.

'They're full up in LA with on-going investigations and . . .' his smile began to broaden '. . . I believe their offices are being redecorated.'

Ron stared at Willard for a moment, then turned to Carol.

'See if we can set up a field office by tomorrow. With the DOT, the FAA, the Justice Department, an empty hangar at LAX . . . wherever.'

Carol just nodded. No use asking questions.

As Ron turned to go, Willard stopped him, grabbing him by the arm. 'You're not serious?' he said tersely.

'We're too isolated here,' replied Ron, breaking free from Willard's grasp.

'You can't do this,' he insisted as Ron walked away.

'Yeah I can,' Ron turned around, 'I am the Investigator-in-Charge here . . . aren't I?' he said, asking himself the question as much as Willard. Willard searched his face for any signs of doubt, then nodded, almost smiling.

'I guess you are.'

Ron's mind was made up. The case was his.

He headed down the corridor, the others following.

Al turned to Bob and asked him, just loud enough for Willard to hear, 'Have they got snakes in LA?'

'Oh, fuck you!' Willard shouted after them.

CORNER OF SUNSET AND VINE, HOLLYWOOD, CA

Julie leant against the wall and spat out the taste of her last trick. She closed her eyes and squeezed the $50 bill she had in her pocket. It was worth it . . . it was worth it, she recited to herself, like a mantra to ward off terrible doubts. The other girls had warned her about it. Don't ever do it without a rubber, they'd tell her. Shit. She had no choice. Rent was due and the landlord was one mean fucker.

She opened her eyes again and was about to leave when a small white car pulled up, crawling to a stop. She looked down the street which was quiet now save for the odd car flashing through the intersect. The other girls had finished for the night and the sidewalk was almost empty. A drunk lay like a heavy sack against a shop doorway, a bottle smashed in shards beside him. Some garbage bum with a trolley was tearing at the slashed seam of a plastic sack outside the old diner.

One more? she asked herself. Might as well. It had been a good night.

She walked over to the car, her high heels stabbing the concrete. The window was down and the man inside was staring straight ahead.

'Ten bucks and I'll give you hand,' she began, 'forty for the full bacon and fifty for a blow. The back door is shut though, honey, you'll have to try out by the airport for that kinda shit.'

He remained quiet, gazing ahead as if mulling over the options in his head.

'The silent type, huh? Well, screw you, buddy,' she said and was about to take off when he turned, smiled and produced two wrinkled twenties from his jacket. He leant over and clicked open the door. Julie paused for a second before getting in, looking down the street once more. The tail lights of other cars faded away like red eyes in the distance, dissolving in the city's sullen gloom.

FEDERAL BUILDING, WILSHIRE BLVD, LOS ANGELES, CA

Carol led the way, carrying a box of her favourite desk items: her Rolodex, pen carrier, framed photograph of her little niece and a postcard of a half-naked Adonis on a beach in Crete. Ron and Al followed, struggling under heavy boxes of paperwork.

'How did you manage this?' Al asked, looking around the splendid interior of the foyer.

Ron didn't know. 'Ask Carol, she arranged it all.'

'This was the only Federal office space available,' she answered. 'Besides a girlfriend of mine is a PA to the Deputy Director.'

'Well, however you swung it, well done,' Ron congratulated her.

Carol had an uncanny knack for seeking things out: finding crucial reports from the seemingly impossible labyrinth of technical archives which the investigators needed for research; getting them the best motels in the most out of the way places.

A tall man in a white shirt, dark tie and pants, an ensemble which seemed to be the uniform of all the people in the building, came towards them with a well-practised smile.

'You must be from the NTSB?' he greeted them, taking Carol's box from her.

'How did you know?' asked Al. 'All the paperwork?

There's a van load of it outside,' he said, his voice shaky from the weight of his box.

The well-dressed man just smiled.

'I'm Special Agent Jones. On behalf of Assistant Director in Charge Foley I'd like to welcome you to the Federal Building,' he said, like a charming maître d'.

'Sounds like a friggin' hotel,' Al whispered to Ron.

'Ron Carter,' he said, managing to extend his hand.

Jones led them to the elevator. 'Please follow me and I'll show you to your new home.'

The seventeenth floor of the building was covered in a deep blue carpet which imbued the FBI offices with a atmosphere of hushed silence almost like a church. Ron, Al and Carol followed Jones, looking like tourists gazing up at the splendour of the Sistine Chapel.

'So this is where all the federal funding goes,' remarked Al, vaguely resentful.

'I think I'll put in for a transfer to the FBI,' said Carol, watching Jones from behind

'Here we are.' He stopped. 'I hope you'll be comfortable.'

The office was spacious, immaculately clean, with polished desks and potted yuccas by the wall.

Carol sat down at the desk in the middle of the floor and ran her fingers over the keys of a spanking white computer terminal. She began unpacking immediately, making the place her own.

'This is your office, Mr Carter.' Jones directed Ron to a smaller room in the corner. 'I thought you might like the view,' he added.

Ron placed his box of files on the desk and looked out of the tinted glass. A bright haze hung over the city, stretching a light golden veil from the Palisades to the basin of Long Beach. Here – here he felt he could start finding the right answers, or at least start asking the right questions.

He watched the aircraft gliding in from the sea to LAX like heavy metallic birds, their silver wings glinting in the sunlight.

'I'll be just down the hall if you need anything,' Jones said as he turned out of the door.

'Thanks,' Ron said and opened the box on his desk.

Lying on top of the files was the picture of Captain Luis Juarez.

OLD OAK ROAD, GLENDALE, CA

Morning in LA opened with a light drizzle which slicked the roads in a thin oily lather. Ron had forgotten how big this city was. He checked the address once more and halted the car outside a large bungalow partially obscured by a lush overhang of palms which dripped with rainwater.

On the porch lay a black Labrador, eyeing the stranger with nothing more than a mildly inquisitive look before dozing off again.

After pressing the door bell Ron could hear movement inside, someone coming down the stairs. The latch snapped and a dark-haired woman appeared from behind the door. Dressed in a thick gown, her hair tumbling in knots about her shoulders, Ron realised he had gotten her out of bed. She looked at him as if trying to recognise an old friend through a crowd.

'Mrs Juarez?' Ron asked.

She nodded vaguely.

'I'm Ron Carter, with the NTSB. I talked to you on the phone yesterday,' he said as gently and politely as he could.

She nodded again and forced a weak smile. Her face was pale but quite beautiful, her skin tight and drawn over her fine features. Her eyes were dark, sunken, with red rims as if stung by many tears.

'Of course, Mr Carter, please . . .'
She opened the door wide to let him in.

The house was dim, the blinds drawn on most of the windows, almost as if it hadn't been lived in for some time.

'Please sit down, Mr Carter.' She directed him to a chair by the fireplace in the living room.

'Thank you,' he said politely.

'Can I get you anything? Coffee? Tea? Some juice?' she asked, her voice weak with exhaustion.

'No, thank you,' Ron replied, 'I'm sorry to have disturbed you so early.'

'No, no,' she insisted, 'I'm usually up well before now, it's just . . .' She paused. 'I'm not sleeping very well these nights and my younger son is staying with my sister at the moment. He's still in school,' she said as she went out to the kitchen.

Feeling uncomfortable and strangely nervous Ron stood up and looked about the room. The pine shelves were lined with pilot's manuals and navigation books. A glass cabinet under the window displayed a legion of trophies, many with little silver airplanes on the top. Standing on the mantelpiece over the fireplace there was a small model of an old Sopwith Camel, finely carved in wood, complete with nylon struts and rubber wheels. Next to it was a picture of the family. Ron picked it up, staring at Juarez, his wife and their two sons, smiling out at the world.

'Are they going to blame Luis for the crash?' Mrs

Juarez asked blankly as she came back in, a cup of steaming black coffee in one hand, a packet of cigarettes in the other.

She sat down, carefully placing her cup on the carpet. Ron was caught a bit off guard, not really knowing what to say in reply.

She looked up at him, her eyes narrowed, intense, pleading.

'Are they going to blame him?' she asked again.

Ron felt she deserved an honest answer.

'I don't know,' he said.

She looked away, searching her pockets for a match.

'They seem to think he did it,' she said, lighting up.

'Who?' Ron asked.

She smiled at him, wondering if he was playing stupid or just innocent.

'The news people,' she replied wearily, 'the FAA, the airline, the families . . . you.'

She took a deep drag, knowing he wouldn't have an answer. Ron shook his head, avoiding her gaze.

'Nothing has been proven,' he mumbled.

He shouldn't be here, he thought to himself. Another bad idea.

'He was a good pilot,' she announced, suddenly standing up and taking the photograph from the mantelpiece. 'Wasn't easy to live with,' she went on, 'could be a son of a bitch sometimes. But then, I was no saint myself,' she added, her smile falling away.

Ron was looking at another photograph. An old

black and white of a group of young men in jump suits with thick hairstyles from the seventies.

'Where's this?' he asked, picking it up.

Mrs Juarez came closer to him and stared at the old photograph in his hands.

'Flying school,' she confirmed, pointing to a sign behind the group.

'GOLD WINGS FLYING CLUB,' Ron read out the words.

Her face began to brighten, fond memories seeping back.

'The happiest days of his life, I reckon. He was always talking about them. That's where he first learnt to fly.'

Ron examined the planes in the background, old Cessnas and Air Force trainers, lined up in formation on a sandy strip.

'Where was it? The club?'

Mrs Juarez shrugged, pulling on her cigarette.

'Don't know exactly. Somewhere out in the desert, near Barstow, I think.'

Ron stared at the photo, remembering his own early flying days.

'May I borrow this?' he asked, not really knowing why he wanted it.

She thought about it for a moment, looking about the room, at the books, the trophies and the model planes.

She smiled sadly. 'You can keep it if you want,' she said. 'It's no use to me.'

INTERSTATE 15, BETWEEN BARSTOW AND BAKER, CA

Ron was glad to extricate himself from the convoy of eighteen-wheelers that thundered along the highway like racing metal monsters devouring the miles of road. His Buick glided down an off-ramp, its tyres sticking to the clammy tar. The clouds had melted away leaving only an empty gold-white sky and the road ahead, straight and narrowing to the horizon, seemed to swim beneath a shimmering tide of heat waves. The land was a reflection of the sky, a pale sandy brown, dotted by a few large oil tanks and a lurid Exxon sign over a filling station.

'Shit!' Ron said, glancing at his map and wiping a line of sweat from his forehead. Not long to Christmas and this place was like an oven. A sign indicating the Gold Wings Flying Club floated by, attached rather precariously to a scorched wooden post. Above him he could hear the drone of a heavy turbo-prop, its engines biting the pallid desert sky. He knew he was getting close.

The car phone purred, its shrill startling Ron from the daze which the hot monotony of the endless road was luring him into.

'Hello,' he said hoarsely, snatching the phone from its holder.

It was Carol, her voice distant and crackling. She

wanted to know where he was – there were messages from Washington, Willard hadn't stopped calling wondering what the hell was going on, Bob and Al were looking for him, as were Greg and Pete down in Mexico, and a reporter from ANN had called several times.

'Everyone's been looking for you,' she said, annoyed she didn't have an answer for them.

'I'm in hell,' Ron answered, not joking.

'Where?' Carol asked, the line bad.

Ron followed another sign which pointed up a dry dirt track. He could see a few sheds huddled together, a tower sticking up out of the middle of them. The sun was reflected in sparks of light on the fuselages of small planes that lined an airstrip.

'I'm not sure what time I'll be back, maybe tonight,' he said hastily. 'I'll get on to them tomorrow,' he added, swinging the car off the dirt track, the wheels grinding through the hard sand.

'Okay, Ron,' was all Carol said. 'I'll talk to you tomorrow.'

The line went dead and he halted the car. Turning the engine off, he could hear a slight wind sifting through the buildings, whistling through the cracks in the windows. There was something cinematic about the place. He fully expected Clint Eastwood to round the corner in a swirl of dust, his guns smoking. He got out of the car and walked behind the buildings. A door creaked with the wrenching sound of rusted metal. There were a dozen or so planes in various stages of neglect, old crop dusters and a couple of well-used Cherokees. He was reminded of the boneyards of Arizona where thousands of aircraft from Starfighters to B-52s lined the desert, slowly dying in the vapid air, grounded spirits of a phantom air force. The wind died down as he reached the hangar door. Some flies buzzed, weaving a ball of dirty air above a black plaque of oil shored in the dirt. He could hear banging from inside the blackness of the hangar.

'Hello!' he shouted, his voice cutting the dark dusty air. The banging stopped for a moment then continued. Ron walked further into the sweltering blackness, his eyes taking their time to adjust. The metal corrugated roof seemed to tick, expanding in the heat of the pulsing sun.

'Hello? Anyone here?' he cried.

The banging stopped again and a muffled voice shouted back. 'Under here,' it said.

In the corner, gleaming under the few shafts of light that penetrated the roof, stood the scowling shape of a P-51, an old World War II fighter, complete with painted white teeth and a red tongue grinning behind the propeller blades.

'Hello,' said the voice again as two legs clad in oil-stained overalls slid out from beneath the under-carriage.

A man in his sixties stood up, his face black-brown from years of sun, two silver wings of hair flanking the sides of his bald head.

'Come to rent a plane?' the man asked, his eyes hopeful. 'I've got a Cherokee, an Islander, and if you think you can manage it a P-47 . . .' He stopped himself for a moment. 'Though she might need a new carb and a squirt of oil,' he added, suddenly remembering the plane hadn't flown in over two years and would need more than an oil change.

'No,' Ron replied, 'I'm not here to rent a plane.'

The man plucked a filthy old rag from his pocket and began rubbing his hands.

'So what can I do for you?'

Ron looked at the plane. He wasn't sure how to answer the question.

'An old P-51, huh?' he asked.

The man smiled and patted the silver wing.

'Yep,' he replied. 'A North American P-51D Mustang, 430 miles per hour, climb rate 3,475 feet per minute, have you here to the ceiling in no time,' he rattled like a second-hand car salesman. 'Could be a little rough on the turn, though,' he remarked, as if forgiving a lover a slight indiscretion, 'but deadly on the level,' he said, planing out his hands like wings.

He turned to Ron again.

'So what do you want?'

He smiled civilly. 'Ron Carter, NTSB.'

'NTSB?' the man repeated. 'A tin kicker, eh?' He grinned and extended his oil-covered hand.

'I'm Skid Mortensen, Chief Instructor . . . well, only instructor.'

'Pleased to meet you.' Ron shook his hand. 'I'd like

to talk to you about an old pupil of yours, if you don't mind?'

Skid nodded.

'Luis Juarez?'

Ron was amazed.

'Yes, Captain Luis Juarez . . .'

''I heard about it on the news. Tragic, just tragic,' said Skid, shaking his head sadly. 'Come on into my office.'

He led Ron to a small room in the corner of the hangar crammed with old files, manuals and bits of aircraft engine. A single 60-watt bulb illuminated the room, infusing it with a dim yellow glow.

'Care for a drink?' Skid pulled out a drawer from beneath the desk and held up a bottle of bourbon.

'No, thanks,' Ron responded, not wishing to get any more dehydrated than he already was. 'Got any water?'

Skid leant under the desk and opened the door of a small fridge. He threw Ron a cold bottle of sparkling water, beads of condensation dripping down the plastic.

'Thanks,' he said, cracking open the top.

'So what do ya wanna know?' asked Skid as he watched Ron gulp his water down.

He wiped his mouth. 'Juarez . . . what was he like, as a pilot, a student, as a man?'

Skid sat down behind the desk and put his feet up. Ron leant against the wall, careful not to disturb a shelf load of spare parts which threatened an avalanche if disturbed.

'Well, he was just a kid when he was here,' Skid began, 'but he was one hell of a good pilot. One of the best we ever had. Top of his class, in fact, if memory serves . . . and it was a very good class, the class of '75, just one failure that year.'

'Did he have any weaknesses in his training? Navigation? His math?' Ron enquired.

Skid was already shaking his head before Ron finished.

'None that we could see,' he confirmed, and swung his creaky old chair around to a shelf tight with folders.

'Let me see . . .' he said tracking along the files. 'Ah!' He plucked one of the brown manila folders out and swivelled around on his chair again to face Ron.

He announced, 'The class of '75!' and opened the folder. On top was a black and white photo. He handed it to Ron.

'There they are,' he pointed out.

Ron took the photo and looked at the same faces that were in the shot at Mrs Juarez had given him. Their pose was the same, all the smiling faces looking into the camera, but this time each young cadet was holding out a small badge, their silver wings.

'When was this taken?'

Skid looked up at the ceiling, stroking his rough chin, the rewind button pressed full.

'It woulda been . . . about . . . September '75. Yeah,' he nodded, 'they'd just got their wings.'

He pulled two sheets of thin pink paper from the file.

'That's young Juarez' report.' He handed it to Ron. 'As you can see, almost full marks in everything.'

He flicked through the pages, brittle with age, detailing Juarez' performance as an eighteen-year-old pilot: instrumentation, navigation, flight principles, weather, ratings, everything down to the size of his flight suit and boots.

'They're blaming him for the crash, aren't they?' Skid asked, pouring himself a glass of bourbon.

'Some people are talking pilot error,' replied Ron, still looking at the pages.

Skid shook his head again.

'A shame, such a damn' shame,' he said over and over.

'Do you mind if I hang on to these?' Ron asked, holding the old photo and Juarez' file under his arm as Skid led him out to his car.

'Sure, so long as we get it back.'

Skid glanced about at the old planes lined on the fringe of the airstrip, his face saddening. 'I know the place looks like shit,' he continued, 'but we don't like to throw anything out 'round here. Just let the desert gently eat it away.'

'Don't worry,' Ron assured him, 'I'll get it back to

you. Besides it'll give me an excuse to come back and visit.'

A smile returned to Skid's face.

'Yeah, maybe we could wheel out the old P-51 and grab some sky.'

GENAIR OFFICE BLOCK, EL SEGUNDO, CA

Al watched as Ron paced up and down the deep burgundy carpet of the GenAir reception area. The secretary behind the desk, with a mane of white-blonde hair, would occasionally look up from her work and smile patiently. The walls were a light blue and lined with photographs of past presidents of the company and some of the noteworthy shareholders. Ron stopped and examined the picture of a minor tennis star in a phoney embrace with what looked like one of the company's head suits, a director or the CEO.

'Where the hell were you yesterday?' asked Al.

Ron went on to consider another photo. This time of a group of men, all looking like Texan oil barons, holding up their share certificates for the camera.

'The desert,' he replied, 'Juarez' old flying school.'

Al just shook his head. He was beginning to think Ron was concentrating on the pilot too much. There were many other factors involved which needed their attention.

'They've a lot of powerful shareholders here,' remarked Ron, looking at another shot of some businessmen and a couple of politicians he vaguely recognised. Someone had mentioned that an ex-President was once on the GenAir board, Reagan or

Bush maybe, but it was probably just Washington talk.

Al leant back in his comfortable chair, sighing with impatience. 'We seem to spend most of our lives waiting outside other people's offices,' he complained.

The secretary's phone beeped and she picked it up, nodded, put it down again and turned to Ron, smiling.

'Gentlemen, Mr Roseman will see you now.'

'Thanks,' Ron said, and followed her to the wood-panelled door next to the reception desk. Al followed, bounding up from his chair.

'Mr Carter and Mr Martinez,' she announced as she led them inside.

Roseman stood up from behind his desk, an expansive smile running from ear to ear.

By the window Jack Taylor stood motionless, arms folded, barely acknowledging Ron and Al's presence.

'Gentlemen, please . . .' Roseman said, motioning for them to sit down in the seats in front of his desk.

Ron shook hands with him. Alarmed by the weakness of the other man's grip he quickly withdrew his hand.

'Would you like anything?' asked Roseman. 'Coffee? . . . Tea?'

'No, thank you,' said Ron.

'I'm fine too,' Al added, taking a seat.

Roseman smiled at his secretary.

'Thank you, Cathy.'

She smiled back and left the office.

Roseman sat down again.

'I think you already know Jack Taylor,' he said, 'our Director of Engineering.'

'Yes,' Ron replied, nodding at Taylor.

'Nice to see you again, gentlemen,' he said without smiling, his features maintaining an expression of mild hostility.

But Roseman kept on smiling through the awkward moment of silence as no one knew exactly where to start.

'So,' he said, 'what can we do for you?'

Ron came straight to the point.

'We're here,' he began, 'as a matter of courtesy, Mr Roseman.'

Roseman just nodded, not really knowing what that meant.

'We would like to talk to the men who worked on 248 the day of the crash . . . Edmunsen and Marx.'

Ron knew it would be wise to get permission from the company before he talked to any of its employees. It would avoid any claims of under-handedness being levelled at the investigation team by the company later. Best to keep everyone on side for as long as possible.

'I thought they already gave their statements,' Taylor cut in, almost growling.

'They did,' Al replied. He had interviewed them

himself. 'But we just have a few things we'd like to clarify,' he explained.

Ron turned to Roseman.

'Only with your permission, of course . . .'

Roseman stared at Ron for a second, his gracious smile fixed on his face as if stuck somehow, unable to loosen itself from his features.

'Of course,' he replied. 'Please be assured that we will co-operate as fully as we can in the investigation. We are as interested as you in finding out what was behind the accident. It was most upsetting,' he added, turning his smile into a serious frown.

Taylor seemed uncomfortable, shooting his boss a warning look.

'I'm very glad to hear it,' Ron said. 'Our work relies very heavily on the assistance of the interested parties. We really appreciate it.'

He wondered if he had overcooked it a bit. Everyone knew that it was a battle, a battle for information. Every company had something to hide. They may have been totally without blame in the accident but the airlines, the builders and especially the maintenance companies were rarely comfortable with the idea of investigators sniffing around their operations or asking their people awkward questions.

Taylor unfolded his arms and moved his large frame closer to where Ron was sitting. Al instinctively sat up straight in his seat, sensing that Taylor's aggression towards them might actually become physical.

'Are you investigating the airline?' he asked, containing his anger. 'The engine people? The pilots?'

Ron remained calm.

'We're giving every aspect of the case careful consideration.'

Taylor put both his huge hands on the desk and leant close to Ron. 'I've been thirty years in the business,' he said, 'never lost a bird. But I've seen accidents, and most of the time it's the fly boys who come along and just hop in, thinking the plane looks after itself, like magic. But everybody,' he raised his voice, '*everybody* blames the mechanics when something goes wrong.'

Roseman shifted uncomfortably in his seat.

'All right, Jack, I'm sure Mr Carter is doing all he can,' he said, trying to cool the situation.

Ron had heard this before. The pilots always thought everyone blamed them when something went wrong and the mechanics were the same, thinking they were always unfairly the target of the finger of suspicion.

Ron looked the big man in the eye and began speaking calmly.

'Mr Taylor, we're interested only in finding the cause or causes of this accident so that we may prevent it from happening again.'

Taylor closed his eyes and turned away again, not wanting to hear it. But Ron continued.

'We're not trying to give anyone or any particular company a hard time . . . we're gonna' give *everyone* a hard time,' he said suddenly, matching Taylor's hostility.

Al looked at Ron, surprised by his forcefulness.

'It's our job,' he added finally.

Roseman held up his hand, like a referee trying to intervene.

'I'm sorry, gentlemen,' he said to Ron and Al as Taylor retreated to his side of the room.

'I think what Jack is trying to say,' he continued, 'is that we are a little concerned that the investigation seems to be singling us out for,' he paused, 'special attention.'

Ron had calmed down and felt grateful for Roseman's level-headedness. If they wanted to find out what happened they would need all the cooperation they could get.

'We simply need to clarify some points with your men,' he said.

Roseman nodded his head in compliance.

'Of course,' he said, 'the accident has shaken us all up. As you will understand, we feel a little guarded.'

'Indeed,' Ron said, knowing exactly what he meant.

Taylor suddenly spoke but kept his back to the room, just looking out of the window over the complex. 'You'll find Edmunsen in hangar 2.'

'Er . . . thanks,' Ron replied. 'And what about Marx?'

'He has taken some days off and is resting at home,' answered Roseman. 'It has been hardest of all on him, as you can imagine.'

'Yes, of course,' said Al, once a maintenance engineer himself. 'It's not easy to cope with such a tragedy.'

Roseman smiled at him for a second before turning to Ron again.

'Cathy will arrange for security passes for you. We try to keep the hangars off-limits to the public.'

'We won't be long,' Ron assured him. 'Thank you for your assistance.'

GENAIR MAINTENANCE HANGAR 2, EL SEGUNDO, CA

A vast cathedral of steel and concrete, the hangar echoed with a dissonant symphony of hammers, drills and air compressors. Ron and Al tagged on the visitor badges that were left for them at reception. VISITOR – RESTRICTED ACCESS ran the words in bright red across each badge, making them feel somehow inadequate, like a couple of kids on a school tour. They followed the trail of yellow lines which would lead them safely through the hangar and keep them away from the aircraft which were in various states of disrepair. A sign on the wall reminded them that if they strayed off the designated path they would be ejected from the facility.

'Pretty tight,' remarked Al, impressed with the security.

Ron looked anxiously around as mechanics worked on the aircraft, all dressed in white overalls, the GenAir logo blazoned on the back.

'Can you see him?' he asked.

'Nope,' replied Al, 'they all look the same . . . hold on.' He stopped by the wing of a Boeing 737, a similar type aircraft to the BD-12.

'That him?' Ron asked. All he could make out was a figure on a ladder leaning inside the open covers of one of the jet's engines.

Al squinted at the mechanic.

'Yeah, I think so,' he said, vaguely recognising the man.

Since the morning when he'd heard of the crash Paul Edmunsen had busied himself as much as he possibly could. Management insisted he take a week off from work during which time he nearly drove himself and his girlfriend mad. He was tempted to break things around the house just so he'd have to fix them and give himself something to do, taking his mind off the crash. The investigation had concentrated more on Marx the senior mechanic but Edmunsen could not escape the sheer pressure of being discreetly scrutinised by the company, the crash investigators, and of course himself. He would always wonder if he had done something wrong – left a bolt untightened, a wire loose or a fuel line unchecked.

'Paul!' Al shouted over the noise of a drill. 'Paul!'

Edmunsen popped his head up from the engine and turned around. He could see Ron and Al waiting below.

Christ, not more questions, he thought to himself.

'Can we have a few words?' Al shouted up to him.

Edmunsen nodded and descended the metal steps. He wiped his hands on his overalls and greeted the two investigators as pleasantly as he could.

'How ya doin', Mr Martinez?' he said and shook Al's hand.

'Fine, Paul, and you?'

Edmunsen tried to be convincing.

'Oh, not so bad.' He smiled thinly.

Al introduced Ron.

'This is Mr Carter, he's the Investigator In Charge of the 248 case.'

Edmunsen shook hands with Ron also.

'How do you do, Mr Carter?'

Ron smiled, 'Please, it's Ron.'

Al took out some papers from the little black satchel he always carried on interviews.

'Listen, Paul,' he began, quickly casting an eye over Edmunsen's previous statement, 'when I first interviewed you, you said there were three people in or around the plane the evening of the accident.'

Edmunsen narrowed his eyes, trying to remember.

Al continued, 'You, Marx, and another unidentified man.'

Edmunsen nodded in confirmation. 'Yes, that's right, as far as I can recall.'

Ron asked, 'Can you tell us anything about this third man?'

Edmunsen laughed, more out of nervousness than from amusement.

'Hey,' he said, 'sometimes there can be a lot of guys around the aircraft at any one time, guys you don't know, people you've never even seen before.'

He glanced about the huge hangar as if to illustrate his point.

'I mean, it's a big place. There are personnel from the engine companies, avionics guys, FAA inspectors, cleaners, airline officials, a lotta people.'

Al poised his pen over the margin of Edmunsen's statement.

'You're saying you didn't know him, you'd never seen him before?'

Edmunsen felt a tightening of tension again, as if each word he uttered could be used against him. He briefly wondered if he should call for Taylor or the company lawyer. Taking a deep breath, he calmed himself. 'No,' he affirmed his position, 'I'd never seen him before.' He paused for a moment. 'Or at least, I don't think so.'

Al stopped writing.

'How do you mean?' asked Ron.

'Well,' Edmunsen began, 'to be honest, I really didn't get that much of a look at him. I mean, I wasn't taking any notice. I just don't know who it was.'

'He could have been another mechanic?' proposed Ron.

'Coulda been,' said Edmunsen vaguely, 'but more likely he was with the cleaning contractors.'

'Why do you think that?' Ron asked.

'Blue overalls,' said Edmunsen. 'He was wearing blue overalls, same as the cleaning guys.'

Ron and Al traded glances. Why the hell couldn't he have mentioned this before?

Edmunsen noticed their puzzled expressions. 'I just

wasn't that concerned about him,' he said earnestly. 'Like I said, there can be a lot of people coming and going around here and besides . . .' he hesitated once more, panicking slightly, not sure if he should continue.

'And besides what?' Ron asked gently, detecting Edmunsen's nervousness.

'Well, I think Marx might have known him.'

Al stopped scribbling and looked up from his notes.

'What makes you say that?'

'I think that Marx had a few words with him. Like I said, I wasn't taking too much notice, but I think they were talking.'

'And you couldn't give any sort of description of this man?' Al queried.

'No.' Edmunsen shook his head. 'He had his back to me. All I could see were his hard hat and overalls.'

'Where were you at the time?' asked Ron, trying to get a mental picture of the scene.

Edmunsen pointed to the rear of the 737. 'I was on the ladder raised up under the back of the fuselage, working on the APU.'

Ron walked under the metal hulk of the plane's underbelly and stood beneath the shadow of the tail.

'Marx and the other guy were out under the left wing,' continued Edmunsen, and pointed at the wing to the other side of the plane.

'May I?' asked Ron as he grabbed hold of the ladder, which ran on wheels, and pulled it towards the rear of the plane.

'Er . . . sure,' Edmunsen said, wondering what the point of it was. Ron dragged the ladder right under the tail plane and climbed up to the top rung so that he was no more than a foot under the riveted cone of the rear fuselage. He realised it would be very hard to see anyone under the wing from this vantage point.

'Did Marx say anything about this man?' asked Al.

Edmunsen shook his head, becoming exasperated by the line of questioning.

'Look, I told you guys, I don't know who the hell he was. It coulda been my own brother or the Pope for all I know and I wouldn't have realised. I just . . . couldn't see his face.'

Al realised they may have been pushing a little too hard on the questions and was about to ask Edmunsen if he wanted to get some coffee or something when Ron jumped off the ladder and came up to them.

'Okay,' he said softly, 'we just have to check everything out.'

Edmunsen rubbed his forehead wearily.

'I know,' he said, 'I'm sorry . . . it's all been kind of a strain.'

'Tell me about it,' confided Ron, giving a knowing smile.

'I don't know where the guy went next,' said Edmunsen. 'Anyway, then the pilot came along,' he added.

Ron's eyes widened.

'Juarez?'

'Yeah, he came up this way.' Edmunsen pointed to the other end of the hangar which opened out on to the airfield. 'Marx came over from the other side and they met about here where we're standing,' he said. 'They had *words*.'

'Words?' Ron repeated, picking up on Edmunsen's emphasis.

'Yeah,' he said, 'it got a bit heated.'

'How do you mean?'

Edmunsen explained. 'Well, it happens a lot. You know, the pilot wants to get moving, doesn't want to miss his slot, under pressure from the airline, from the ground controller, dispatch or whatever . . .'

Ron and Al nodded, knowing full well what he meant.

'He was pretty pissed, huh?' said Al.

'Pretty much,' Edmunsen agreed. 'In fact I'd never him seen so angry before, but we still had to hold him up.'

'The APU?' Ron guessed.

'Exactly,' said Edmunsen. 'The damn' thing was playing up again, the detector rod was giving a false warning . . . well, you know all about it.'

Edmunsen realised that they probably knew more about the aircraft's history than he did at that stage.

'We fixed it, of course,' he continued, 'and in accordance with procedure we had to check the other fire detector rods in each of the two engines, and of course the electrics service bay.'

'So, what happened then?' Ron wanted to know.

Edmunsen shrugged again. 'Nothing much,' he said simply. 'Juarez just stormed off, cursing us to high heaven.'

'Marx and Juarez, had they come into conflict before?' asked Ron.

Edmunsen felt as if they were trying to put words in his mouth. Sure Marx and Juarez had crossed each other a few times, even had a couple of screaming matches, but it wasn't that uncommon for pilots and mechanics to fall out. People were under pressure.

'Well ... yeah,' he said, guardedly, 'I suppose they'd had their differences but Marx didn't have it in for Juarez, if that's what you're getting at.'

'We're not suggesting anything,' Ron said, trying to keep Edmunsen friendly, 'we're just . . .'

'. . . checking everything out,' Edmunsen sang like a chorus line.

Ron smiled. 'Sorry for the grilling.'

Edmunsen relaxed again.

'I'd better get back to work.'

'Okay, Paul.' Al put away his paperwork and closed his satchel. 'Thanks for your help.'

But Ron wasn't quite finished. He looked at the open nacelles of the 737's CFM turbofan engines, the nozzles, compressors and innards of the huge powerplants exposed.

'Just one last thing.'

Edmunsen sighed but tried to remain co-operative to the last.

'The aircraft?' asked Ron. 'Was it left unattended for any length of time that evening?'

Edmunsen looked at the ground for a moment, trying to remember.

'After we had checked all the detector rods we had to go and do the sign-offs in the office . . . down there.' He pointed at a large glass enclosure at the other end of the hangar.

'How long?' asked Ron. 'How long were you away from the plane?'

Edmunsen thought about it for a moment.

'Not more than ten minutes,' he estimated. 'Then we did a final check,' he continued, 'closed everything up and rolled her out.'

Ron turned to Al.

'That oughta about do it.'

'Yeah,' agreed Al, glad to be able to leave the young mechanic alone. 'Thanks, Paul,' he said again and they all shook hands.

'Sure hope you find out what happened,' said Edmunsen, 'the whole thing's kinda driving us nuts around here.'

He gave a quick smile and went back to work.

Ron and Al made their way through the rows of cars

at the GenAir car park. Both were quiet, running over in their minds the conversation with Edmunsen.

'Do you think we should check this other guy out?' Al asked.

'Sure, I guess,' said Ron. 'I wonder why Marx hasn't mentioned him.'

'Probably didn't think it important,' said Al. 'I mean, this guy was just a cleaner according to Edmunsen.'

A heavy C130 transporter lumbered in overhead descending slowly over the airfield, its engines drowning out all other sounds for a moment.

Ron could see Al's lips moving.

'What?' he shouted.

'Maybe one of us should go and talk to the cleaning contractors,' Al said loudly.

'And maybe one of us should have a talk with Marx again,' Ron added.

His mobile phone hummed in his breast pocket. It was Bob. He was at the FBI forensics lab in Westwood Park and thought Ron should get there as soon as possible.

'What's up?' Al asked, catching snippets of the conversation.

Ron pocketed his phone again.

'The FBI lab's just finished testing the APU fire detector,' he said, walking quickly towards the car.

'They found something?' asked Al.

'Maybe,' was all Ron could say.

FBI FORENSICS LAB, WESTWOOD PARK, LOS ANGELES, CA

Long thin lines, curling at each end, ran the length of the surface, layered on top of each other like the work of a crazed artist in a fit of rage.

'Looks like it's been scratched by iron wool,' said Ron, moving back from the eyepiece.

Magnified four hundred times a section of ACL248's APU fire detector rod, a long thin piece of tubing which shrouded the heat sensor wire, was clamped beneath the imposing eye of the $50,000 compound microscope.

'Striations,' said the thin young man standing with Bob behind the microscope. At twenty-four Dr Andrew Taggart had not been lured by the generous salary and benefit package offered by the Bureau as he received his doctorate from Ohio University, or indeed by the warm California climate, but by the promise of work on some of the country's most intriguing forensic cases.

The facility itself was only open six months. Though still seen as inferior in both equipment and in the experience of its personnel to the FBI's national lab in the J. Edgar Hoover Building in Washington it was hoped that in time Westwood would take over most of the FBI's terrorism-related forensic studies. Since his arrival at the Materials and Devices Unit Taggart had run UV tests on minute pieces of a letter in which a tiny bomb had been placed and sent to a director of an abortion clinic in Atlanta and had even worked on a piece of plaster from the ruins of the Alfred P. Murrah Building, Oklahoma City.

He possessed the air of smugness which seemed to be a common characteristic among the bright young graduates recruited by the FBI.

'. . . oblique impact abrasions,' he continued. 'Not an unusual occurrence, I'd say. At impact there's a lot of hot metal moving about, a lot of grinding.'

'Is the rest of the rod like this?' asked Ron, curious.

The young man's expression changed to one of serious contemplation.

'No,' he replied, 'and that is a little unusual, I think . . .'

'You think?' Bob asked, concerned by the element of doubt in the young scientist's tone.

'I would have thought the whole surface area of the rod would show similar signs of contact damage,' replied Taggart.

'And they don't?' Bob said.

Taggart shook his head. 'No.'

Ron leant close and looked through the eyepiece, seeing once again the surface of the rod, like a landscape of tightly packed streams and canals.

'Do you think the marks were caused before the impact?' he asked, standing back again from the microscope.

Taggart thought about it for a moment, considering the possibility carefully.

'It's unlikely,' he decided, 'but we'd know a lot more if we did a comparative test with the other components that were in proximity to the rod before the impact. If they show the same pattern then we could extrapolate that the damage was due to the major event.'

'Major event?' Ron said.

'The crash,' Taggart said casually.

'And if they're different?' asked Bob, trying to make some sense of it all.

Taggart smiled. 'Well, it might indicate a separate event.'

'Hold on a second,' Bob interrupted, 'have you done a chemical?'

Taggart put his hands in his lab coat pocket and walked to a plotter next to a computer screen that was plastered with little yellow post-its.

He handed Bob a print out of a simple bar chart, each bar labelled with a chemical symbol.

'Analysis has shown up traces of mercuric oxide, some crystalline structures and groups of benzene and nitrobenzene.'

'Benzene and nitrobenzene?' Ron repeated, not sure what the significance was.

A woman's voice made the men turn around.

'Aromatic hydrocarbons!' she said.

It was Nancy Kronziac.

'Don't they teach you chemistry at the NTSB?' She

smiled. The men were all a bit too surprised to reply. 'I'm sorry,' she said, and introduced herself. 'Special Agent Kronziac, Domestic Terrorism Unit.'

Ron remembered her only too well.

'Hi,' he said. 'Ron Carter, Investigator In Charge.'

She took his hand and held it momentarily in a firm handshake.

'Congratulations.'

'This is Bob Tunamachier,' Ron introduced his colleague.

Bob just smiled and nodded at her. The situation seemed slightly awkward for some reason nobody could really explain.

'I thought you'd have your own people running the tests,' said Kronziac, glancing at Taggart who looked away and pretended to busy himself at his computer.

Ron felt caught out, unable to think of an answer.

'Ron thought it'd save time,' said Bob, trying to put him on the spot.

'It would waste valuable time to ship everything back to Washington,' he explained. 'Besides your people seem to be most competent.'

He suddenly felt utterly stupid for having made such a patronising remark.

'I hope you don't mind,' he added limply.

Kronziac's expression changed from one of mild amusement to utmost seriousness.

'Can I speak to you outside for a moment?' she said to Ron.

He glanced at Bob, wondering what he was in for.

'Er, sure,' he replied, and turned to Taggart. 'Can you continue the chem tests?'

Taggart looked at Kronziac for some indication of how he should answer.

'The Bureau will help you in any way it can,' she said and began walking towards the door.

Ron shrugged and followed her. He found himself walking in Kronziac's footsteps through the car park. She hadn't said a word since they'd left the lab.

'Where are we going?' he asked.

Kronziac walked to the driver's side of a black Ford Explorer.

'Get in,' she said.

SAN DIEGO FREEWAY, SOUTHBOUND

Kronziac turned the wheel slowly and gently edged the car off Wilshire and on to the five lanes of traffic which runs like an artery through the heart of the city.

'You do know kidnapping is a federal offence?' Ron joked, trying to provoke some reaction from Kronziac, but she remained motionless behind her dark glasses, concentrating on the traffic.

'Come on,' he said, getting anxious, 'where are we going?'

Kronziac glanced in the mirror and swung the car into the fast lane. Ron gripped the arm rest of his door and hung on tight.

'Have you talked to John Marx yet?' she asked, keeping her eyes on the road.

'Marx?' asked Ron, the last person he'd thought they would be talking about.

'The GenAir mechanic who worked on 248.'

'Yes, I know who he is,' snapped Ron, 'and, no, I haven't talked to him yet . . . what's this all about?'

Kronziac pulled the car to the right, passing an old VW minibus that was struggling along at 55, pumping smoke from its exhaust.

'Piece of shit,' she remarked, 'shouldn't be on the road.'

Ron clung tightly to his arm rest as they thundered down the freeway towards the southern districts of the city.

'He's a member of the Los Altos Aero Modellers' Club,' said Kronziac.

Ron felt for a moment that she may have been mistaking him for someone else.

'Well, that's just great but what's it got to do with me?' he wanted to know.

'We've been . . .' she began, manoeuvring the car to overtake once more.

'Yes?' said Ron, impatiently.

'. . . monitoring them,' she continued.

'Monitoring?' he asked. 'Monitoring who?'

Keeping one hand on the wheel, she reached over and pulled open the glove compartment.

'Look in the envelope.'

Ron stared down at a large white envelope.

'Open it,' she urged him.

Ron slipped open the flap and took out an FBI report and some photographs. At first he was not sure what he was looking at, then turning it right side up realised it was a building, a small white two-storey house, somewhat rundown, with boarded windows and flaking paint. A sign over the door read LOS ALTOS AERO MODELLERS' CLUB.

'We got a tip-off some months ago indicating that the place was being used as a cover for a subversive group simply called The Club.'

'Terrorists?' said Ron, looking closely at the photo.

'Neo-fascists, white supremacists, ultra right, Free-men, Third Position, Children of the White God . . . whatever,' Kronziac contemptuously listed them. 'A lot of the government agencies have been keeping an eye on their web sites, tapping their phone lines here and on the east coast. After Oklahoma every nut with a pair of combats and an NRA card is a suspect. We think the group has ties all over the country and abroad, France and Germany.'

Ron opened the FBI report file, entitled *Militia Movement in the US*, made to the Judiciary Subcommittee on Terrorism, Technology and Government Information – an extensive document. He scanned rapidly through the underlined words, the suggested motivation for these groups: . . . *American immigration control . . . immigrants driving up costs, bring disease . . . calls for immigration reform . . . country under siege . . . World Trade Center bombing, crime levels, Mexican immigrant workforce . . . separatist stance needed . . . America first policy advocates isolationism . . . Christian values . . . imposition of Biblical law . . .*

He closed the report, unable to take it all in, and looked through the attached series of surveillance photos taken at various times.

'I thought you only had these nuts in the south and mid-west,' he remarked.

Kronziac shook her head.

'The fuckers with the ZZ Top beards and snakeskin boots?' she uttered. 'They're just militants, different type of whacko. These guys are organised, political, with a national agenda.'

Ron stopped at one of the photographs. Looking closer he could see a round-faced man with sun glasses and a black polo shirt. He was coming out of the building, walking towards a red pick-up truck. On the breast of the man's shirt Ron could just make out the GenAir logo.

It was John Marx.

'You think Marx is one of them?' he asked, shocked.

'We think he's just a runner, a foot soldier, a believer,' said Kronziac dismissively.

Ron put down the photos for a moment and stared out as the tall buildings of downtown LA drifted by in the hazy sunlight. 'How did you make the connection?' he asked. 'I mean, how did you know it was Marx?'

'We cross-referenced his plates with LAPD,' Kronziac answered.

Of course. Ron nodded his head, a logical step.

'He's been a naughty boy,' she added.

'What do you mean?'

'A bit of a philanderer, our Mr Marx,' she said, overtaking a Porsche.

'What did he do?'

'He was cautioned for soliciting a minor,' Kronziac said, 'a fifteen-year-old runaway from Philly. She'd been working the streets around Hollywood. Her picture's in there.'

Ron pulled out a small poster with a murky photocopied picture of a young black girl. On top in large letters was the word 'Missing'; underneath her name, Julie Townes, missing from South Philadelphia since 18 June. Ron examined her picture. She wore a hair band, smiling just like any other schoolgirl.

'He beat the rap,' lamented Kronziac.

'How?'

'She disappeared before the charges were brought, so he got off with a caution.'

Ron stared at the young girl smiling out at him.

'Maybe she got some sense and went back home, got the hell out of this place,' he suggested.

'You're right on one count,' Kronziac said quietly.

Ron looked at her, dreading what she'd say next.

'She was found in an alley off Sunset.'

Ron closed his eyes, a queasy, empty feeling in his stomach. He fumbled about, looking for the window button. Kronziac pressed it for him on the centre console and the window lowered with an electrical whine.

Ron felt the hot air from the freeway blast against his face, the smell bitter with gasoline and rubber.

'We don't think Marx had anything to do with it,' Kronziac assured him. 'We had a tail on him the night she was killed. She was strangled, not a pretty sight . . . not a very clean job, if you know what I mean.'

Kronziac noticed that Ron was still staring blankly at her.

'I'm sorry,' she said, 'you get a little too used to this sort of thing in my job.'

He just nodded and looked at the poster of the missing girl again.

'How come you're telling me all this?'

'There's more,' she said, nodding at the envelope. 'A transcript.'

Ron reached into the envelope again and picked out a couple of sheets of paper stapled together.

'Read the highlighted area,' Kronziac suggested.

He looked over the papers, searching for the piece underlined.

NATIONAL SECURITY AGENCY

Federal Document Clearing House
Room 509, FANX 5 Building,
SIGINT Operations,
M-Group, Fort Meade, MD

Federal Doc: 141592653/FTP-7896
Copyright restrict total.
Classified – 2

SIGINT Channel exchange tap authorisation FTP-7896
Time: 21:48 (PDT)

CALLER DETAILS	RECEIVER DETAILS
NPA code: 213 (local)	: 213 (local)
Node : 3B	: 3D
CO code : 944	: 970
Tel No. : 944–8976	: 970–9980

Excerpt transcript:

Male: *Hey, Marx, how ya doin', buddy? Listen, I gotta'*
tell you I've given our dago friend Juarez a little
treat, some firecrackers to light up the night and
give the kiddies a fright ... I can't wait to tell ya all
about it ... maybe you could put a word in for me
with Mr Grey ... you know I'm committed ...

Message end.

FBI CLEARED COPY

Ron looked up from the transcript, barely able to take it all in. 'What the hell is this?' he asked desperately.

'The NSA got special clearance to run a tap on the club's phone line,' Kronziac filled him in. 'This is a transcript of a call made from a pay phone.'

'He mentions Juarez . . . the 248 Captain?'

Kronziac nodded. 'Seems like it,' she said. 'That's why I'm telling you all about this. The transcript was sent from the National Signals Intelligence Centre in Fort Meade the day after the crash, November second, and was collated with all the other surveillance reports from around the country at the NSA.'

Ron was reading through the transcript again.

'But don't you get a lot of this sort of thing after a crash? You know, hoaxes, crank calls?'

'Sure,' said Kronziac, easing the car past a goods truck, 'but this one's different.' She added, 'It took me a while to spot it too.'

'Spot what?' Ron squinted at the transcript, looking for something out of the ordinary.

'Look at the time on it,' she told him.

Ron's eyes moved to the top of the front sheet.

'21.48 hours,' he read out the time of the recording, 'so the guy saw it on the news.'

Kronziac pumped the gas pedal and swerved the car across four lanes to exit the freeway on the Culver City off-ramp. Ron had to hold on tight to prevent himself from being flung across the seat.

'Jesus, what's the rush?'

Kronziac kept her eyes on the road, ignoring Ron's concern for the speed they were doing.

'Because of the time difference,' she began calmly, 'we get reports from the NSA clearing house a day late. We received this one on the second as I said, which means it was recorded on the night of the thirty-first: 9.48 Pacific time on the 31 October, Hallowe'en night.'

Ron stared at the time at the top of the page in disbelief.

'Nearly three hours *before* the crash?' he uttered. 'Are you sure?'

'Yeah,' Kronziac said, 'checked it out with the NSA and the tapes confirm the time.'

She turned the car down a quiet street, lined with small office blocks, some apartment buildings, a drug store and a garage with a pile of crashed cars piled up outside.

'We've got to go and talk with Marx!' pleaded Ron.

Kronziac brought the car to a stop by the kerb and parked behind a large white camper van.

'What the hell are we doing down here?' asked Ron, looking around.

Kronziac got out of the car. 'You'll see.'

They were parked outside a bridal shop with three mannequins dressed in white and peach silk standing in the window display. Ron reluctantly unbuckled his seat belt and got out of the car.

Kronziac held out her hand. 'Come on, we don't

want to look out of place.' She smiled and led him by the arm into the shop.

Inside, the shop was full of old and new dresses, with plastic flower arrangements spilling off the shelves and lengths of fabric lining the walls like curtains. A large lady in her fifties behind the counter lifted her eyebrows momentarily above the glasses which perched precariously on the end of her nose. She had a customer, a young Hispanic girl who was excitedly leafing through a bridal catalogue.

Kronziac pulled Ron through the shop like a reluctant groom to a door at the back which led to a set of wooden stairs. He felt totally confused and wondered why he didn't just stop and demand to know what in God's name was going on.

Climbing the narrow staircase to the second floor, they entered a small hallway which was stuffed with boxes of cloth and bags of ribbon that trailed about the floor like the aftermath of a raucous party. As they reached the end of the dark hallway Kronziac rapped her knuckles on a door. After a moment it opened and she went in. Ron hesitated, waiting in the doorway.

Inside the room were four men. One was sitting at a table holding a set of earphones to the side of his head with one hand while slowly turning a dial on what looked like some sort of tuner with the other. Another man sat tapping at a laptop computer while the other two stood by the only window in the room which over looked the street outside. One of the men was looking through a camera with a long telescopic lens, pointing across to the other side of the street. The man stepped back from the camera and turned around.

'You're just in time.' Agent Jones smiled.

'Marx?' asked Kronziac expectantly.

Jones nodded. 'Arrived ten minutes ago.'

He smiled at Ron. 'Hello, Mr Carter.'

Ron nodded and entered the room slowly like a kid unsure of new surroundings.

Kronziac pointed to each of the men in the room and introduced them to Ron.

'Special Agents Phillips, Morris and DiCannio,' she rattled off their names.

Each of the men turned and gave him a polite little nod before returning to their work.

'Has he picked up the messages?' asked Kronziac, looking out of the window.

Phillips, a tall young man with sun-bleached surfer's hair, turned from his audio surveillance equipment.

'Yep,' he confirmed, 'he just got them.'

Ron walked over to the window to see what the others were looking at. Across the street he could see a white building, its windows boarded up, a small sign over the doorway: LOS ALTOS AERO MODELLERS' CLUB. Parked outside was a red pick-up.

'Messages?' he asked, wondering what Kronziac had meant.

'Marx comes to the club twice a week to pick up any messages left on the answering machine,' said Kronziac.

'They leave messages for each other?' he said, struck by the absurdity of it.

Jones was looking through the camera again.

'It's a pretty basic set up,' he said, 'but quite an effective way for them to communicate without being traced. It meant we had to go in and bug the place ourselves.'

'I thought the NSA took care of that?' said Ron.

'They did,' said Kronziac, 'but that was only a tap at the exchange, not a location bug – besides the NSA isn't chartered for domestic surveillance – could be a grey area in a Federal court.'

'We went in ourselves,' added Jones, 'and can now pick up the whole building, not just the phone.'

Kronziac and he smiled at each other.

'A simple insertion,' Jones said proudly, 'wired the whole damn' place.'

'Morris and Phillips went in disguised as Pacific Bell technicians,' Kronziac explained.

Ron laughed, amazed by the corniness of it all.

'Jeez, just like a movie!'

Kronziac and Jones stopped smiling. The movies had indeed glamourised the FBI but many times they were portrayed as either hard-assed weirdos who spend their time chasing serial killers and investigating alien conspiracies or just incompetent government stooges.

'We intercepted a call from a guy we think is the same man who left the message the night of the crash,' Kronziac said. 'He wants to meet with Marx.'

Phillips shifted in his seat, holding the earphones tightly to his ear.

'The subject is leaving the room . . . closing the door . . . and locking it,' he said, giving a running commentary of Marx's movements inside the club building.

Agent Morris, a dark-haired version of Phillips, leant down and turned on a video surveillance camera which was also pointed across the street at the front of the club.

'Should be coming out any minute now,' he said, flicking the record button on the video camera in anticipation.

Ron and Kronziac moved closer to the window, their faces concealed from the outside by Venetian blinds which were open just wide enough for the camera lenses to peer through.

A car cruised by, driven by some youths, its stereo blaring, humming like a trapped giant bee. A kid cycled past on the pavement. Then the door of the Aero Club opened.

'That's him,' Ron cried as he saw the figure of John Marx emerge from the building. Marx locked the door behind him, glanced up and down the street then walked quickly to his pick-up. The reverse lights came on and the truck backed out from its parking spot and sped off down the road. Ron felt an urge to run, to chase after Marx. He was surprised to see Kronziac and Jones so relaxed, so calm.

'Aren't we going to follow him?' he asked.

A slight smile appeared on Kronziac's lips, like a mother humouring an excited child.

'We know where he's going,' she said casually.

6925 HOLLYWOOD BLVD,
WEST HOLLYWOOD, CA

Ron found the ride back up the freeway an uncomfortable journey, troubled by the questions running through his mind. He was relieved when the white camper van came to a halt by the sidewalk. From the outside the van looked quite large and spacious but when crammed with banks of audio and video surveillance equipment, four FBI agents and one slightly confused air crash investigator, the MSU felt like a sardine can.

'Mobile Surveillance Unit,' Jones explained the abbreviation.

Ron began to wonder if the agents had an abbreviation for everything – soon they wouldn't need whole words.

'This the best spot we can get?' Kronziac asked, looking out of the one-way window through which nobody could see inside.

'Can't go any further,' Morris replied as he switched off the engine.

'This'll do fine,' Jones observed as he picked up a pair of binoculars and trained them on the large ornate building on the other side of the street.

The most famous cinema in America, Mann's Chinese Theatre with its pagoda-style architecture, rose into the warm Hollywood air like a Mecca for star-gazers and tourists, a holy place for movie freaks. Here in 1953 Marilyn Monroe and Jane Russell knelt together smiling for the cameras as they pressed their hands in the wet cement, leaving their stellar imprints for posterity. Clint Eastwood scribbled 'Thanks for making my day', Gene Autry's horse stuck his hooves in and Jimmy Durante left an impression of his famous nose. Meryl Streep left her mark there, Tom Cruise too, but the place was filling up, not much room for today's movie idols.

'Must be someone coming,' Jones remarked, pointing at a crowd of fans outside the entrance to the theatre which was cordoned off by ropes and the mountainous figures of security men dressed in tuxedos. A deep red carpet was laid down, leading from the kerb side to the door of the theatre.

'That's not going to help,' Kronziac cursed.

'A lot of tourists too,' Jones added, shaking his head.

Ron watched as groups of holiday makers milled about the courtyard of the theatre, staring at the ground, trying to match their hands and feet with the prints of Cary Grant, Elizabeth Taylor or Steve McQueen.

'Is this where Marx is meeting the other guy?' Ron asked.

'Yeah,' replied Kronziac, looking at her watch, 'he's late.'

'No, he isn't,' Jones said suddenly, following a figure coming up the street.

It was Marx.

'Right, guys, let's go to it!' Kronziac shouted and Jones pulled out a seat underneath the surveillance console. He flicked a few buttons and a row of monitors came to life with live pictures of the outside of the theatre. Kronziac pressed a mike switch and over two small speakers inside the van they could now hear a dissonant chorus of voices from the crowd around the theatre. Morris and Phillips began taking off their shoes, putting on trainers and T-shirts to make themselves look like tourists. They each picked up a small digital camcorder and turned them on.

'Okay, ready for a test?' Jones asked, watching the screens.

'I'm on,' Morris confirmed, a little red light flickering on his camcorder. He turned the camera around and made a face at the lens. On one of the monitors he appeared, smiling.

'Yeah, you're on,' said Jones. 'Phillips?'

Agent Phillips, struggling into a white T-shirt complete with a Mickey Mouse motif, pointed his camcorder at himself and likewise his face appeared on a monitor next to Morris's image.

'Are the cameras radio linked?' Ron asked, noticing there were no cables running from them.

'Up to a thousand-metre range,' Kronziac nodded, 'and we've got one on the roof concealed in the air vent, 25mm when wide, 500mm when fully zoomed in.'

On a larger monitor above the console Jones

was zooming the roof camera in on Marx as he approached the theatre.

'Subject is approaching from west side and is approximately twenty metres from the entrance,' he said.

They watched as Marx made his way slowly to the theatre.

'He's nearly there,' crooned Kronziac, her voice urging Marx to go in.

On the large monitor they could see him stopping just outside the theatre. He looked up and down the street, furtively, like a man on the run. Finally he turned and disappeared behind the growing crowd outside the courtyard.

'That's it!' Jones cried. 'Time to rock.'

Morris and Phillips stuffed tiny earphones into their ears, opened up the back door of the camper and jumped out on to the street. Through the window Ron watched as the two agents made their way through the busy traffic to the other side of the road. Phillips held up his camcorder to his cheek.

'Can you hear me?' his voiced hissed over a speaker in the van.

Kronziac put on a headset and drew the mouthpiece to her lips. 'Loud and clear,' she replied, watching the monitors closely. 'Act natural,' she urged them, 'you could be two hicks from Muskratville, Kentucky, first time in LA.'

Morris began pointing the camera at the ground. On the monitor in the van they could see Barbra

Streisand's bronze star sunk in a pink terazzo square of pavement. He tilted up and they could just see a line of stars stretching down the length of the Hollywood sidewalk.

'Where the hell's Jimmy Cagney?' Phillips asked.

'Dunno, where's Julia Roberts? That's what I want to know,' said Morris, his camera searching the ground.

'Time to split up, fellas,' said Kronziac into her mike. 'Phillips, you follow him into the courtyard, but stay back among the crowds.'

'Okay,' complied Phillips as he made his way into the front area of the theatre.

'How about me?' Morris asked over the speakers.

'Stay on the other side of the crowd, to the right,' Kronziac told him.

'On my way,' he said and moved in the opposite direction to his colleague around the crowd which was swelling to a noisy mass of excited fans, mostly teenage girls.

On the video monitor with Phillips' live feed Ron could see the courtyard of the theatre with the foot and hand prints sunk in the concrete, tourists standing around them taking photographs.

'Anyone see him yet?' asked Phillips, moving slowly forward, panning his camera over the yard.

In the van they watched all the video monitors closely for any signs of Marx.

On the monitor which was linked to the camera on top of the camper van itself the image was slowly zooming in, the people across the street steadily increasing in size.

Jones gently turned the camera to the right and then to the left, searching for their target. He suddenly stopped the camera, seeing a man with the familiar round face and balding head of John Marx.

'There!' Jones cried as Marx ambled across the screen among the other tourists.

Kronziac looked at the monitor and began directing her agents into position.

'Phillips, he's about thirty feet ahead of you on your ten.'

'All right,' he replied, panning his camera to the left. 'Got him,' he said, as he saw Marx through the eyepiece. 'I'll just keep the camera moving around so he won't suspect anything.'

'We've got an eye on him from here anyway,' said Jones, glued to the big screen.

'I can see him too,' said Morris.

On his monitor they could also see Marx, but further away, partially obscured behind the crowd of fans on the near side.

'Any sign of the other guy?' Ron asked, unable to contain his impatience to see who Marx was supposed to meet.

'How about him?' he said, pointing to a tall man in his fifties who had walked up beside Marx and was looking at the ground.

Kronziac seemed doubtful. 'Doesn't seem right,' she said, shaking her head.

Sure enough the other man drifted away from where Marx was standing, just another tourist.

'Marx is getting a little anxious,' remarked Jones. They could see him looking at his watch and glancing around the crowd.

Ron looked at his watch also: 3.25 p.m. He had spent most of the day with Kronziac and her crew.

'Hold on a minute,' said Morris, his voice tense on the speaker, as if trying hard to concentrate on something.

'See the guy in the jacket and cap . . .'

Jones zoomed out a little and on the wide angle of the main camera those in the van could see the figure of a man in a blue jacket and a yellow peak-cap walk close to Marx, then stop and stare at the ground.

'Can't see his face,' Jones said, zooming in again to get a closer look.

'Turn on your rifle mikes,' ordered Kronziac.

'Okay,' said Phillips, and switched on the powerful microphone which was attached to his camera.

Ron leant closer to Kronziac, trying to get a good look at the man on the screen standing next to Marx.

'What's going on?' he whispered.

Kronziac began slowly turning a dial on the console and spilling out of the speakers came all the voices and sounds of the theatre courtyard being picked up by the microphone on Phillips' camera.

'They've got high-powered mikes on their cameras,' she said, concentrating, 'we can zoom them in and pick out individual sounds from the background noise.'

'Like an egg-scrambler?' said Ron, remembering Gordie's little gizmo back in the NTSB sound lab.

'Yeah, sort of,' Kronziac nodded, 'puts us within earshot of the subject,' she added, still turning the dial slowly.

'They're conversing,' said Jones, zooming the camera in on the side of Marx's head. They could see his lips moving, his jaw muscles pulsing. Jones panned the camera slightly to the other man, but all they could see was the back of his head, the bright yellow cap covering it.

'Shit,' Jones cursed.

'All right, I'm tracking,' said Kronziac as she continued to turn the dial, a sliding chorus of strange sounds coming through a speaker over the video monitors.

'Can you guys pick up anything yet?' asked Phillips, keeping his camera and microphone trained on Marx and the other man.

'Hold on,' said Kronziac, her voice edgy and strained, as the speaker above her mumbled and hissed, voices fading in and out as if she was changing quickly through the stations on a radio, only they were all chat shows, with voices young and old, male and female.

'There!' she hollered as the frequency picked up Marx's voice, his words matching his lip movements on the screen. They just caught the tail end of a sentence. His voice was tense, angry.

'. . . you know they won't take you in.'

Marx paused and looked at the man next to him, as if waiting for some reaction.

'Come on, come on,' said Kronziac, staring at the screen, hoping the man would turn around so they could get a look at him.

'Morris, can you get a better angle on him?'

He moved further to the right but was losing sight of the men in the crowd which was still growing around the entrance to the theatre.

'No can do, boss,' he said, 'all I can see is his jacket and cap . . . a Lakers cap, I think,' he added, recognising the purple trim on the hat.

'A basketball fan,' remarked Jones, turning to Kronziac, 'that's all we got on him so far.'

But Kronziac was listening intently, tweaking the frequency for the best signal on the voices. The other man's voice suddenly trembled over the speaker, a slow drawl.

'. . . Do you like musicals, Marx?'

Kronziac and Jones exchanged bewildered glances.

'Not especially,' Marx replied, an annoyed tone in his voice.

'My mother loved musicals,' the other man went on. *'She used to take me to see the old ones if they were playing at the movie house. The old ones were the best, you see . . . Rogers . . . Kelly. And of course my ol' buddy Fred Astaire here.'*

On the monitors they could see the man staring at the ground as Marx looked on, shaking his head.

'What the fuck is he doing?' asked Kronziac.

Phillips' voice came over the speakers.

'I think they're standing over Fred Astaire's footprints.'

'This is nuts,' Jones muttered under his breath.

The man's voice burst excitedly over the speaker above the video banks.

'*Well, whadda ya know?*' he cried. '*Same shoe size. My mom always said long, thin feet were a sign of good breedin'.*'

They could see Marx becoming agitated, more and more angry with the other man's rantings about musicals and Fred Astaire. '*Listen, I don't give a shit about your stories or your mother . . . just don't call me or anyone else at The Club no more,*' he said forcefully.

The other man laughed, a thin, squeaky laugh, like an evil dwarf in a Wes Craven flick, mocking its next victim.

'*Did you get the photo, Marx?*' he said, still giggling.

The picture from Phillips' camera suddenly jerked as he bumped into another tourist and for a moment those in the van were looking at the irate face of a disgruntled lady from some Far Eastern country, telling Phillips to watch where he was going. They could hear him apologise, and then the picture of Marx and the other man appeared again. Marx was rubbing his forehead, frustrated with the situation.

'*Jesus Christ! I mean, did you have to kill her?*'

Jones and Kronziac glanced at each other again. At last they were getting to the interesting stuff. Kronziac checked to make sure that all the recording buttons were on, taping the video and audio channels.

Ron stared at Marx's face on the screen, realising that the GenAir mechanic was talking about the girl found in the alleyway off Sunset, just another fifteen-year-old runaway, another sad statistic for the LAPD files. He shook his head in disgust.

The video image bobbed again as a small group of tourists walked around Phillips but he held it steady, training it once again on the two men.

'For Chrissakes, turn around,' Kronziac urged the man in the cap as he appeared with his back to them again.

They could see his shoulders moving. He was laughing again.

'Hey! I was protectin' my ol' buddy,' he said. *'What do you think Mr Grey and the rest of the boys would do if they found out you'd been messing about with some nigra pussy?'*

Marx leaned close to the man, his face tight with anger.

'You shouldn't have killed her, you coulda brought a lotta shit down on top of us,' he snapped.

Ron moved close again to Kronziac.

'Who's Mr Grey?' he whispered, afraid almost that Marx could somehow hear him.

Kronziac shook her head. 'We don't know.'

'Oh, shit,' said Jones suddenly, 'great friggin' timing.'

Ron looked out of the window as a long white limo pulled up outside the theatre. The crowd screamed and pushed forward, straining the barriers. The security men formed a human chain, locking arms to keep the eager fans back.

Some handsome young guy with a mess of long blond hair got out of the limo and waved to the crowds.

The picture from Phillips' camera suddenly jerked wildly as all about him fans rushed from the courtyard of the theatre to see the arrival of the star. He tried desperately to hold the camera steady as Marx and the other man's voices faded in and out. Kronziac struggled to hold the signal, the voices breaking up.

'. . . she was just trash, Marxie boy . . . just like Cap'n Slickback. He always thought he was above us . . . well, I taught him a good lesson in manners . . . he won't be givin' you mouth anymore.'

The video image shifted again as Phillips' camera wheeled up and then down as he was knocked to the ground by a rushing group of tourists.

'What's happened?' cried Kronziac as both the video and audio signals failed.

'It's goddamn' mayhem,' said Jones glancing out of the window. The movie star was making his way with his entourage of bodyguards towards the door of the theatre between two heaving lines of fans who had surged forward once more for a closer glimpse, some reaching out to try and touch him.

Phillips' voice stuttered over the speaker as he crashed to the ground and the picture broke up into snowy interference on the screen and hissing static on the rifle mike – the men's voices lost.

'Shit! Shit!' Phillips gasped saying. 'I've lost them!'

Kronziac reacted quickly, pulling her mouthpiece closer to her lips.

'Okay, Morris!' she shouted. 'Move in as close as you can, see if you can get a shot of them!'

'I'm on it,' he replied, moving around the back of the crowd to see if he could get Marx and the other man within sights of his camera. On the monitor all they could see were the contorted faces of hysterical girls with outstretched hands, screaming.

'There!' Jones exclaimed. 'In the background!'

'I see them,' Morris shouted. He had found a small pocket of space cordoned off by two heavy bodyguards just before the door to the theatre. Morris zoomed the camera in and on a monitor in the van they could see Marx and the man in the cap still talking. Marx was obviously in a rage, berating the other man.

'We still can't see his face,' Ron cursed as the man in the bright yellow Lakers cap remained with his back to them.

Kronziac tried desperately to retune the frequency.

'Just keep it there,' she told Morris.

'I'll try,' he replied, voice breathless on the speaker.

The star was near the door and the crowd began to swell around where Morris was standing.

Kronziac picked up their voices again, carefully tweaking the tuning dial.

'. . . *We can't meet any more,*' Marx was saying. '*Do you hear? And don't leave any more messages at The Club . . . you're too fucking dangerous . . . too fucking crazy . . . WE DON'T WANT YOU, GOT IT?*'

The other man suddenly grabbed Marx by the arm, his voice trembling with rage.

'*Don't you talk to me like that. I've earned the right to be in The Club . . . look what I did for the cause . . . you . . . you owe me!*'

Marx broke free and turned away from the man. The image on Morris' camera began to waver as the crowd surged once again while the star made his way towards the door of the theatre.

The audio signal began to break up, with only scraps of Marx's voice getting through as he walked away from the man in the yellow cap.

'*You're fucking crazy!*' he shouted with a dismissive wave of his hand.

The man with the cap began to turn around, screaming after him: '*You need me, Marxie boy, you need me!*'

Jones stared at the screen, watching the man in the cap closely.

'Come on, come on,' he urged, 'turn around, you son-of-a-bitch.'

Morris had to move as the crowd jockeyed about

him, filling the screen with waving arms and excited faces. The star moved closer to the door and gave one last wave to his adoring fans.

Ron, Kronziac and Jones watched the screen intently as the man in the cap turned fully around to shout after Marx once more.

Everything went black.

Instinctively Jones reached for the controls to see if there was something wrong with the equipment; maybe someone had pressed the wrong button in all the excitement.

The black shape on the screen moved like a huge monster with five tentacles. A muffled voice came over Morris' radio link.

'I'm sorry, sir, you'll have to move back . . .'

One of the star's bodyguards was covering the lens of Morris' camera with his hand and pushing the FBI agent back with the rest of the crowd.

'Oh, shit!' Jones cursed, realising what had happened. He turned to the lever which controlled the camera on the camper roof and swung it left and right, zooming it in and out, but could not see Marx or the other man.

'He's going to get away!' cried Ron, peering out the window to see if he could find the man in the cap through the crowds outside the theatre.

As the star swept by into the entrance the bodyguard pushed harder against Morris and the rest of the fans around him, totally obscuring any view of the other side of the courtyard.

'I've lost him! I've lost him!' cried Morris over the speaker.

Kronziac pulled her microphone close again.

'Phillips! Phillips! Go in, go in, we've got to get him!' she shouted before pulling off her headset and rushing to the back of the van. Jones did likewise, swinging open the back door of the camper and jumping on to the street.

Ron followed without hesitating, running across the road dodging between the traffic.

Outside the door of the theatre Morris reached into his pocket for his ID but the bodyguards thought he might be reaching for a weapon and leapt on top of him, wrestling him to the ground despite his cries of protest. The crowd screamed as the star gave one final wave and disappeared through the door.

On the other side of the courtyard Phillips frantically ran about, searching for the man in the cap. Near the back, amid a group of tourists, he caught a glimpse of a man in a blue jacket and a bright yellow peak-cap.

He drew his gun slowly and moved forward towards the man in the jacket until he was less than twenty feet away.

'Stop!' he shouted. 'FBI!'

This scattered the crowd in a million directions, shouting and screaming, some diving to the ground, others just looking around in bewilderment.

The man in the blue jacket stopped in his tracks and turned around slowly as Phillips ordered him to put his hands in the air. Jones and Kronziac arrived, their guns drawn also, Ron just behind them. But they came just in time to see Phillips lower his gun slowly, realising in disgust that he had cornered a seventy-year-old tourist who was now trembling with fear, babbling in excited Japanese.

'Fuck!' Kronziac stamped the ground and holstered her gun.

'He's gone,' said Jones, looking around at the shocked crowd, some people picking themselves up off the ground.

'We still don't even know what he looks like,' added Ron.

A small group of fans had rushed over from the entrance of the theatre to see the spectacle. Some of them began clapping and whistling, thinking it was all part of the show.

Kronziac looked about her, 'Goddamn' Hollywood.' She shrugged and shook her head in disbelief.

NTSB TEMPORARY FIELD OFFICE, FEDERAL BUILDING, WILSHIRE BLVD

It had been a long and restless night. Ron had tossed and turned in his hotel bed before finally falling asleep at about five. The events of the day in Hollywood with Kronziac and Jones had left him physically and emotionally exhausted. He yawned widely as he opened the door to their temporary office.

Carol was at her station, humming a little tune to herself like she always did, something by Tony Bennett or Sinatra.

'Morning, Ron,' she said chirpily.

But his mind was back on the case.

'Anything from the forensics lab?'

She shook her head.

'How about Gordie?' he asked, stopping by her desk to check for any faxes or e-mails in the message tray. Carol had been careful to try and make the office run just like their home in Washington.

''Fraid not,' she answered, 'he's still working on it.'

Ron nodded and threw some faxes from Washington in the bin – probably demands from Willard for reports and updates.

'Oh . . .' Carol remembered, '. . . that reporter from ANN, Mary Shaw. She's called several times. Wants to know if you'd give her an interview?'

Ron didn't reply, reading some paperwork from Jerry regarding the engines.

'I told her you were busy,' added Carol, feeling as if she was just talking to herself.

He nodded distractedly.

'Okay,' was all he said and he walked towards his new office.

Carol returned to her own work, muttering to herself, 'Morning, Carol, nice to see you, thanks for all the hard work you're doing, we really appreciate it.'

Ron stopped just before entering his office.

'Carol!'

She looked up, surprised, thinking he may have overheard her.

'Find out what shoe size Fred Astaire was, will you?'

As Ron closed the door behind him he was shocked to see Willard sitting in his chair reading through some of the files on the desk.

Willard looked up and gave one of his condescending little smiles. 'Morning, Ron,' he said and glanced about him. 'Nice office. I hope you're not getting too comfortable.'

'What are you doing here?' he asked wearily, too tired for another confrontation.

Willard stood up from the desk as Ron gathered the files he'd been reading.

'Spying now part of your job spec?'

Willard held up his hands.

'Look, I didn't come all the way out here just to fight with you.'

'So,' said Ron, sitting down, 'what did you come here for?'

Willard began pacing about the room, looking at the shelves, checking the view out of the window.

'The Board back in DC is getting concerned that there seems to be little or no progress being made in the investigation. We haven't heard anything from you in almost a week.'

He looked out over the city, LA basking in the early-morning sun.

'They think you might be losing your way,' he said by way of a caution, 'enjoying the California sunshine a bit too much perhaps.'

He turned and looked at Ron, adding, 'Though I have to say, you look like shit.'

'Thanks.' Ron smiled back and rubbed his eyes. 'So you've been sent out to keep tabs on me?'

'I'm here to help you,' Willard assured him. He walked over to Ron's desk and rested his hands on top.

'Look the Board, the FAA, the media . . . they want to know what's going on. They have a right. We need to be giving out the information through the proper channels, in the correct manner, not whenever it suits you.'

Ron nodded, smiling like an insolent pupil, and put his arms behind his head.

'You really like procedure, don't you, Willard? Correct departmental procedure at all times.'

Willard stood up straight again.

'I believe it's necessary for any organisation to run smoothly.'

Ron leant forward.

'Well then,' he said, 'since you're such an expert you should know that under the Department of Transportation Act of 1967, I . . .' he tapped his chest '. . . an investigating official of the NTSB, do not report to the Department of Transportation, the Federal Aviation Administration or the goddamn' media.' His voice was rising angrily. 'I report to the Safety Board and to Congress itself, so don't give me your departmental procedure or any bureaucratic bullshit!'

Willard swung around. If he didn't turn away he might be tempted to land one right on Ron's chin, knock the cocky little shit off his big chair.

'Oh, God,' he retorted, 'spare me the one-good-cop routine. Everything *is* bureaucracy, just like everything is politics, and don't think you're immune!' He pointed his finger at Ron.

The phone beeped. End of round one.

Ron stabbed the speaker button.

'Yeah?' he barked.

Carol's voice sounded coy, hesitant. She could hear them arguing from outside.

'Excuse me, Ron, but Jerry's calling from Mexico. He's on line one. Seems pretty urgent.'

Willard retreated to the window again.

Ron calmed himself down, loosened his collar and picked up the phone.

'Hi, Jerry, how ya doin'?'

Jerry's voice was distant, the line poor.

'Hello, Ron . . . can you hear me?'

'Just about,' he replied, straining his ears.

'I haven't got much time . . .'

'Where are you?'

'I'm in a small village, about twenty miles north of the crash site. It's pretty . . . well . . . let's just say facilities are basic.'

'Have you got any news for me?' Ron asked.

'I think so . . .'

The signal wavered as Jerry's voice tailed off.

'Jerry! Jerry, can you hear me?' Ron shouted again.

'Yeah, I can, just about. We think we may have found something . . .'

'What?'

'A piece of the engine, Ron,' said Jerry, the line getting worse.

Ron made up his mind there and then.

'Okay, Jerry, hold tight I'm coming down there,' he said. 'Keep everything under wraps, okay?'

'Okay!' was all Jerry could say before the line went dead.

Ron got up from his desk and began gathering his files.

'Now where the hell are you going?' demanded Willard.

Ron stuffed the files into a briefcase.

'Weren't you listening?' he said. 'Mexico.'

'But we need to sit down and compile a report for the Board.'

Ron had opened the door and was about to leave.

'You do it, Willard. There's plenty of paper around here, go shuffle some.'

'I told you before, Ron, I can have you removed from this investigation, you arrogant son-of-a-bitch . . . and it's a procedure I would take great delight in implementing.'

Ron stopped and turned around. The rest of the people on the floor could now hear the two men.

'I've got a procedure for you,' he said.

Willard smiled, waiting for it.

'Yeah, what?'

Ron looked at him and smiled back.

'Go fuck yourself . . . standard procedure for assholes!'

WESTCHESTER RECREATION PARK, WESTCHESTER, LOS ANGELES

People were enjoying the unseasonal heat wave. Mothers walked in pairs, wearing sweats and shorts, pushing their kids in buggies. A group of school children played soft ball on the grass. Couples necked under the shade of the oak trees.

At the eastern edge of the park in a large playing field John Marx stood alone. He was lucky, he thought to himself, nobody else around in the field, just perfect for him to test out his new model plane. Holding the radio-control unit with both hands he watched as the little plane circled about twenty feet above the trees and thick bushes that cordoned off the field from the rest of the park. The model plane executed smooth banking turns and dips in accordance with the deft movements of his fingers on the controls.

For a few calm peaceful moments he blotted out of his mind the events of the past few weeks. He couldn't talk to his wife about things any more. He had loved her once, a long time ago; now he could hardly bear to watch her as she picked over dinner or listen to her as she talked about her silly friends from the Rotary Club. For a moment he forgot about ACL248, its mangled wreckage, the unknown faces of its passengers, the kids, whole families wiped out, people he would never know. He forgot about Juarez, his angry face staring at him, blaming him, accusing him of all their deaths. For a brief moment he forgot it all – even the girl. He watched as the plane swung low over his head, its little engine buzzing, carving through the bright evening air.

He wasn't the only one watching.

Morris held his pen over three empty boxes of the crossword puzzle of the *LA Times*. He rubbed his temple, trying to get his mind going.

'Colour . . . three letters,' he said, mulling over the clue.

Beside him Phillips raised a pair of binoculars to his eyes and watched the model plane circle above the trees in the distance. He tilted them down and could see Marx slowly walking backwards, his eyes firmly fixed on the circling plane.

Phillips and Morris had been put on permanent surveillance of Marx and the Aero Club so they had to follow his every move.

Since he was not at work and had spent most of the time tinkering in his shed it had been a long tedious day for them. They had positioned their car in a small clearing above the park. While at a safe distance they could keep a close eye on their subject.

'My kid wants one of those things for Christmas,' remarked Phillips, watching the plane circling the field, around and around, buzzing like an annoying insect. 'The noise would bug the shit out of me though,' he added, watching Marx through the binoculars as he continued to walk backwards until he was almost out of sight behind the trees.

'Hue,' said Phillips suddenly, his binoculars still on Marx and the model plane.

'What?' asked Morris, looking at the crossword.

'Hue,' Phillips repeated, 'colour . . . three letters . . . hue.'

Morris squinted at the crossword, seeing if the letters would tie up.

'Spell it,' he said, still doubtful.

'H . . . U . . . Shit!' cried Phillips as he could see the plane suddenly dive and smash into the tree tops, its white wings splintering and falling apart. 'He's crashed.'

'I hope Marx is a better mechanic than he is a pilot,' said Morris, looking up from the crossword in time to see pieces of the plane falling to the ground.

Phillips scanned the field with his binoculars for Marx, but the mechanic had disappeared out of sight behind the trees.

400 FEET OVER BARRANCA DEL CORBE, SIERRA MADRE, NORTHERN MEXICO

The Mexican Air Force Huey hugged the contours of the land, rising with the ridges and falling with the slopes, keeping a steady altitude. The morning sunlight flickered in the cabin of the chopper under the clattering blades. Below the Urique river stretched its silver sinews away from the foothills into the level plains like a stream of mercury.

Colonel Pinchon tapped Ron's shoulder and pointed to a huddle of buildings which clung like mould to the foothills of one of the canyons. Behind the little village rose a parched clay-red hill with a clearing on top.

'This is it,' shouted Pinchon.

Ron nodded.

As they neared the hill he could see the local townspeople – mostly Tarahumara Indians – scrambling up the side like ants. At the top stood the unmistakable figure of Jerry Wojowski, holding a hand over his eyes, watching as they came in to land. Ron waved but Jerry couldn't yet see him. As the chopper touched down all the kids shielded their eyes against the blizzard of dust under the blades.

The rotors slowly wound down and Ron climbed out, followed by Pinchon. Jerry held out his hand in greeting, a broad smile on his face.

'Good to see you, Ron.'

Jerry was coated in a thin film of dust, his jeans and jacket were mud-stained and he sported a week's growth of beard.

'Shit, you look like hell!' said Ron, laughing.

'I feel like hell.' Jerry smiled back. 'Welcome to the Mother Mountains.'

Jerry led Ron and Pinchon down the hill to a waiting jeep which looked as if it might have seen service at Iwo Jima.

'Sorry about the transport,' said Jerry, hopping in.

Ron climbed into the passenger seat while Pinchon got in the back.

'How far is it?' asked Ron.

'About twenty miles,' Jerry replied and turned on the engine which coughed sickly into life. 'Up hill,' he added with a grin and took off.

It took them nearly an hour to cover the twenty miles of winding track which brought them up the foothills of the mountain range through a changing landscape of papaya, yucca and cactus to the ponderosa pine groves of the upper reaches. A headache pulsed between Ron's temples, a symptom of fatigue, the heat and the rarefied air. Pinchon managed to doze off during the journey and Jerry remained silent as it was too noisy in the jeep to talk.

They finally reached a clearing in the trees. Ron glimpsed the walls of a shack which nestled under a thick growth of brush. The jeep's engine struggled up the stony track to the house, squealing around the corners like a distressed animal.

'How did you find this place?' Ron asked, looking around at the yard in front of the shack which was filled with bits of timber, rope and pieces of metal. An old truck from the fifties, a Dodge, Ron thought, was slowly decaying in the corner of the yard, being eaten by an orange swathe of rust.

'Well, we did what you told us to do,' said Jerry, getting out. 'We searched along the flight path and asked a lot of questions . . . got no answers till we came here.'

The three men walked up to the door of the shack. The porch was hung with baskets filled with corn and kapok and two dead deer dangled by their back legs on a hook, slowly twisting in the light breeze.

Jerry knocked on the door.

Ron saw movement behind a window, the curtain drawing back slightly, revealing the face of an old man. He looked the men up and down then smiled with a mouth full of gap teeth.

'Can he speak any English?' whispered Ron.

Jerry shook his head.

'Not a word, but his Spanish is pretty good.'

The door opened, creaking and shaking on its hinges, and the old man appeared.

'Hey, amigo!' Jerry greeted him. '*Que pasa?*'

The old man nodded and motioned for the men

to come in. At least eighty, his skin was a deep chocolate brown and shiny like well-worn leather.

Jerry first introduced Ron and then Pinchon who exchanged pleasantries with the old man in Spanish.

Inside, the shack was dark and smoky with an open fire glowing on one side of the single room. A small hole in the roof acted as a chimney through which the acrid smoke drifted. Over a table in the centre a small gas lamp burned, lighting the shack with a dim warm glow. The old man reminded Ron a lot of Skid Mortensen out in Barstow and, now he came to think of it, the shack was not in much worse a state than Skid's old hangar.

They sat down around the table and the old man placed some tin cups in front of them and went to a cabinet nailed to the wall. Jerry blew a cloud of dust out of his cup while they waited for their host to come back to the table. The walls were decorated with pots and pans, hooks and dried animal skins; the shelves warping under a weight of tins and dried fruits.

'A trapper,' Pinchon said, looking around him. 'Probably a retired prospector.'

'Ever see the film *Treasure of the Sierra Madre*?' Jerry asked. 'With Humphrey Bogart.'

'Was that the one where they all killed each other?' Ron said, vaguely trying to remember.

The old man came back to the table with a bottle of what looked like milky water and was probably powerful liquor, Ron thought to himself – moon-shine.

The old man uttered something as he filled their cups. Pinchon translated.

'He says we will drink to good health.'

Ron asked, 'What exactly is this stuff?'

'*Tesguino*,' Pinchon replied.

Jerry grinned. 'Tarahumara version of Budweiser,' he said, and held up his cup.

The old man sat down and filled his own, draining the last drops from the bottle.

'It is customary before a deal is struck,' said Pinchon, urging Ron to drink.

He picked up his cup slowly, raised it at the old man and smiled. 'Well, down the hatch,' he said, and they all put back their heads and gulped down the harsh alcohol.

Jerry finished first, banging the cup on the table as he gasped and shook his head.

Ron coughed and spluttered as the *tesguino* burned down his throat, his eyes watering, stinging from the sharp taste.

Pinchon and the old man smiled as they coolly finished their drink, as if taking nothing more powerful than a cold soda.

As Ron placed his cup on the table, still coughing, he decided it was time to get down to business and turned to Pinchon.

'Can he tell us what happened, the night of the crash?'

Pinchon nodded and addressed the question to the old man in Spanish. He looked at Ron for a moment before talking slowly, his voice rough and gravelly with age and probably too much *tesguino*.

'He says it was not a very cold night,' translated Pinchon, 'the sky was full of cloud. He heard something overhead, a loud crack, like a big tree breaking. A while later he heard another crack, this time much louder, like thunder. It seemed to be coming from far off, in the distance, over the mountains.'

The old man pointed out of the window in the general direction of the range.

Jerry leant close to Ron.

'The impact,' he whispered.

The old man continued, his voice growing faster.

'He went outside,' Pinchon continued with the translation, 'and could see the glow of fire on the mountain tops. He did not know what to think at first, what had caused it. He thought maybe they had begun blasting the hills for the mines. It was not until the next day when he was checking his traps that he found the piece.'

'Where? Where did he find it?' Ron interrupted.

Pinchon turned to the old man and asked him. He nodded and pointed out of the window once more.

'About a mile from here, further up the mountain,' said Pinchon, translating the old man's answer. 'He dragged it here using his two mules.'

Jerry handed Ron a map of the area which he

spread out on the table and asked the man to show them where he had made his discovery. He understood what Ron was saying without Pinchon having to translate. He studied the map for a moment then ran his finger along the contours of the slopes until he stopped and tapped his finger.

'About here?' Ron asked.

The old man nodded.

'Yeah,' said Jerry looking at the area which the old man had pointed out, 'right under the flight path, about fifteen miles from where she went down.'

The old man began talking again, this time asking Ron a question. He looked at Pinchon for the translation.

'He wonders if the piece is a sacred object from the heavens.'

Ron smiled. 'Tell him it's from an engine, one that keeps an airplane flying in the air.'

As Pinchon passed on what Ron had said the old man began laughing and said something which he seemed to find very funny.

Pinchon smiled too.

'He says it must be a piece of junk if it just fell out of the sky.'

They all laughed for a moment, more out of courtesy than actually finding it humorous. But the old man said something else which stopped Pinchon smiling. He asked the old man to repeat what he had said.

'What is it?' asked Jerry.

Pinchon turned to the two investigators.

'He said the other men must have thought it was valuable too.'

Ron and Jerry exchanged puzzled glances.

'Other men?' said Ron. 'Did we have other guys down here?' he asked Jerry.

But he just shook his head.

'I was the only one around this area. Greg was at the other side of the range.'

'Ask him if he had any idea who they were.'

Pinchon put the question to the old man who answered immediately. 'He says they were Gringo . . . American,' the Colonel translated. 'They came looking for the same thing you're looking for, just a couple of days after the crash.'

The old man finished his sentence with a hoarse laugh.

'He did not tell them that he found it.'

Jerry asked, 'Can he describe these men?'

The old man pulled at his grey-white strands of thinning hair. 'He says one had hair this colour, only cropped tight, and the other wore glasses on his eyes,' said Pinchon. 'They were both big, strong-looking.'

The old man shook his head and uttered something dismissive as if he was mildly repelled.

'He did not like them,' said Pinchon.

'Why not?' asked Ron, intrigued.

Pinchon asked the old man who began smiling again. Turning back to Ron, Pinchon shrugged.

'They had nothing to trade, *senõr*,' he explained. 'He is a trader, he will only deal with you if you have something of worth to trade. He says all the other men had was money, dollars and a ring. He has no use for such things. Money is too heavy in his pocket.'

The old man began staring at Ron's watch and said something.

'He says time is the only precious thing to him,' Pinchon translated.

'Tell him I'm sure he has plenty of years left in him,' Ron replied, smiling.

'No, *senõr*,' Pinchon shook his head. 'He wants your Rolex.'

Jerry laughed. 'Go on, you'd better give it to him,' he said as the old man sat there eyeing Ron's watch covetously. 'Maybe you could claim it on expenses.'

'Son-of-a-bitch,' Ron uttered under his breath as he slid off his beloved timepiece and handed it to the old man who in turn smiled and muttered something back.

'He says you are most generous,' Pinchon said, amused.

'Suckered more like,' said Ron, feeling almost naked without it, 'Right,' he said, 'tell him to show us where it is.'

The old man didn't even wait for Pinchon to translate. Getting up from the table, he went to the back door of the shack and opened it. A shaft of late-morning sun flooded in, the smoke of the fire curling slowly in its golden brilliance. The old man motioned for them to follow.

The back yard was much like the front only more crammed with junk and bric-à-brac. The mountain air was thin and the men's clothes stuck to their skin in a lather of sweat. The trees swayed in a light breeze which brought them some relief. The old man led them quickly through the maze of junk, bits of timber, cartwheels, old bicycles and a mound of paint tins. Finally as they reached the back of the yard he stopped at the rusted skeleton of an old car – no tyres, no interior fittings, just a dull red shell.

He turned around, laughed and said something which Pinchon again translated.

'This is where he hid it from the other Gringos.'

Ron and Jerry came close, looking inside the empty car. They were now breathing heavily, their lungs unaccustomed to the thin air. The old man went around to the back of the car and after some effort pulled up the boot lid, its hinges grinding open. The old man stood back as the others came around to the rear of the car and looked inside.

Twisted and black with scorch marks, a long steel rod lay before them. At the top a circle of blades spread like an umbrella's spokes from the titanium fan disk, all bent and charred at the edges. One of the blades was severed, only a stump left attached to the disk.

Ron knelt down and touched the cold metal.

He smiled and nodded slowly to himself. It was the missing fan blade section from ACL248's No. 1 engine.

FBI FORENSICS LAB, WESTWOOD PARK

Ron had managed to persuade Pinchon to commandeer a military transport truck and take the fan blade section to Chihuahua Airport about 150 miles away where it was flown to LA in the cargo hold of a FedEx MD-11 SkyTruck. From LAX he drove the broken blade to the FBI forensic facility, laying it, carefully wrapped in polythene, in the back seat of his FBI issue car.

The severed blade, having been carefully detached from the fan disk, was about six inches long. Gently they placed it beneath the incisive eye of Taggart's microscope, like a sacred relic awaiting verification. Ron had called Bob as soon as he'd arrived with the blade. But Bob had berated him, saying that the whole section should be shipped along with the APU detector rod to the NTSB lab in Washington for analysis there. But Ron didn't want to waste time in getting the pieces back east.

Bob shook his head. 'They ain't gonna' like this back home.'

Taggart hooked up the microscope to a small monitor so Ron and Bob could have a good look at the blade magnified by a factor of 500. The scientist then slowly focused the powerful optics on the surface of the blade, which was curved like a twisted boomerang. As the surface came into view

213

Ron looked closely at the little pock marks which appeared near the point of fracture. A pattern of these covered the surface. It reminded him of a lunar landscape.

'Cratering,' he observed. 'Any idea why?'

It was unusual to have such a pattern of markings. Usually a fan blade should be smooth, burnt and badly gashed perhaps, but the consistency should be that of polished titanium, built to handle the enormous pressures it would experience while rotating in the blast of a jet engine.

Bob just shook his head. 'Could be anything. Maybe . . .' He was about to say that probably the impact or the post-impact fire had caused the markings until he remembered this section did not crash with the plane but was jettisoned before the main impact.

Taggart cleared his throat as if something was on his mind.

'What is it?' Ron urged him to speak.

Taggart pointed at the little craters on the monitor.

'Well, maybe it's because we come across a lot of these patterns in this particular lab,' he began reluctantly, 'but these markings are usually associated with a close-impact detonation.'

Ron nodded in agreement. He didn't want to come out with it himself first but Taggart had confirmed his own suspicions. He had seen this pattern before.

Bob frowned at the screen.

'Come on, guys, it's a bit early,' he said, unconvinced.

Taggart agreed. 'You're right, it's way too early to tell. I'll have to run a chemical.'

Ron kept his thoughts to himself. A close-impact detonation meant an explosion of some kind – a spark, a fuel ignition, an electrical short or a bomb. The word itself was enough to start a chain-reaction of hysteria and speculation.

'Yeah, let's run a chemical on it,' he said casually, shrugging off the possible implications.

Bob still wore a worried frown. He was afraid to think about it. It presented a whole new range of problems for them to solve.

Taggart stood up.

'Speaking of a chem exam,' he said, walking over to his computer, 'I've got more results on the APU rod. I think you'll find them interesting,' he added, purposely muting his own excitement.

He tapped at the keyboard and drove the mouse over the mat, calling up a bar chart on the screen.

'Each bar denotes a detected chemical trace group,' he explained, pointing at the bars of various colours and size on the chart.

He stopped the cursor over a small bar, coloured bright yellow with the chemical symbol HgO on it next to a large blue bar.

'Here we have the traces of mercuric oxide tagged to traces of zinc,' he said.

Bob wasn't in the mood for unexplained chemical terminology especially from some lab-head twenty years his junior.

'So?' he said.

Taggart strained his eyes at the bar chart, almost as if trying to see something he had missed before.

'Well,' he said, 'on their own they mean very little but together . . .' Again he was reluctant to go on.

Ron was getting impatient also.

'Go on.'

'Together they would constitute a major part of a dry cell battery,' he stated.

Ron looked at Bob whose frown was deepening again.

'This is way off,' he muttered.

'What else have you found?' asked Ron.

Taggart pointed to a large red box on the chart. 'Those crystalline structures have been ID'd as nematic liquid crystals. You see, they possess a uni-directional molecular structure . . .' he added, thrilled by his own discovery.

Ron interrupted him.

'Hold up, what are they exactly? Should they be there? Where do they come from?'

Taggart shrugged as if the answer should be obvious to everyone.

'Oh, usually they come from your calculator, pocket organiser, digital watch . . . any LCD – Liquid Crystal Display,' he explained. Bob just shook his head, not knowing what it all really meant. Taggart began to smile, relishing the chemical mystery in front of him.

'Here,' he pointed at a green bar, 'we have the most interesting piece of the jigsaw.'

Ron recognised the symbols, all ending with the letters – CH_2. 'These the hydrocarbons?'

Taggart nodded, confirming Ron's guess.

'Yes,' he said. 'Most of them are by-products and residuals but we've isolated the basic propellant,' he added nonchalantly.

'Propellant?' cried Bob.

Pressing a key Taggart brought up a window on which a nebulous cell structure rotated like a swirling set of spheres, some huddled in small clusters, others like giant planets, all dancing about each other to the forces of chemical bonding.

'Gentlemen, I present to you 2,4,6 trinitrotoluene,' Taggart announced, as if introducing tonight's special guest.

'What the fuck is that?' growled Bob, becoming increasingly irritated by the young scientist's theatrics.

Ron drew back from the screen.

'TNT,' he said quietly.

Bob heard him but still cried, '*What?*'

Taggart watched the little chemical monster turn slowly on the screen, its elements stretching out like bulbous tentacles. 'Yep . . . Mr Bang,' he said, marvelling at it.

NTSB TEMPORARY FIELD OFFICE, FEDERAL BUILDING, WILSHIRE BLVD

Bob kept at it all the way back: in the car, in the elevator, in the office.

'You're not going to take that little snot-nose seriously, are you? Been watching too many *X-Files* . . . and you've been hanging around with the FBI too much. The guys back in Washington ain't gonna buy this crap . . .'

Ron just smiled. Bob always ranted and raved when something unexpected turned up in an investigation; the more mysterious it was the more it irritated his sense of logic and order. He hated surprises.

'Look, we have to keep an open mind on this,' said Ron calmly as he swung open the doors into the office. 'Gotta watch all the angles.'

Bob was still shaking his head as he walked off to his own desk. 'We should move the operation back east where we belong. This whole city is nuts . . .'

For a moment Ron was inclined to agree. Ever since they'd got here things had just grown weirder and weirder.

'Ron!' Carol said, catching his attention. 'Agent Kronziac is waiting for you in your office.'

'Good.'

He had something to tell her.

'Mr Willard has also been looking for you again.'

'Yeah, I'm sure he has,' Ron replied, not too concerned.

'And that reporter keeps calling . . .' Carol added.

Ron checked for any messages in the tray and walked towards his office.

'. . . and he wore size 10½!' Carol shouted after him.

Ron turned around, a look of bewilderment on his face.

'Fred Astaire,' she reminded him. 'His shoe size was 10½, thin feet – a sign good breeding.'

Ron nodded, remembering.

'A sign of good breeding,' he said quietly to himself. 'Okay, thanks, Carol, nice work.'

Kronziac stood at the window, her arms folded, looking out over the city. Her long black hair hung loose about her shoulders, her head held at a slight angle like someone lost in a daydream.

'Hey, Kronziac,' Ron said, bustling in, 'just the person I wanted to see. Your boy at the Forensics lab has found something interesting . . .'

Kronziac turned around. The expression on her face did not show any great enthusiasm for the lab tests.

'What's up?' Ron asked.

She spoke quietly.

'Marx,' was all she said.

LA COUNTY MORGUE, USC MEDICAL CENTRE, MARENGO ST

The walls of the corridor were a pale sterile green, exactly the colour of the scrubs worn by the pathologist Ron and Kronziac followed to the 'cold' room, where the bodies were kept. The strip lighting overhead was bright, the bulbs buzzing with static in their perspex casings. It was the only sound, except for the low hum of the ventilation system and the squeaking of their shoes on the pristine tiles. At the end of the corridor the pathologist stopped and swung open a heavy door. Ron and Kronziac followed him in. Silent as a crypt, the large room was just a few points above freezing with rows of steel drawers lining the walls like giant filing cabinets. In the centre of the room was a single autopsy table, a heavy stainless steel bench which sparkled under the fluorescent light. Above it hung weighing scales, again of shining steel. Underneath the table stood a squat steel bucket on the smoothly polished floor. A super clean butcher's shop, Ron thought to himself, shivering.

Kronziac gathered her jacket about her and folded her arms. These places always gave her the creeps though she had been in nearly every morgue in the country.

The pathologist, whom Kronziac had introduced

as Dr Vesoles, was a rather handsome middle-aged man with thick dark brows and brown eyes that glanced periodically at a small clipboard he carried with him, clipped to his waist. He spoke in a very quiet, calm voice. When Ron thought about it he reckoned carrying out an autopsy must be one of the less stressful surgical procedures as the risk of something going wrong was not really a factor.

Vesoles pulled on one of the large handles, rolling out a drawer with the shape of a human body covered in a white sheet lying on it. The pathologist took off the veil, revealing the ashen face of GenAir's chief mechanic, John Marx.

'Philips and Morris found him,' Kronziac said. 'He was in his local park . . . broad daylight,' she added, hardly believing what had happened.

Vesoles unhitched his clipboard and ran his eyes over the autopsy notes.

'The laryngeal cartilages are extensively fractured and the victim's heart and lungs exhibited signs of haemorrhaging due to extreme pressure being exerted on the vagus nerve,' he read. 'This strangulation caused cardiac arrest and eventual suffocation.'

Ron turned to Kronziac. 'Just like the girl.'

She remained silent.

'I thought you had your people watching him at all times?'

'He went out of view for a few seconds. By the time they got to him it was done, all over,' she retorted. But she was angry with herself more than anyone else and, if the truth be told, she wasn't angry because Marx was dead but because her agents had let it happen, weren't quick enough. Now she might lose her chance of nailing The Club and its more senior members. Marx, after all, was just a foot soldier.

Vesoles gave a little smile, like a chaplain consoling the relatives of a fallen son.

'If it's any comfort, he died very quickly.'

Kronziac asked, 'Have you found any foreign traces?'

Vesoles looked at the body.

'The killer was very clean and precise. He or she attacked from behind and there wasn't much of a struggle. We have found some traces of latex around the neck which almost certainly suggest the assailant wore some sort of glove.'

'And that's it?' Kronziac said, appalled at the lack of any clues to work with.

Vesoles looked closer at Marx's throat.

'This is really only a secondary observation,' he remarked, pointing at a small purple lesion around the windpipe, 'but we have a tiny vertical contusion distinct and roughly perpendicular to the digital bruising on the neck strap muscles caused by the assailant's hands.'

'A ring?' Kronziac speculated.

The pathologist nodded.

'It could mean the attacker wore a ring. On one of the middle fingers, I would say, of the left hand.'

'A ring?' Ron said, feeling a little lost.

Kronziac threw her eyes up.

'Great,' she said cynically, 'the killer was married. That narrows it down.'

Vesoles covered Marx again and pushed the drawer back.

'Sorry. Like I said, it was a very clean job.'

Kronziac was glad to be out in the sunshine as they walked to her car. Ron followed slowly behind, an idea running through his head. He wondered if Kronziac had considered the same thing.

'You think it was Cap Man?' he asked tentatively.

'Cap Man?' said Kronziac.

'The guy we lost in Hollywood, in the Lakers cap.'

'Jesus . . . *Cap Man!* You should be writing scripts for Oliver Stone.'

'Were you able to get any leads on him?' Ron asked hopefully.

Kronziac shook her head.

'Ran through the surveillance video with a fine tooth-comb but still no clues.'

Ron had another idea.

'I'd like someone to take a look at it,' he suggested. 'Might help.'

Kronziac stopped by her car.

'Hold it, Carter,' she said. 'This, strictly speaking, is FBI business. I shouldn't have even brought you down here. Shit, I got my boss Foley on my back already for using up valuable resources at the lab.'

'Come on,' he pleaded, 'we're all on the same side. The new era of inter-departmental co-operation and all that crap. We're both looking for the same answer.'

Kronziac opened the door of the car.

'Are we?' she wondered aloud. 'I'm not even sure I know what the question is.'

RESTROOM, FBI OFFICES, FEDERAL BUILDING, WILSHIRE BLVD

Ron turned the tap and tepid water ran over his hands. He glanced up at the marble walls, almost sparkling in the low-key lighting. He looked at the floor, its tiles coated in a smooth sheen of polish, a sweet, alpine fragrance rising from it. The taps looked as if they were made of gold, for Christ's sake. He shook his head. The FBI sure had it made.

In the mirror he could see the door swing open, a man in a dark suit marching in.

Ron bowed his head and sighed wearily.

Shit. What now?

'Carol said I'd find you in here,' Willard said brightly, walking up to one of the white porcelain urinals.

Ron smiled at him in the mirror.

'You know, Willard, I'm beginning to think you've got a crush on me.'

Willard laughed, the sound echoing about the marble walls.

'You really are a funny guy,' he cackled, 'a regular fucking comic. Plays by his own rules, don't need anyone else, a real maverick. Yeah, a wise-crackin' maverick. That's how you see yourself, isn't it, Ron?'

The drain beneath his urinal gurgled.

'What the fuck do you want, Willard?' Ron asked as he stepped to the hand dryer and punched the on button.

'What do I want . . . what *do* I want?' he chanted, and zipped himself up. 'The question is Ron – what do *you* want?'

He reached into his breast pocket and took out a letter.

'This is your last chance,' he said, holding it up. 'Are you really too fuckin' stupid to take it?'

Ron laughed.

'You came all the way out here to give me a letter? I mean, haven't you heard of Federal Express?'

He took the white envelope from Willard and was about to crumple it up into a ball and chuck it in the bin.

'Another one of your memos on procedure, huh?'

'I wouldn't advise that.' Willard smiled, half warning, half daring Ron. 'It's not from me.'

He looked at the letter, puzzled.

'Well then, what is it? A Christmas card from the Chairman?'

Willard's smile broadened. He was clearly enjoying himself.

'Close.'

Ron became more annoyed.

'Come on, Willard, stop fucking around. What is it?'

He just shook his head and smiled a little more.

'I told you you were pissing them off,' he said

and turned to walk away, heels clicking on the marble tiles.

'You forgot to wash your hands!' Ron shouted after him but Willard continued out of the door.

Ron looked at the letter and then quickly tore it open. There was a short simple message inside.

INTERNAL MEMO

TO: MR RON CARTER – Office of Aviation Safety
FROM: JAMES CLARKE
RE: ACL248 – PROGRESS REPORT

Dear Ron,

Despite repeated requests for the above the Board has not yet been in receipt of proper information regarding the ongoing investigation. Therefore we request that you attend a closed meeting with an Accident Report Review Committee on the 4 January at the NTSB Board room at 9.00 a.m.

May I remind you that failure to appear may render you subject to departmental disciplinary action and possible suspension from duties.

Please bring all relevant findings.

Signed,

Jim Clarke
Chairman
(Washington DC)

VIDEO ROOM, FEDERAL BUILDING, WILSHIRE BLVD

Kronziac pressed the rewind button and the tape shuffled back with the figures of Marx and Cap Man making jerky movements in fast motion.

Ron and she were reviewing the surveillance footage they had taken of Marx and the other man outside the Chinese Theatre in Hollywood. Kronziac had the footage from each of the three cameras playing simultaneously on a split screen. She froze the footage as all three screens presented a different angle of Cap Man grabbing Marx by the arm.

Ron was staring blankly at the screens.

'You okay?' Kronziac asked, noticing he hadn't said anything much since he'd entered the room.

'Yeah, I'm okay,' he replied unconvincingly. 'Let's get on with it.'

Kronziac nodded, and didn't ask any more about it. She pressed a key on the console and one of the screens zoomed in on Cap Man's left hand. Through the magnification the picture became fuzzy and pixelated but was clear enough for them to tell.

'No ring,' Ron said, disappointed.

Kronziac zoomed out again.

'Could have taken it off, I suppose,' she said half-heartedly.

The phone bleeped next to the video console. Ron picked it up. It was Carol upstairs.

'Sorry to interrupt, Ron, but Fred Stranski has arrived.'

'Good, send him down. I hope you don't mind,' he turned to Kronziac, 'but I think he might be able to help us out in trying to get a profile on this guy. His name is Fred Stranski, he's a psychologist with the FAA, one of the best in the business . . . and very discreet. We can trust him.'

Kronziac stared at the screen and smiled to herself. 'I know.'

There was a knock on the door and Ron got up to answer.

'Hi, Fred,' he said as Stranski appeared.

'Hello, Ron.' He gave his usual goofy smile.

'Had a good flight?'

'Yeah, just fine. Sat next to a very interesting man with an unresolved Oedipal complex.'

Ron pitied the poor passenger unfortunate enough to be stuck next to Fred Stranski on a five-hour flight. By the time he got off he was probably ready to check himself into a therapy programme for psychological problems he was previously unaware of.

Kronziac stood up to say hello as Ron introduced her.

'This is Special Agent Kronziac.'

Stranski took her hand and smiled broadly.

'Nancy,' he said, 'nice to see you again.'

Kronziac smiled back. 'Dr Stranski, it's good to see you too.'

Ron was shocked, had no idea they knew each other. Kronziac, noticing his expression of surprise, explained.

'Dr Stranski taught me Criminal Investigative Analysis at Quantico.'

'Came top of your class,' he recalled, 'if I remember right.'

It was the first time Ron ever saw Kronziac blush or heard anyone call her Nancy.

'Teachers never forget their best pupils,' Stranski added charmingly.

Kronziac just smiled and blushed a bit more.

'So what have you got for me?' he asked, seeing the surveillance video on the screens.

They all sat down as Kronziac rewound to the start. Stranski took out his notebook and watched carefully.

As the third screen went dead and Morris' camera fell to the ground in the scramble with the bodyguards, Stranski began shaking his head.

'You were most unlucky not to get a shot of the man's face,' he lamented, 'there's not that much to go on.'

The others knew it only too well and stared at the dead screens glumly.

'Come on, Fred, you gotta find something on who this guy might be,' pleaded Ron, hoping Stranski's renowned powers of observation might provide them with a clue as to Cap Man's identity.

The psychologist looked doubtfully at the few notes he had scribbled in his pad.

'Okay, let's begin with the basics,' he said. 'He's in his mid- to late-forties, five-eight, five-nine, 150 pounds. Accent is south-west, Texas–New Mexico border, I'd say. Vocabulary suggests a poor rural background, not university educated, but possibly skilled in some technical area. He may be unemployed or a shift worker given their meeting was in the middle of the day. Or,' he looked up, 'he may just have had a day off.' He shrugged, faintly embarrassed by the lack of anything concrete in his appraisal.

Kronziac asked, 'Do you think the reference to his mother is significant?'

Stranski considered it for a moment, pinching his bottom lip with his teeth.

'Possibly,' he replied and threw the problem back, testing her. 'What do you think?'

'Single-parent family,' she suggested, 'abandoned by the father maybe.'

Ron intervened.

'Maybe he just didn't get on with his dad.'

Stranski nodded solemnly.

'Yeah, could be. Might be something, might be nothing at all. That kind of thing is hard to call.'

'Anything else?' wondered Ron, taking out his own notebook to write down any clues. 'Anything at all?'

Stranski turned over another leaf in his notes

and read the two scrawled words on the otherwise empty page.

'He does show the classic signs of the "Lost Dog" profile,' he observed.

Ron, intrigued by the words, repeated them.

'Lost Dog?'

Kronziac answered, herself thinking the same thing as Stranski.

'Will do anything to join the pack,' she explained, 'and quite vicious when running with the group. Usually becomes the most unstable, most aggressive, most crazy – even too crazy for Marx and his buddies.'

Stranski was nodding in agreement, smiling proudly at his former pupil's assessment.

'Many of these right-wing groups and extreme elements appeal to such individuals,' he elaborated, 'lost, angry, full of hatred for themselves and the rest of the world. They seek comfort in a shared belief system. This reinforces their deeply held convictions and prejudices.'

Ron was finding it all a bit hard to take in.

'His racism?' he said.

Stranski nodded. 'His attraction for this type of group is enhanced by his inherent racist tendencies which have possibly stemmed from childhood.'

'His reference to Juarez and the dead black girl?' Ron asked

'Yes. He talks about Juarez as always thinking he was more important. The word *always* is crucial here. It suggests that he knew Juarez at some time in the past and perhaps,' he paused, realising he was wandering into a tenuous realm of psychological theory, '*perhaps* the resentment points to a moment or event when Juarez succeeded where he failed.'

Stranski closed his pad, leaving his suggestion hanging in the air for the others to mull over. Ron looked at his own scribbled notes, trying to find some connection.

Kronziac turned to her old teacher.

'Do you think he was capable of doing . . .' she could hardly bring herself to ask the question '. . . what he said he had done? I mean, causing an airplane to crash just to impress someone?'

Stranski shook his head gravely.

'You can never underestimate the lengths someone will go to, to be accepted, to be loved. I don't know if he did what he said or whether he was just bragging. But I do know people are capable of anything, especially people like this.'

Kronziac turned back to the video equipment, rewound the tape and froze a picture of the back of Cap Man's head. She stared at the screen and prayed for a clue.

Ron circled some of the words in his notebook: *past . . . failed . . . Juarez succeeds . . .*

He turned to Stranski.

'You said a teacher never forgets his best pupils,' he said. 'What about the bad ones?'

Stranski and Kronziac glanced at each other, wondering what he was getting at.

119TH STREET, HAWTHORNE, SOUTHWEST LOS ANGELES

Paula Alvarez was trying to do several things at once. Her right eyelashes flickered as she applied the last strokes of mascara, her left foot wrestled with a new shoe, struggling to get itself in. She glanced at the clock and managed a quick sip of coffee, trying hard not to smudge her fresh lipstick.

This morning she could not be late. It was her first day at Union Pacific Bank. Goodbye to Mr Max and his shitty, greasy little garage.

She could hear Jordan out in the garden, calling her. 'Be there in a minute, honey!' she shouted back.

She finished her make-up and smiled at herself in the mirror above the fridge.

'Not bad, lady . . . not bad at all, Miss Alvarez,' she said to herself.

She glanced at the clock again. Goddamn!

She hurried around the kitchen, danced about the stools, throwing the dirty dishes in the sink, giving the table a quick wipe, picking up Jordan's toys which seemed to spread themselves across the floor whenever she turned her back.

'Right, just the bin left,' she panted, and pulled out the liner.

She found Jordan in the garden standing on the

patio. He was looking up at the balcony on the apartment above.

'What is it, darling?' she asked him.

He shook his head.

'Lucy won't come down, Mom,' he said sadly.

Paula herself looked up at the balcony but there was no sign of the cat, just the twittering of small birds nesting. She turned away quickly, preferring not to be seen looking up – she couldn't put her finger on it but the guy who lived in the upstairs apartment gave her the creeps.

'Come on, darling.' She put her hand around her son's shoulder and led him down the garden. 'Help Mommy put the trash out.'

But Jordan kept looking back as they made their way down to the trash disposal near the back gate.

'Is Lucy going to leave us?' he sobbed.

'No, honey,' his mother reassured him, 'she just likes playing with the birds in the tree.'

This did nothing to console Jordan as he became progressively more tearful.

'Come on, help Mommy open up the big can,' she said, trying to distract him. 'Hold your breath, it's very smelly.' She smiled and pinched her nose, making a disgusted-looking face.

Jordan began laughing at his mother as she lifted up the lid of the big bin. But she did not throw the bag in. Just froze, her smile dropping off her face.

A heavy stink blasted from the refuse, almost making her vomit.

Bill Murphy

'What is it, Mom? . . . What is it?'

The body of a cat lay stiffly on top of a mound of cans and rotten vegetables, its white fur streaked with scarlet daubs of blood, neck twisted and broken.

GOLD WINGS FLYING SCHOOL, BARSTOW, CA

Ron found Skid Mortensen under the old P-51 again. The plane looked in about the same condition as when he'd last visited, maybe even worse as some of the flaps and aileron assemblies dangled from their anchors, their control cables trailing on the ground. The engine cowling was opened out, spilling a limp bunch of leads and pipes.

'Hello, Skid,' said Ron, bending down.

He slid out from beneath the plane, face smeared with black smudges like war paint.

'Ah, Mr Carter!' His face lit up. 'How ya doing?'

'Not bad, not bad,' replied Ron, standing up again. 'How's she coming along?' he asked, running his hand along the wing's leading edge. 'Nearly ready to take to the skies?'

Skid stood up and, wiping his hands with a rag, looked forlornly at the plane. 'Someday, maybe . . . someday.' He turned back to Ron. 'What brings you back here anyways?'

Ron let go of the wing and wiped his hands together. 'Class of '75,' he said. 'You said there was one failure . . .'

Skid rifled through the shelves and pulled out one of the hundreds of faded brown manila folders that covered the back wall of his office. He slid the folder across the desk to Ron.

'Robert Jimenez,' he said and opened out the drawer beneath his desk. 'How's about a drink, wet the whistle?' he offered, holding up a newly opened bottle of bourbon, trying to tempt Ron.

But Ron was staring at the file on the desk. He shook his head and picked up the folder. Skid shrugged and poured himself a drink, giving the stained glass a quick rub on his sleeve.

Ron opened the file and began looking through the thin sheets of pink paper that had the same sort of details that were on Juarez' file which Skid had given him last time. Only this was slightly thinner. All the remarks and comments on the reports indicated an unremarkable student with low scores in flight control and navigation.

Skid held his drink poised about three inches below his nose.

'I still remember him,' he said, 'sitting where you are now, when I told him he wasn't going to make it, wasn't going to get his wings . . . shit, I can remember every young face we had in this place, must have been damn' near hundreds of cadets got their wings with us.'

Ron looked up. Skid was staring at some indefinite point on the desk, seeing the past.

'What happened? How come he failed?' inquired Ron.

Skid took a drink, a deep swig from his glass.

'He was good at the theoretical side of things,' he said, 'but theory can't fly a plane. That takes a pilot and he just didn't have it.' He shook his head. 'Broke his heart.'

Skid took another drink as Ron waited for him to continue.

'All the young fellas that came here, wanting to be the next Chuck Yeager . . . we didn't have so many but those who failed, – it kinda broke them. They had to leave straight away.'

Skid emptied his glass, swallowing hard.

'You know,' he continued, 'like in a ball team, if one of the players takes an injury or gets cut coming up to the big game, well, they get him right out of there, in case he brings the rest of them down. Doubt is the worst enemy of a flyer.'

'How did Jimenez take it?' asked Ron as Skid opened the bottle again and began pouring another drink.

'Oh, he just cried and cried . . . got a little nasty actually. He was a strange kid. Don't remember that much,' Skid confessed, 'but I do remember he was a strange fish. Kinda bitter.' He held up the bottle again. 'Sure I can't tempt you?'

Ron just smiled. 'Not just now, thanks.' He looked through the file. Stapled to one of the sheets was a small photograph of Jimenez. He seemed younger-looking than the other cadets with light, delicate features.

'You had flight suits for each of the cadets,' Ron

remarked, looking at Jimenez' bright orange flying suit with the Gold Wings Flying School insignia.

'Sure,' Skid answered proudly, 'suits, goggles, boots . . . the whole kit. We ran a slick operation here in those days.'

'You wouldn't have his measurements, would you, by any chance?' Ron asked, glancing hopefully at the crammed shelves.

Skid did not answer, just swung around his chair and ran his eye along the stacks of paperwork.

'Class of '75 . . . class of '75 . . .' he repeated to himself, searching for the right one. 'Here we go,' he said.

'Flight suit: chest 38, waist 28 – small; gloves – small too. Yeah, he was a little guy.'

'What about shoe size?' Ron asked, trying to peer at the folder.

Skid ran his finger down the page and stopped.

'Size 10½.'

Ron nodded and began smiling to himself.

NTSB TEMPORARY FIELD OFFICE, FEDERAL BUILDING, WILSHIRE BLVD

They had gathered in Ron's office. Jones sat in front of the desk reading from a fax that had just come in from NCHS State Records in Santa Fe. Kronziac paced up and down the room, her arms folded, a posture she would assume each time she heard something she found hard to believe or was not backed up by sufficient evidence.

Ron watched her. He knew she was doubtful about the whole thing, and she was right to be, but he couldn't help himself. There were, he thought, just too many coincidences.

'Okay,' Jones began reading the fax, 'date of birth August tenth, 1957, in Deming, New Mexico. Robert James Jimenez – born Robert James Kelsey.'

Ron put his hand up to stop Jones going on.

'Hold it,' he said. 'He changed his name?'

Jones looked down the fax sheet.

'His father, Brian Arthur Kelsey, was killed in Vietnam in 1967, shot down over the Mekong – an F4 pilot. The mother, Louise, remarried in 1970 to an Ernesto Jimenez, a ranch foreman, and they took on his name.'

Kronziac stopped pacing for a moment.

'The kid mustn't have liked it much,' she suggested, 'if he changed his name back.'

Jones went on, 'On his twenty-first birthday, New Mexico state registry records that he changed his name back to Kelsey by deed poll.'

Ron asked, 'Have you found anything on a Jimenez or Kelsey here in LA?'

Jones shook his head.

'Not yet.'

'He could be living under another name for all we know,' added Kronziac.

Ron was inclined to agree. He could be anyone, anywhere. There was a sharp knock on the door as Al appeared, carrying a small cardboard box.

'Sorry, Ron,' he said, interrupting, 'but I think you might want to see this.'

'What is it?' asked Ron, looking dubiously at the box.

'I went to the cleaning company, the contractors who work on the Aero Centrale fleet, and asked a few questions,' he explained as he opened the box, showing a pair of overalls inside.

'Blue overalls!' Ron exclaimed, 'The guy Edmunsen saw?'

'Maybe.' Al smiled. 'They found these by the perimeter fence the night of the crash.'

Kronziac came over and picked up the overalls with a pen, turning them around to examine them.

Al handed Ron an extra pair of thin evidence-handling gloves.

'And boots!' he said like a magician pulling a

surprise out of a hat as he took two heavy-looking work shoes from the box.

'Surely they have a record of who it was?' Kronziac commented.

'They would,' Al answered, 'if it was one of their workers. But everyone checks out. They don't know who these belongs to. No ID found on the overalls,' he said. 'All their workers carry an ID badge – it's the only way they can get into the GenAir compound to clean the planes.'

Kronziac turned over one of the boots to examine the thick rubber sole. On it was the measurement stamp.

'Size 10½,' she said quietly.

'So how did he get into the hangar?' Ron wondered.

Al stuck his hand into one of the deep pockets on the overalls and picked out a small laminated security tag.

'Remember these?' he said. 'We got one when we went to see Edmunsen.'

'Yeah,' nodded Ron.

'Only this one is all-areas, unrestricted,' Al said. 'We had to stay on the yellow lines. This guy could go anywhere he wanted. Only special guests of the company get them.'

Al handed the little badge to Ron. It looked like a credit card with the GenAir logo on it.

'Anything else on it?' asked Jones.

Ron turned it over and examined it closely.

'Some numbers, like a code and a name,' he said, reading it out. 'Cleared by C. Dickenson.'

'C. Dickenson?' Ron repeated the name. 'Ring any bells?'

Al shrugged. 'Don't know who it is.'

Ron moved suddenly, grabbing the phone.

'Let's see if we can find out.'

'General AirFactors, good afternoon,' a woman's high-pitched voice answered.

Ron responded, 'Good afternoon.'

'How may I help you?' the woman said quickly. A busy day on the switchboard.

'I wonder, can you give me an extension for C. Dickenson, please?'

'Would that be Charles Dickenson or Catherine Dickenson?' the woman asked.

He was stumped for a moment.

'Er . . .' he stuttered, '. . . I would like to enquire about a visitor's pass to the maintenance facility?'

'For what purpose, sir?'

Ron had to think quickly again.

'I'm a tenth-grade teacher and would like to organise a field trip for my students to see how they work with planes. It's sort of a project they're working on.'

Al, Kronziac and Jones all looked at each other, wondering what the hell Ron was up to.

There was silence at the other end of the phone and Ron began to curse himself for coming up with such a lame story.

The woman came back on.

'Please hold, sir,' she said. 'I'll put you through to Miss Dickenson.'

The phone clicked.

Another woman's voice answered. A cool, calm tone. 'Director of Operations' office . . . Catherine Dickenson speaking.'

Ron couldn't say anything, his mind was racing too much.

It was Roseman's office.

'Hello, can I help you?' Dickenson asked her silent caller. 'Hello,' she said again.

He cleared his throat.

'Good afternoon,' he said, trying to steady his voice. 'Can I speak with Mr Roseman, please?'

Al exchanged a quizzical look with Kronziac, who just shook her head and came nearer.

'Who may I say is calling, sir?'

Ron tried desperately to think of something to say.

'Hello . . . hello . . . sir, who may I say is calling?'

The words had come out before he could stop them. 'Tell him it's Mr Grey,' he said as slowly and as calmly as he could.

As Dickenson put him on hold Ron looked up and found Kronziac glaring at him with a murderous expression. She punched the mute button.

'What the fuck are you doing?'

Ron had no answer. It was just a hunch, an impulse. He pressed the speaker phone and gently lowered the handset on to the desk, waiting for Roseman to come on the line. Al was about to ask another question but before the first word could leave his lips Kronziac shot up her finger in front of him. He said nothing and retreated to a chair at the other side of the room.

'I'm hanging up,' said Kronziac and was about to press the clear button on the phone when Roseman's voice came on the speaker.

'Hello? . . . Hello, Mr Grey?' he said in a rather panicky voice, not the cool and diplomatic GenAir executive Ron and Al had met previously.

'I wasn't expecting to hear from you . . .' He paused. 'Hello? . . . Hello? . . .'

Ron and Kronziac looked at each other.

'Who is this?—' Roseman shouted.

Then the phone went dead, the line beeping vacantly.

'What the fuck was that all about?' Al asked, looking at the others, checking their faces for any clue as to what was going on.

Kronziac moved back from the desk. This had thrown her, really thrown her.

Jones piped up, unable to keep his conclusion to himself. 'Roseman knows who Grey is,' he said, shocked.

Al was shaking his head again.

'Yeah, and who in the name of fuck is this Mr Grey anyway?'

Good question.

Carol popped her head around the door.

'Ron!' she cried, smiling broadly. 'It's Gordie.'

He looked up at her. 'The FDR?' he asked excitedly.

'Showing all data streams,' she confirmed, 'and he's got the movie.'

The movie was a computer-generated animation of a flight using the information from the plane's Flight Data Recorder. It showed a model plane, cloud formations and terrain – replicating electronically the movements of the aircraft throughout the flight, right from take-off to the point of impact if necessary. It would be a potent tool in showing the events prior to the crash of Flight ACL248.

Ron looked at Carol and Al. 'Okay, guys, I guess it's time to go home,' he said with a mixed sense of relief and dread.

VEHICLE PERFORMANCE DIVISION LAB, INDEPENDENCE AVE, WASHINGTON DC

Ron sat rubbing his bleary eyes. Just in from LA, he found readjusting to the cold Washington air both draining and depressing. A grey night-fog rested on the roots of the city. The old building seemed dreary and desolate.

'You up to this?' asked Gordie, as he prepped his equipment for the preview.

'Oh, you better believe it,' replied Ron. 'I've been waiting a long time for this.'

Gordie keyed up his graphics program on the large twenty-inch computer screen and clicked the play mode with the mouse.

'Get your popcorn,' he said as the digitised shapes of the mountains crept slowly across the screen.

'Do we have to watch the whole thing?' asked Ron, rubbing his neck. He hadn't much time – tomorrow he would have to appear before the Board's Report Review committee.

'No,' Gordie shook his head, 'just the highlights. I'm going to start it just before the APU warning flashed up.'

He keyed in more commands and on a smaller monitor a graphic representation of a BD-12 flight instrument panel flickered on screen. Like a flight simulator the instruments would appear as they

248

had looked to Hunter and Juarez on the night of the crash.

Across the large screen a grey BD-12 floated into view, flying at 35,000 feet over the fake Mexican terrain. The computer took its point of view from just behind the tail plane so the viewer could see the whole of the aircraft.

'Here's the APU,' Gordie pointed out as the fire-warning light flashed on the instrument panel.

'I'll speed up the action a bit,' he said, shuttling quickly through. The plane made jerky little movements on the screen as the movie fast forwarded, the instruments quickly flickering. Gordie slowed it down again to real-time playback and pointed at the instrument panel.

'Here comes the second event,' he warned.

Another red light flashed on the instrument panel.

'Electrical failure,' said Ron, recognising instantly the warning light.

'Look at the time,' urged Gordie, tapping with his finger the top right-hand corner of the screen. '00.05 hours,' he said, 'exactly ten minutes after the APU warning flashed up.'

Gordie looked at Ron for some sort of reaction but he remained silent, taking note, keeping his opinions to himself. Perhaps it was just a coincidence that the two events were exactly ten minutes apart. He had to remain cautious.

'What sort of failure is it?' he asked. 'Power loss? A short?'

'It coincides with that unidentified click we picked up on the CVR,' replied Gordie.

'Yeah . . . and?'

'I found a match after nearly a thousand runs through the egg-scrambler,' answered Gordie, proud of his own exhaustive detective work. 'Frequency, wave and acoustic lines all correspond.'

'Well? What was it?' asked Ron impatiently.

'A circuit breaker on Panel 6,' confirmed Gordie.

Ron looked about him, searching frantically for something. He was about to get up and dash upstairs when Gordie reached under the desk and lifted up a thick binder, stamped on it in gold letters the words 'Drayton Industries – Electrical Schematics – BD-12 Series B'. The aircraft's electrical manual.

He handed it to Ron who took it eagerly and began riffling through the pages.

'It's got a yellow sticker on the right page,' Gordie pointed out, amused at his excitement.

Ron opened the page which was headed 'Main AC Load Control Center – Component Location'.

A series of boxes indicated the different panels of electrical circuit breakers located on one of the large racks behind the co-pilot's seat on the flight deck. Ron ran his finger down the page to the box marked 'P6'.

'That's the AC subsystem,' he exclaimed and turned quickly to the index, finding the page number for the aircraft's overview schematic of the AC power subsystem. On page 6.11 he found it. An outline of a

BD-12, its AC electrical system running throughout like an arterial network feeding electrical power to the lights, fans and instruments. He ran his finger along the main line and stopped at a point on the fuselage that indicated 'Open-Access' – the electrics service bay – the only part by which the AC electrical system could be accessed from outside the plane.

'Here's the third event,' Gordie said, and tapped Ron on the shoulder. 'Look at the screen.'

He watched as the model plane flew peacefully through the dark pixelated sky.

Gordie kept an eye on the clock which had just turned 00.15. 'Now!' he said.

From the plane's left engine a thin, elongated shape shot out from the exhaust and fell away from the plane.

'The fan blade section,' Ron whispered to himself.

The plane began descending, lunging downwards. Ron had seen enough.

'Can you synch up the CVR with the movie?' he asked

Gordie rubbed his neck and nodded, half yawning.

'Yeah, should be no problem. I can synch up an audio channel from the CVR with the graphics. When do you need it for?'

Ron looked at him, pleadingly.

'Tomorrow,' he said as if the word hurt. 'First thing.'

Gordie paused. He would have to work through the night.

'Okay . . . Jesus, Ron,' he said, shaking his head. 'Thanks.'

'I'll have the whole thing ready by the morning, complete with sound.'

Ron heaved a sigh of relief.

'I owe you one.'

'Owe me *one*?' Gordie raised an inquisitive brow.

But Ron was already on his way out of the door. He checked his watch: 10 p.m. which meant it was 8 p.m. in Mexico. Time to make a phone call.

WRECKAGE RECOVERY HANGAR, HIDALGO DEL PIERO AFB, SINALOA, MEXICO

Jerry put down the phone and stared at the note scribbled on his hand. The line was bad and Ron had almost to roar down the phone: '*Electrics Service Bay – 28V AC subsystem wiring*'.

Jerry glanced up at a large diagram of a BD-12 aircraft on the wall of the hangar office, eyes running down the fuselage to an area beneath the forward entry door of the plane.

'Why does he want that?' he wondered aloud. He stepped out of the office on to the hangar floor. It was quiet, not a single sound, the high roof cooling and darkening with the onset of evening.

Where the hell would he start?

Ron had told him he needed a wiring sample from the 28V AC subsystem as soon as possible and to send it to the FBI lab in Los Angeles for immediate analysis.

Jerry walked down the hangar, his footsteps echoing about the half-acre of enclosed steel and concrete. Spread before him lay the remains of ACL248, broken into several thousand pieces.

NTSB BOARD ROOM,
490 L'ENFANT PLAZA, WASHINGTON DC

Ron waited outside. Peeping through the door he could see the members of the Accident Report Review Committee sitting in a line in the middle of the room, chatting to each other. They had heard rumours of conspiracy theories, bombs, FBI involvement and terrorist groups. Now, they hoped, Ron would deliver them the real story of the investigation and where it was leading.

Sitting in the middle was Chairman James Clarke, a former Allied Airline Pilots' Association president with nearly thirty years' flying experience. After several years as Administrator for Government and Industry Affairs with the FAA, Clarke was appointed to the Safety Board with Clinton's re-election. A careful, thoughtful man, he guarded the well-respected integrity and autonomy of the Board with an almost religious fervour.

He listened carefully as Vice Chairman Richard Smyth, sitting to his left, described how he'd birdied the thirteenth at the Evergreen Country Club, his weekend haunt near the Bull Run Mountains. New to the Board, this was Smyth's first real investigation. With a background in political administration, he had worked in various departments of the Illinois State Transportation Planning Office before entering

Washington as a lobbyist for some large mid-west industrial concerns.

On Clarke's right sat an official from the FAA, whose presence Chairman Clarke had tried to discourage but had to allow in the interests of improving relations between the Board and the FAA. Too many times in the past differences between the two bodies had led to tension which was not helpful when they tried to get the FAA to carry out recommendations from the Safety Board. Geraldine O'Meara, an Assistant Administrator from the FAA's Office of Regulation and Certification, sat silently next to him, tapping her notepad, waiting for the show to begin.

Behind the three members of the Committee sat Bob and Al, both looking about nervously, wondering what Ron was going to say. Bob reckoned he had only one real choice – declare the investigation undetermined in its conclusions so far due to insufficient evidence. That way at least, he thought, it would buy the team more time to carry out tests in the Washington lab.

Al, for his part, just hoped Ron wouldn't refer to Kronziac or the FBI's involvement. A mere mention of the Bureau could spook the Committee into having Ron's findings quashed and a new investigation team being set up. It had never happened before but they'd come close a couple of times.

At the top of the room Gordie had set up three video monitors with one large screen in the middle and two smaller TVs, one on each side. He placed a DVD in the drive containing the movie, data streams and instrument graphics which he had copied from the hard drive in his graphics workstation in the lab. He tapped in a few commands on his laptop computer. On the large monitor in the middle the three-dimensional movie of the BD-12 flying through the air would appear. On the other monitors the cockpit instruments would show up as well as the data streams, running like lines of computer code, giving an electronic commentary on the plane's systems during the flight – all extrapolated from the Flight Data Recorder.

Ron waited outside the room checking all his paperwork. He took a deep breath and instinctively looked at his wrist, forgetting he had handed over his watch to the old man in Mexico. He wondered what Kronziac was up to. Had she any lead on Kelsey, any idea how to find him? Even if she had he doubted that she would call – he had compromised the whole FBI operation enough and she could possibly lose her command on the case. He shook the doubts from his mind. No time for that now.

He felt a hand on his shoulder.

'Cutting it pretty fine, Ron,' said Willard, pointing at his watch.

Ron just nodded.

'Shall we?' asked Willard, gesturing towards the open door of the boardroom.

'Yeah, I guess it's time.'

It was only as they entered the room that Ron realised McKenzie was there, sitting at the back with Bob and Al. Now fully recovered from his heart attack, he had taken a few weeks' sabbatical from the job but was as eager as anyone to hear how Ron had fared with the investigation.

As Willard went to take his seat just behind O'Meara he turned and, with an expression reserved only for the damned, wished Ron the best of luck.

Ron stood there smiling awkwardly as the hum of chatter lowered to a hushed silence. Gordie sat at his AV equipment, ready for his signal to go.

'Good morning, Mr Carter,' said Chairman Clarke, noting Ron's composure.

'Morning, Mr Chairman,' he replied with polite formality. 'Vice Chairman . . . Ms O'Meara.' He saluted them in turn, the members of this little kangaroo court. They each nodded back, O'Meara regarding him with cold dispassion, Smyth with a weak smile.

Clarke glanced about the room, like the starter at the Indy 500 making sure everything and everyone was in place.

'Shall we proceed?' he suggested.

'Yes, of course,' said Ron as he put his large black pilot's case on the desk at the top of the room and took out four copies of his report. He tried to lighten the heavy atmosphere in the room by apologising for any typos which would probably appear in the text of his report.

'I'm afraid I typed it up myself during the night,' he explained.

Before he began reading out the report he caught Al's eye and received a little nod in support. Bob, beside him, smiled nervously, wishing Ron the best but fearing the worst.

Leafing through the document and noting the abundance of technical terminology, O'Meara looked up at Ron.

'Please remember, Mr Carter, we're not all engineers or pilots here so you might have to explain some of the more technical aspects of your report.'

'Of course,' he said. 'I've kept it as concise as I could, given the . . .' he hesitated, not wanting to appear a smart ass '. . . time constraint.'

One night to write an investigation report – what did they expect?

Vice Chairman Smyth held up his copy and, turning to his colleagues, regarded the document with raised eyebrows.

'It is rather slim,' he remarked, 'it must be very concise indeed. Or perhaps thin on facts,' he added with a smirk.

Before Ron could tell the VC to go fuck himself – which he would have dearly loved to do – Chairman Clarke's impatience saved him.

'Let's begin,' said Clarke sitting up and leaning closely over his copy of the report.

And so Ron began.

'Ladies and gentlemen, I would like to present

to you my provisional report on the circumstances and causal factors which led to the crash of flight ACL248 and the loss of one hundred and forty-eight lives. This is a culmination of over two months' investigative work in various locations here and on the west coast as well as at the crash site.

'Aero Centrale Flight 248, a Drayton BD-12, registered N379AZ, was a chartered flight operated on an instrument flight rules flight plan under Title 14, Code of Federal Regulation Act 121 . . .'

He went on to give the pilots' names and an account of the delay resulting from the anomalous fire detector rod before the flight was finally cleared for take-off from LAX at 22.05 hours.

'The plane completed the first three sectors of the flight plan without incident,' he continued. 'However, as they reached about 700 nautical miles out of Mexico City and west of the Sierra Madre mountain range something happened . . .'

Ron let the words hang in the air, tantalising his audience as he took a sip of water from a glass on the desk before him. He had felt his mouth getting drier and drier.

'Gordie here has set up the animation of the flight and we have graphic representation using information taken from the Flight Data Recorder as well as on-screen replication of the aircraft's flight instruments and systems schematics.'

Gordie did his stuff, artfully keying in the commands which ushered the video screens into life.

The large monitor in the centre blinked as it showed Flight 248 manoeuvring through the sky above the black mountainous terrain, while one of the other screens displayed all the cockpit instruments. The third monitor showed a 3D skeletal image of the aircraft, illustrating its electrical, pneumatic and hydraulic systems.

'Nearly two hours into the flight, at 23.55 hours, a fire-warning light for the Auxiliary Power Unit was illuminated on the light shield.' Ron pointed at a little button flashing red on the instrument panel. 'This problem had occurred several times on previous flights,' he added, 'and in accordance with standard procedure the Captain ordered the APU to be disabled by the fuel shut-off valve.'

On the screen with the instrument panel Gordie placed a flashing circle, like a halo, over the APU fire-warning light. The model BD-12 on the large monitor maintained a steady flight path, the landscape barely moving below it.

'Here we'll bring in the pilots' voices from the Cockpit Voice Recorder,' said Ron, as Gordie cued up an audio channel from the CVR and began playing it for the committee.

Large speakers to either side of the video monitors hissed as the voice of Captain Luis Juarez came to life again. Running parallel with the audio tracks the pilots speech was fed out on one corner of the large screen in text form:

CVR TRANSCRIPT – TIME CODE
RELATE PROTOCOL
– 'HAL' NTSB – DCB-00-G-021

JUAREZ: . . . pretty dense . . . hope it clears before
we make descent . . .

HUNTER: . . . have you moved out?

JUAREZ: . . . yeah, my brother's got a place in
Marina del Rey . . . it's small but the view's
nice . . .

<SOUND # 001 – CHIME –
'FIRE-WARN INDICATOR'>

JUAREZ: . . . what is it? . . .

HUNTER: . . . we've got a fire-warn . . .

JUAREZ: . . . what system? . . .

HUNTER: . . . auxiliary power unit . . .

'The aircraft continued on autopilot,' Ron went on
with his commentary, 'maintaining a correct flight
path with all systems functioning as normal while
the pilots shut down the APU. However at 00.05
hours the FDR signalled a failure in the 28-volt AC
bus which was being powered by the generator on
the No. 2 starboard engine.

'This caused a momentary loss of some cabin
lighting and power,' explained Ron, 'as well as some
non flight-essential instrumentation.'

HUNTER: . . . so he replied, 'Yeah, I've got the Fokker underneath me' . . .

<SOUND # 002 – HIGH AMP. SIG – CLICK – PANEL 6 ELECTRICS AC SUB 28V TRIP>

HUNTER: . . . hey . . . what the . . .

JUAREZ: . . . what? . . .

HUNTER: . . . some of the instruments . . . I don't know . . .

JUAREZ: . . . mine are okay . . .

HUNTER: . . . no . . . flight instruments are fine . . . it's the engine monitors . . .

Clarke and Smyth took particular note of this, realising anything interfering with instrumentation, no matter how temporary, was a significant occurrence.

On the instrument panel a button marked NO. 2 GEN – 28V Bus flashed off while the button next to it NO. 1 GEN – 28V Bus came on. Ron pointed this out. 'Power was restored as the automatic transfer bus crossed to feed power from the No.1 generator on the port engine . . . AC electrical power was now coming from the left engine,' he emphasised, trying to add significance to the point.

The others in the room watched Ron intently, struggling to understand the alarming train of mechanical failures.

'Everything remained as normal for the next ten

minutes, the aircraft's systems stable, the plane keeping course. However at 00.15 hrs . . .' Ron pointed to the top right-hand corner of the large screen which was counting out the time of the flight '. . . the FDR clearly shows a failure in engine No 1 itself.'

From the plane's left side engine a tiny shape shot out of the exhaust cone.

'Not a complete blow out,' Ron admitted, 'but a fan blade had ruptured and was ejected. This failure compromised the Constant Speed Drive and so the No.1 AC generator bus tripped – again depriving the plane of 28V AC power.'

Chairman Clarke furrowed his brow as his eyes darted between the screens and the written report in front of him. Smyth remained expressionless, detached, watching Ron's performance with cold incredulity.

O'Meara was shaking her head.

'I'm sorry, Mr Carter,' she interrupted, 'the . . . the what do you call it? . . . the Constant . . .'

'. . . Constant Speed Drive, the CSD,' Ron finished her sentence for her.

'I don't understand,' she confessed, overwhelmed by the intricacies of the plane's engines and their role in feeding the rest of the aircraft with electrical power. 'What is it? What does it do exactly, this CSD?'

'The CSD,' he began, 'is a hydraulic gear differential device that converts varying engine velocities to a constant generator speed of 6000 revolutions per minute, thus providing a set generator frequency of 400 hertz.'

O'Meara stared at him blankly. Only McKenzie, Bob and Al were able to fully understand what Ron was talking about.

He stumbled, looking for the right words.

'Like a heart regulator,' he tried to explain, 'or a pacemaker, it keeps the generator revolving at a constant rate so there is no fluctuation in the electrical frequency. Without it the power would be too unstable.'

O'Meara began nodding slowly, glimpsing some sort of sense amid the confusing terminology.

'However,' Ron began ominously, 'as the engine had suffered physical damage the CSD disconnected and again the plane was without 28V AC power . . . and now a vicious circle of malfunctions placed the plane on an ultimately fatal course.'

'Couldn't the pilots simply isolate the left engine?' asked Smyth, feeling it an obvious question which no one else seemed willing to ask.

'Sure,' Ron answered directly, 'if they knew that it was indeed the left engine in which the problem had actually occurred.'

'I don't follow,' said Smyth, sensing that Ron was somehow enjoying leading his audience through the maze of events.

'The pilots could not be aware of which engine had failed as their engine monitoring systems had gone down when the CSD automatically shut off

power from the left engine, and as the generator on the right engine had already been cut, as
well as the APU, there was no back up for this
power.'

On the instrument panels some of the dials zeroed
out while on the CVR Hunter was noticing the power
loss:

HUNTER: . . . AC power down . . .

JUAREZ: . . . mmm . . . I think I can get a
vibration . . .

HUNTER: . . . engine failure, you think?

JUAREZ: . . . yeah . . . but which one?

HUNTER: . . . no EGT or vibration reads . . .
which one . . . which one's down?

'This would also have caused the cabin lights to fail
momentarily,' added Ron.

Al looked over at McKenzie as they both pictured
the unrest which would by then have been growing
among the passengers.

O'Meara interrupted again.

'Excuse my slowness on this matter, Mr Carter. But
did the aircraft have electrical power or not at this
point?'

'Yes, ma'am,' answered Ron, 'The essential systems
which kept the aircraft flying were fully serviceable
and were powered by the DC electrical system. All
hydraulic and pneumatic systems were in a normal

status and the plane was under control. It was
the AC electrical power not the main DC power
which was lost and this caused some of the secondary instrumentation to fail. This instrumentation
included the engine monitors – which keep an eye
on the EGT or exhaust gas temperature, oil pressure
and vibration. Any variation in the ratio between
these levels would have warned the pilots of a possible problem in an engine.'

Ron pointed at the engine monitor dials on
the second screen – all their needles resting at
zero.

'So at this point,' he concluded, 'they could not
know which engine had experienced the fan blade
failure.'

The three members of the committee stared at
their copies of the report with intense concern.
Whether or not they could allow themselves to
believe him, they waited with bated breath to hear
the rest of the report.

'Please continue,' Chairman Clarke said.

'In the situation where one powerplant of a multi-
engined aircraft fails but the actual engine in which
the failure has occurred is not determined standard
procedure requires the flight crew to proceed by trial
and error so that the errant engine can be isolated
to prevent the possible risk of fire. The captain also
wanted to descend to a lower altitude so that the
richer oxygen level would aspirate the remaining
engine more effectively. So as you can hear, Captain

Juarez had to take her off auto-pilot and commence this procedure.'

> JUAREZ: ... all right ... taking her off auto ... you have control ...
>
> HUNTER: ... I have control ...
>
> JUAREZ: ... we're going to have to trial and error ... shut off No. 2 and throttle back on No. 1 to thirty percent ...
>
> HUNTER: ... shutting off No. 2 ... cut back 1 ...
>
> JUAREZ: ... I'll get on the horn and request diversion to nearest airfield ...
>
> HUNTER: ... altitude three-one-five-0 ... and 350 knots ...
>
> JUAREZ: ... Center this is Aero Centrale 248 we have a single engine shutdown. ... Request descent to one-four-0 and divert to nearest suitable field ...
>
> ATC: ... Roger Aero Centrale 248 ... Mazatlan closed for runway repair ... Be advised Torreon International open approximately 300 nautical miles south-east of your position. ... Make left on to heading one-two-zero and descend and maintain minimum one-four-0. High terrain at 10,000 ...

JUAREZ: . . . Roger, turning left on to heading one two zero, descend and maintain minimum flight level one four 0 . . . Aware high terrain at 10,000 feet . . .

HUNTER: . . . altitude passing through two-seven-five . . . vertical speed . . . minus 2,900 feet per minute . . .

On the big screen the plane banked gently, leaning left on to its new heading, but still falling rapidly.

'Captain Juarez chose to shut down engine No. 2, the starboard engine, and lower the power in No. 1 to 30 percent N1. This loss of thrust meant they would lose considerable altitude but they had been cleared by ATC for a rapid descent to 14,000ft.'

'How would he know if he'd shut down the problem engine?' asked Smyth, looking hard at Ron.

'Well, if vibration subsided and they were able to maintain thrust, it would be reasonable to assume that the engine they were running on was in good order. When your instruments have failed it's a case of good old common sense,' he added with a brief smile, which no one else in the room returned.

He moved on quickly.

'However,' he pointed at the model plane on the larger screen as it banked through the dark blue night sky, 'at that time the plane was also executing a left-handed turn and they had lowered the throttle on engine No.1 . . . these concurrent manoeuvres could mask the real problem which was, in fact, in that engine.'

'But wouldn't it fail, now having to carry the whole aircraft, so to speak?' asked Clarke.

Ron did not answer immediately. He knew himself it was a question that could not be fully answered.

'They were in a descent and the engine was under as much stress as it was previously, so it basically . . . hung on.'

'Hung on?' asked O'Meara sceptically. 'I'm sorry but again I'm finding it hard to keep up with all of this. I'm afraid I just find it all too . . . well, implausible.' She glanced at her colleagues on the Committee. 'And I'm sure I'm not the only one.'

Ron nodded, in full agreement with O'Meara which surprised the FAA representative.

'Yes, you're not the only one,' he said calmly, 'but by now you might understand what it was like for the pilots . . . and they didn't have the luxury of time.'

On the big screen the BD-12's fuselage was rapidly descending, its nose pointing towards the dark triangles of the mountains below – their tops now fuzzy and indistinct, obscured by cloud. The room remained silent as Ron gestured to Gordie to play the next portion of the CVR.

'And one last element seemed to have sealed their fate,' he said. 'When flight attendant Rosa Velasquez reported to the Captain . . .'

R.VELASQUEZ: . . . excuse me, Captain . . .

JUAREZ: . . . what is it, Rosa? . . .

R.VELASQUEZ: . . . a passenger reported seeing sparks coming from one of the engines . . . I don't know if it's important . . . but I thought it best to tell you . . .

JUAREZ: . . . which side? . . .

R.VELASQUEZ: . . . er . . . the right . . .

JUAREZ: . . . yeah . . . we've just shut it down . . . we're changing course and diverting to Torreon . . .

HUNTER: . . . we're getting into cloud . . .

JUAREZ: . . . don't worry . . . the other engine will get us there just fine . . .

They all listened to the recording intently, everyone in the room realising the dire significance of what Rosa Velasquez had said. On the screen a thick bank of cloud engulfed the plane.

'Why would she say the right engine when it was the left one from which the sparks presumably came?' asked Smyth.

Another question Ron really had no answer for either – only those who'd died on 248 could say for sure.

'I don't know, sir.' He shrugged. 'Sometimes people can have a different perception of events, depending on their point of view. What's left and what's right can easily become confused.'

He turned back to the screens. The plane was descending quickly, this time no sky, no black mountains – just grey-white cloud folding in sheets about the fuselage. The data streams were running frantically, showing the aircraft systems at work as they fought with the sharpening descent. On the instruments panel the altimeter was running down the altitude in hundreds of feet per second.

'The aircraft had descended past its minimum flight level of 14,000 feet and was going down fast.'

JUAREZ: . . . we need to get this mother up . . . give me flaps . . .

HUNTER: . . . flaps down . . .

<SOUND # 012A – LOW FREQ SIG. –
EXTERNAL – FLAP EXTENSION>

HUNTER: . . . still nothing . . . we're clearing below the clouds . . .

JUAREZ: . . . height?

HUNTER: . . . ten five . . . we're in the mountains . . .

The sharp black edges of the mountains emerged through the wispy base of the cloud bank which began to dissolve about the plane like a ghostly veil.

Ron stood next to the big screen as Gordie kept a

close eye on his equipment, keying in the commands on Ron's signal.

'At this point,' said Ron, 'Juarez decided to apply full power to the remaining engine in the hope of gaining some height.'

JUAREZ: ... this shouldn't be ... this shouldn't be ... give me full throttle ...

HUNTER: ... full throttle on No. 1 ...

<SOUND# 013 – HIGH AMP SIG – ENGINE WHINE – POWER APPLICATION – A-CURVE ANOMALY>

<SOUND# 014 – SUDDEN – 'LOW BANG' – CONSISTENT WITH 'BLOW OUT'>

<SOUND# 015 – CONT. LOW FREQ SIG – ASYNCHRONOUS ENGINE REV FREQ>

<HIGH-LOW TAIL OFF – ENGINE REV FAIL – THRUST DECREASE – 'WHINE OUT'>

HUNTER: ... shit ... what the? ...

'With the increase in throttle power the damaged engine flamed out. By this I mean,' Ron began to explain, 'that the rest of the fan blade section collapsed under the increased pressure and the fan disk and part of the shaft section was jettisoned out of the engine unit.'

A bright red glow burned out from the port engine as the fan disk spumed from the rear and fell away from the plummeting jet. The white cloud had completely disappeared, revealing the harsh landscape of the Sierra Madre mountain range.

'We found the fan disk and shaft at a point 15 miles north-west of the main impact site,' said Ron, showing a point on a map of the area a couple of inches away from the big red X of the crash site.

JUAREZ: . . . engine flame out! . . . we're on the wrong one . . . the wrong engine . . .

<SOUND#016 – 'STICK SHAKER' – CONTINUOUS>

<SOUND#016A – GPW SIREN – CONTINUOUS>

JUAREZ: . . . start up No. 2 . . . start up No. 2 . . .

In the background of the CVR audio the first stage of the plane's Ground Proximity Warning system had triggered a whooping siren to warn the pilots of the plane's dangerous closeness to the ground.

'As you can hear,' Ron said, 'they realised at this moment that they had indeed been flying on the damaged engine all along. Captain Juarez ordered an immediate start-up of No. 2. But as the APU was shut off they had no power of ignition – so they had to go to battery. But time was . . .' He didn't finish, letting the CVR conclude the final moments of flight 248.

HUNTER: . . . APU's shut off . . . going to battery

*<SOUND # 017 – GPW – 'PULL UP –
PULL UP'>*

JUAREZ: . . . got to get her . . . gotta get her up
. . . come on, baby . . . come on . . .

The screen was now in almost total blackness, the grey model plane stalling, fighting for height.

On the CVR a third voice registered, an electronic voice, trapped in a tin box: 'Pull Up! . . . Pull up! . . . PULL UP!' it repeated. This final warning from the plane's Ground Proximity Warning system had triggered as the on-board radar detected solid ground and knew it wasn't a runway. Still the siren bleated away, ringing in the ears, like the aircraft itself pleading to be saved.

Hunter's voice shook, a high wavering tone, on the verge of terrified panic.

HUNTER: . . . too late . . . it's too late . . . sweet
Jesus . . . we're going down . . . we're going
down . . .
JUAREZ: . . . I know it . . . I know it . . .

<SOUND#018–HIGHFREQ'IMPACTBANG'>
Spool trip 10Q/y45th ++++++++++END

A muffled thud – a millisecond of high-pitched crunch, metal screaming against rock then sliced into silence.

The grey BD-12 froze on the screen, its nose touching the vast blackness of the mountainside. The data streams ceased, the cursor pulsing at the end of the last line, waiting for further signs of life. The dials and read-outs on the instrument panels had fallen dead, their real-life counterparts smashed to pieces with the impact.

The others in the room waited silently, as if each of them was waiting for the two dead pilots somehow to speak, to emerge once again as if climbing out of a simulator after an impossible test. To wipe their brow and thank God it wasn't for real.

McKenzie closed his eyes. He felt exhausted again. Al and Bob stared at the ground. They had heard the CVR several times now but each time felt that the pilots were talking to them directly, somehow trying to impart a clue to help solve the many mysteries of flight ACL248. Willard gave Ron a little nod and the faintest hint of a job well done. But it wasn't over yet. Ron had tried to show what had happened and that was difficult enough, now he would have to explain *why* it happened.

Chairman Clarke closed his copy of the report and laid it carefully on the desk in front of him.

'Thank you, Ron,' he said solemnly. 'I think we all realise that this was a most difficult investigation and for you particularly, given that you were dropped in it suddenly, so to speak, by being made IIC. We appreciate the efforts you and your team put into this and it was certainly the most . . .' he gave a slight, uncertain head movement '. . . interesting case I have ever heard since being appointed to the Board.'

Interesting? Al thought to himself. INTERESTING! That was the weirdest set of events he had ever come across to befall a commercial airliner.

Ron's heart sank as he listened to the Chairman's comments. He felt like the candidate who did a good interview but still didn't get the job.

'Before this Committee takes your report into consideration we will need to hear your findings on what actually brought about these highly unusual and tragic events,' said Clarke, knowing this was going to be the really tough part for Ron.

O'Meara and Smyth nodded eagerly, keen to hear the rest of the story.

'Yes, I agree,' said Ron, 'the circumstances are most unusual.'

'We could take a small break for coffee and give you time to prepare,' suggested Clarke. But everyone in the room remained still and unresponsive, wishing to get on with it.

'I would prefer, sir, to proceed, if that's all right?'

Clarke briefly consulted the other members who were all in agreement.

'Very well,' he said. 'Please proceed.'

Ron took a deep breath once more, opened his mouth and delivered the damning line.

'It is my belief that this aircraft was sabotaged.'

Clarke, Smyth and O'Meara stared incredulously at him. McKenzie shut his eyes again, shaking his head. Willard folded his arms and waited for the rest of it.

'Oh, shit,' whispered Bob.

But Al was smiling. Go on, kid.

'Sabotaged?' Clarke repeated, barely able to bring himself to repeat the word.

'Yes, sir,' said Ron boldly, trying to sound as firm and as cool as possible.

Vice Chairman Smyth leaned forward, looking at Ron as if he was someone who had suddenly lost his wits.

'Do you realise what you're saying?'

'Yes, sir,' Ron maintained, his voice a little shaky, his mouth dry again.

'You do know, Mr Carter,' O'Meara reminded him, 'that this Committee can only consider reports based on hard fact, backed up by evidence . . . not theory or personal hearsay?'

'Yes, ma'am, I'm aware of that,' he replied, still standing his ground.

Clarke sighed. 'All right, what have you got for us that can prove this plane was brought down deliberately?'

Ron handed each of the Committee members

some sheets of paper, stapled together insecurely.

'What's this?' asked Smyth, holding the papers gingerly.

'A chemical analysis report compiled by the FBI forensics lab in Los Angeles.'

'FBI?' Chairman Clarke raised one eyebrow.

Smyth immediately joined in. 'What's wrong with our own lab here in Washington?'

Al leant close to Bob and whispered, 'Not a good start.' Bob nodded. He had warned Ron about mentioning the FBI.

'The FBI, I believe, are better equipped and more experienced to carry out this type of testing. And I didn't want to waste valuable time by having to ship all the samples back here. LA was much more convenient.'

'Mmm . . . for whom?' remarked Smyth, unconvinced.

Ron waved the report in his hand.

'The first page gives the results on the fractographic and chemical analysis carried out on the APU fire detector rod. As you can see the tests clearly indicate the presence of striations – marks caused by a close-impact detonation.'

'Detonation?' said Clarke, staring incredulously at the lab report.

'Yes, sir. Analysis indicates the presence of vapourised explosive residues and dried liquid crystals from a timer device. In fact,' Ron went on, 'these timing devices have been identified as coming from an intervalometer for a Canon EOS 1 35mm SLR camera.'

'What is that?' asked O'Meara. 'An intervalometer?'

'It's a device you attach to the back of a stills camera. Linked to the shutter release it can automatically trip the shutter at a pre-programmed time – basically it's a delayed triggering device,' Ron said, and turned to the next page of the lab report.

'On page two you will see that the same tests run on the broken fan blade, which caused the failure in engine No. 1, display microscopic surface markings known as cratering – this again suggests close-impact detonation and . . .' he paused, allowing it all to sink in '. . . the same explosive and timer device residues were also found to be present.'

'What sort of devices are we talking about?' enquired O'Meara.

'They're known as firecrackers,' replied Ron, 'high-intensity TNT explosives which cause localised damage only. They're usually no bigger than your pen, but a hell of a lot more powerful than what kids use on Hallowe'en.'

O'Meara looked at her ballpoint for a second, pondering the possibilities.

Clarke was studying the results carefully. Everything was detailed with utmost precision – but what did it all mean?

'How do these . . . devices relate to the eventual crash of 248?'

Ron nodded to Gordie who called up the electrical

schematic of the BD-12 on the large screen, its various subsystems drawn in different colours.

'The crash was caused by three related contributory events,' he stated, and pointed to the rear of the plane, under the fuselage. 'Here a small detonation on the APU fire detector rod signalled a fire-warning for the APU in the cockpit.'

On the instrument panel, still on one of the small screens, Gordie highlighted the APU FIRE-WARN indicator.

'This caused the pilots to shut down the Auxiliary Power Unit.'

A red line running from the APU at the rear of the plane to the cockpit flashed on the screen.

'The second event occurred at 00.05 hours, which caused the AC power, which was being generated by engine No.2, to fail and so the automatic transfer bus tripped to engine No.1. We found this as one of the sounds, number 002 on the CVR, was identified in analysis as a breaker trip on Panel 6 on the electrical board behind the co-pilot's seat.

'At 00.15 hours, exactly *ten* minutes later, again a small fan blade failure occurred in engine No.1.'

Gordie pressed a button on his keyboard and a blue spark flashed on the port engine.

'This was also caused by a small device being attached to one of the fan blades.'

In the top right-hand corner of the big screen a box opened up, showing the long conical shape of one of the plane's Juno XD104 engines, its fan blades slowly rotating, an airflow running through the exhaust chamber. A small fan blade broke in two and was ejected through the exhaust.

'Now the aircraft was without the vital back-up power system and had one bad engine. Though serviceable, it would not stand up to much stress being placed on it . . . the bad visibility and high terrain were the final factors which brought about the tragedy,' Ron added finally.

O'Meara immediately spoke up, several questions clearly preying on her mind.

'I'm intrigued,' she began, 'as to how anyone could possibly plant these devices in such various locations around the plane?'

Ron had been waiting for that one.

'I believe there was an opportunity just hours prior to 248's departure from LAX,' he replied. 'Because of recurrent maintenance problems with the APU detector rod, the maintenance mechanics had to carry out checks on all the aircraft's fire detectors in accordance with FAA directives.'

O'Meara smiled, acknowledging Ron's reference to her organisation.

'This meant that crucial areas of the plane were exposed,' he continued, 'the APU, both engines and the electrics service bay.'

On the large screen these four areas were indicated; the APU at the rear, the two engines and the electrics service bay on the fuselage, just behind the flight deck.

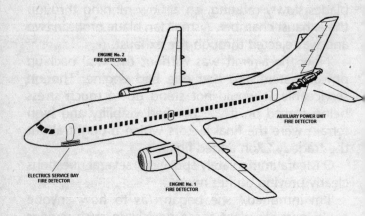

'Are you saying one of the mechanics placed these devices on the plane?' asked Smyth, appalled at the idea.

Ron referred to his notes on Edmunsen's statement.

'No,' he answered, 'but they had to leave the aircraft unattended for a few minutes to sign off the work on the maintenance log. It was during these few minutes that someone would have had the chance to plant the . . . firecrackers.'

Ron could see Willard staring at him, an expression of disbelief frozen on his face.

'Did any of the mechanics report seeing anyone near the plane?' asked Clarke. 'Surely they would have seen someone?'

Ron looked at Edmunsen's statement.

'The junior mechanic, Paul Edmunsen, testified that he saw an unidentified man in blue overalls talking to chief mechanic John Marx that night in the hangar.'

'Did you get to talk to Marx about this man?' asked Smyth.

'No, sir,' Ron said blankly, waiting for the inevitable follow-up.

And it came.

'No?' said Smyth. 'Why not?'

'Never got a chance to,' said Ron, 'John Marx was murdered three days ago.'

The room was shocked into silence, the members of the Committee exchanging sharp glances. Bob and Al knew about it, of course, but the news came as a shock to the others in the room – and in a way added a little credibility to Ron's sabotage theory or at least was in keeping with the sinister nature of the whole case.

Vice Chairman Smyth picked up his copy of the lab report.

'Mr Carter, something concerns me,' he said, as if about to uncover something that would derail the whole theory. 'You say that there was a device in the 28volt AC system?'

'Yes, sir, on the wiring in the electrics service bay.' Ron pointed at the aircraft schematic on the screen with the service bay shown.

Smyth held the report, pinching it like someone holding up a dirty rag. 'Yet there doesn't seem to be any chemical analysis, test results, or anything in reference to the wiring in your report.'

Ron tried to think fast as the room waited for his answer. Bob and Al knew he didn't have the chemical report.

'Not yet,' he confessed flatly.

'*Not yet?*' Smyth queried in disbelief.

'No, sir, I have instructed our field investigator at the site to send the AC wiring samples from the service bay to the lab in Los Angeles . . . I'm still awaiting the results.'

They all looked at Ron for a moment, expecting him to come back with more than that, another unlikely reason or outlandish explanation for the delay. But suddenly the weeks of travelling, the chasing, the probing, the lack of sleep, the worry and now this inquisition seemed to catch up with Ron as he slumped, exhausted, against the desk. He had no more answers.

'Is that all?' asked Clarke.

Ron nodded. 'That's it.'

Clarke rose to his feet and addressed everyone in the room. It was all strangely anti-climactic.

'All right, everyone,' he said, 'in view of the extraordinary nature of this crash report we will be taking the investigation findings under careful deliberation for a couple of days before making any public statement. I hope that you all realise that everything said here today is strictly confidential. I need not remind you,' he warned, 'what the press would do with this.'

He turned to Ron finally.

'Thank you, Mr Carter.'

The three Committee members rose in unison and retreated from the room like judges leaving a court. As they went out Vice Chairman Smyth stooped and whispered something into McKenzie's ear. Ron couldn't help wondering what he was saying. He remained leaning against the desk.

Gordie clapped him on the back.

'Well done,' he said earnestly before turning to gather up his equipment. Before he went Ron stopped him.

'Can you give me a copy of the movie?'

Gordie pursed his lips.

'Yeah, sure, I'll run you up a copy,' he said, finally.

'Get some sleep, chief!' urged Bob, seeing Ron's pale face.

'Yeah, you look like shit,' added Al, smiling.

Willard's reaction surprised Ron the most. He'd expected him to give some smart remark or to laugh slyly at his imminent dismissal as IIC.

'Jesus, Ron,' he began, shaking his head, 'that was . . . unbelievable.'

Perhaps not the right word but his tone suggested he was genuinely impressed.

But Ron still didn't trust him.

McKenzie was the last to approach him. The grave expression on his face did not auger well.

'Can I see you for a moment?' he asked.

Ron shrugged. 'Sure.'

*   *   *

'Shut the door,' said McKenzie as they entered the Vice Chairman's office.

It was bad. These were the first words he had said since they'd come up from the boardroom on the fifth floor.

'Nice office,' said Ron, looking wearily around.

McKenzie closed his eyes and held his head between his hands as if suffering from a severe headache.

'You okay, Bill?' asked Ron, leaning towards his old friend.

McKenzie looked up sharply.

'What the fuck was that?' he barked, almost knocking Ron back into his seat. 'Jesus!' he shouted again. 'You're an investigating official with the NTSB – not fucking James Bond!'

Ron was too shocked to say anything.

'You've been too busy running around with the FBI out in California when you should have been here conducting a proper and thorough investigation!' McKenzie raged.

Ron, stunned, couldn't get a word in.

'We have to base our findings on the facts as we find them, not crackpot sabotage theories!'

He had never seen McKenzie so angry. Many times he had seen him lose his temper but this was different, ominous.

'Come on,' pleaded Ron, trying to defend himself, 'too many things went wrong with that plane to be just an accident.'

'You don't even have a lab test for the electrical system you claimed was tampered with!' McKenzie cried accusingly.

Ron was about to defend himself further when McKenzie put up his hand. He suddenly calmed himself down, the rage in his face subsiding.

'Look, Ron,' he said, low-voiced, 'you know you've always been one of my favourites . . . It sounds like phoney crap but you were almost like a son to me.'

'Were?' Ron said, feeling as if he was about to be banished from the family.

McKenzie ignored him.

'What I heard in there today sounded like some twisted fucking fantasy.'

'It's not, Bill,' he said quietly. 'People are being murdered, for Christ's sake . . . the whole thing stinks to high heaven. There's something bigger here, I can feel it, and given the time I can prove it.'

A look of disgust crossed McKenzie's face.

'You can *feel* it?' he said. 'You can fucking feel it? It's not your job to *feel* anything – your job is to investigate the facts.'

Ron was tired of arguing, tired of trying to convince everyone, tired of feeling like an outsider, a nut.

'What do you suggest I do?' he said coldly.

McKenzie warmed a little. Perhaps Ron had come to his senses.

'Stay close to home,' he urged, 'slow down, run those tests again. But here, in our own labs, with our own people.'

Ron listened, nodding as if taking it all in.

'You saw how they looked at you, Clarke and Smyth and that FAA woman. They're probably talking about you right now . . .'

'. . . and what a fruitcake I am?' Ron interrupted angrily.

McKenzie looked at him straight.

'You could hand over the case,' he suggested. 'Let someone else take the shit.'

'And if I don't?'

'Well, they could take you off it.'

'They?' said Ron. 'Who exactly are *they*?'

There was sudden banging on the door as Al appeared, excitedly babbling something about Kronziac and the FBI.

'What is it?' asked Ron, turning around.

'Just got a call from Kronziac in LA,' he blurted out. 'They found Kelsey.'

Ron shot out of his seat.

'Where?'

'I don't know,' said Al, 'but they're staking him out.'

Ron turned to McKenzie, who stared at him intently, pleading, knowing this was the last chance.

'I'm sorry, Bill, I've got to see it through,' Ron told him.

McKenzie shook his head and sank back into his chair. As Ron and Al rushed out, he reached for the phone.

REAGAN NATIONAL AIRPORT, WASHINGTON DC

Rain drew a dark curtain over the airport, driven in sheets by a north-westerly gust that roared down the Potomac. The landing-strip lights disappeared into the distance, the control tower beacon slowly swinging through the gloom like a lighthouse over looking treacherous seas.

'It's here,' said Ron, halting the car at the FAA compound gates and peering at the sleek shape of the LearJet through the wire fencing, parked at the hangar door. They waited as the security man put on his hat and raincoat in the check-point cabin.

'Hi, John,' said Ron as the security man came out. 'Nasty evening.'

He bent down to the open window, the freezing rain thrumming heavily on his hat.

'Sure is, Mr Carter, might even close the airport. Hello Mr Martinez.' He tipped his cap, noticing Al in the passenger seat.

Ron felt something was up. Usually John would just open the gate and let them in immediately, maybe shout hello and a few words as they went by. But he just stood there, the rain battering his shoulders.

'Is the jet ready? . . . I called earlier to see if it was

available,' Ron said, trying to hint to him to open the gate.

He nodded.

'It's ready, Mr Carter, has been fuelled up an' all, but . . .'

'What is it, John?' asked Ron, sensing there was something definitely wrong.

'I'm sorry but I can't let you in.'

'What?' said Ron calmly, thinking it was some sort of wind-up. He knew sometimes the FAA were careful about the plane but when an NTSB IIC requested to use it, as part of an active investigation, there was never any question.

John just shook his head.

'Orders . . . from the brass.'

Al leant over.

'Who? Whose orders?' he demanded to know. 'Was it that prick Willard?'

'No, sir, I don't think so.'

'Then who?' asked Ron.

John didn't answer, jerking his head back suddenly to see who was coming as another car pulled up to the checkpoint.

'Excuse me,' he said, and he walked back to it.

They looked in the mirror but could only see a dark figure behind the wheel of the car.

'Who is it?' Al asked.

'Beats me,' said Ron, watching in the mirror as John stood back from the car behind and walked past them to the cabin. He seemed agitated, cursing angrily beneath his breath as he punched the big green button on the barrier and the gate clunked and then slowly raised itself into the air.

'Can we go through now?' Ron shouted at him through the rain.

'Go on, go ahead,' John barked back, not at all happy.

'What are we waiting for?' said Al, and urged Ron to go.

But he was looking again in his side mirror at the car behind. The driver's door swung open and a familiar figure got out. He pulled up the collar of his raincoat, walked up to Ron's car and leant in the window.

'I'm getting sick of always chasing you around the place,' he said, his dark face streaming with rain.

It was Willard.

'This time you ain't going without me.'

Ron ran through a pre-flight check list in the cramped cockpit of the LearJet as they waited on the runway. Al, in the right-hand seat, ran his pen over a flight plan which would take them across the country and into Los Angeles. He jotted down a few fuel calculations and kept an ear on the weather bulletins over the radio.

'No fuel stops,' he announced, almost triumphantly, enjoying acting as co-pilot. 'Sure glad this Lear's a long-ranger.'

'Are you sure we should be taking off in this

weather?' asked Willard, tightening his belt in the jump seat behind. He stared out through the rain streaked visor, the runway lights threading into the distance, narrowing into the teeming darkness.

'We'll be fine,' Al assured him. 'Ron loves flying in this,' he added, smiling.

'Once we get through the cloud we'll have a straight run,' said Ron, gripping the control column with both his hands, waiting for clearance from the tower.

Al turned around to Willard.

'What did you say to him anyway, to get him to let us in?'

Willard shrugged, acting all innocent.

'Oh, I just quoted a lot of procedure . . .' he said casually. 'And threatened to have him fired.'

Ron turned around as well, surprised at Willard.

'You threatened him?'

'Told him he'd be obstructing the law,' Willard added, giddy with newfound impulsiveness.

Al narrowed his eyes.

'But someone from the FAA or the Board must have called earlier to tell John not to let us in,' he said. 'Someone high up . . . one of your bosses.'

'Yeah, I think it was probably O'Meara.'

Al glanced at Ron.

'That bitch had it in for you,' he said, not missing the opportunity to take a crack at another FAA official. Not his favourite people, the suits at the FAA.

'Though I think she might have gotten the order from higher up,' remarked Willard without explaining any further.

'How high?' asked Al.

But he just shook his head. 'Don't know.'

Over the radio a little voice from ground control warned of cross winds gusting through the airfield. Ron checked his instruments, making slight adjustments to ready the plane for take-off clearance.

'You both should realise we might lose our jobs,' he warned.

Willard and Al didn't say anything for a moment, just stared out at the runway and the darkness beyond. Sheets of rain gusted and billowed like sails across the airport, the lights of the tenders flickering amber and green by the terminals.

'One hundred and forty-eight people were killed,' Willard said quietly, 'and if there is some nut out there responsible for that, then it's our job to stop him.'

'Whoah, wait up, Wyatt Earp,' said Ron. 'Why the sudden change of heart? You called me an arrogant son of a bitch for saying something similar, remember?'

'Yeah, I remember,' Willard nodded, 'and I still think you're an arrogant and *irresponsible* son of a bitch,' he added for good measure. 'But what I saw in that room today took guts. Maybe it was all a barrel of shit what you were saying . . . but what if, just what if, it's true? And besides, I don't think they gave you a fair hearing. That's something I know about,' he added.

'What are you going to tell your bosses?' asked Al.

Willard thought about it for a moment.

'Might tell 'em to go fuck themselves,' he said. 'Standard procedure for assholes, I believe.'

'We'll make a tin kicker of him yet,' laughed Al.

The radio crackled into life as the tower cleared them for take-off.

'Okay, guys, buckle up,' said Ron and placed his right hand on the throttles, pushing them gently forward.

The engines wound up, screaming into life as the plane moved forward, rolling over the wet asphalt, gathering power for the take-off.

Willard gripped his seat tight and closed his eyes as the jet roared towards the dark.

TERMINAL 1 DEPARTURES HALL,
LOS ANGELES INTERNATIONAL AIRPORT

They were taking down the big Christmas tree in the centre of the concourse, its branches bare and beginning to shed their dry needles. Things had quietened down a little since the holidays but the everyday hustle and bustle of the early-morning domestic flights continued; businessmen and women in suits, families, tourists, and just about every member of every race, religion and creed drifted through the airport, usually in the high state of tension and excitement which seems to affect just about everyone who travels by air.

The check-in girl at the Allied Air ticket desk tapped repeatedly on the enter button of her computer terminal.

'I booked by e-mail,' the man on the other side of the counter informed her for the fourth time.

'Yes, sir,' she said, remaining patient, still trying to call up the confirmation from the central booking office on screen.

'You must have it,' he insisted, running a shaky finger along his thin moustache. 'I got a reply confirming it from your people just last night.'

'Here it is, sir,' she said, relieved, and read through his flight details on the screen.

'Flight ALD419, departing 9.45, arriving Washington Dulles 18.06 eastern.'

She pressed another button on her keyboard to print out his boarding pass and ticket.

'Seat 25A,' she told him, 'and you will be boarding at gate 13 in fifteen minutes. Have you any luggage, sir?'

He held up a small green hold-all.

'Just a carry-on,' he replied, adding with a little grin, 'a short stay.'

She smiled back and handed him his ticket and pass.

'Here you go, Mr Kelsey, have a pleasant flight.'

Putting his ticket in his jacket pocket, he widened his grin. 'I'm sure I will,' he said, and walked down the concourse towards the departure gates.

At the south side of the airport Ron stretched his arms as he emerged from the LearJet. It had been a long flight. Al had slept most of the way while Willard sat frozen to his seat, his heart jumping each time Ron banked the plane.

As Al talked to the mechanics at the LAX FAA hangar, a car pulled up outside the perimeter fence. A black Explorer.

Ron went over to the fence as Jones got out of the car.

'I wasn't sure if you'd got my message.'

'We had to think about it,' confessed Jones, 'this is FBI business.'

'I understand that, but . . . you have no idea how badly I want to nail this guy and I don't give a damn who gets the credit. I've just gotta see him.'

Jones nodded.

'That's what Kronziac thought.' He smiled. 'And that's why I'm here . . . so we can keep an eye on you, keep you from fucking up our operation.'

Ron smiled back. 'How thoughtful. Where is she anyway?'

'At the house,' Jones answered.

'*His* house?'

Jones nodded and headed back into the car.

'Well, what're you waiting for?' he shouted.

As Kelsey neared the security checkpoint in the departures hall he gently eased the straps of his bag off his shoulder and carried it by his side. He joined the long queue of passengers as their hand luggage was passed through the X-ray machine for scrutiny.

'Hold it!' Willard shouted at Ron. 'I told you, you're not going anywhere without me.'

Ron had gone around the other side of the fence to Jones's car. 'Can my guys come with me?' he asked.

Jones shook his head.

'No way, we're not going to the circus, you know.'

But Willard persisted.

'If it wasn't for me you wouldn't even be here,' he reminded Ron.

Al piped up, 'Okay, guys, I'll stay here with the plane. Jeez!' He rolled his eyes. 'You're like a bunch of kids.'

Ron turned to Jones who was growing impatient.

'How about just two of us?'

'Okay, okay,' he relented, 'just get in the damn' car.'

Kelsey carefully laid his bag on the black rubber of the conveyor that ran under the X-ray machine. He watched as it disappeared behind the curtain. Walking forward through the security door, a little bleep stopped him in his tracks. One of the airport security men held out a tray to him. The security man shook his head wearily. The damn' machine was playing oversensitive again. He called it Molly, after his girlfriend.

'Empty your pockets, please, sir.'

Kelsey reached into his jacket and pulled out a set of keys, some coins and a silver pen. He put them on the tray.

The security man nodded for him to go around and come through the door again.

This time he came through unchallenged by the metal detector. Kelsey picked up the keys and the coins as the security man handed him the pen.

'Nice,' he said, turning it in his fingers. Near the top was a small LCD with the time displayed.

'She's a couple of hours out, though,' the security man remarked checking it against his own watch.

'I just use it for writing,' said Kelsey as he took the pen from the security man, 'it was a present from my mother.'

But the security man wasn't really listening, his attention drawn by one of his colleagues, the operator of the X-ray detector. He had seen something in Kelsey's bag as it went through.

'Please, sir, can you come over here and open up your bag?' the security man asked and led him over to a small table behind the X-ray machine.

'What is it?' he enquired nervously, his heart beginning to pound rapidly, his breathing suddenly shallow and laboured.

'We just wanna take a quick look inside,' said the security man as he lifted the bag carefully from the end of the conveyor and on to the table.

Kelsey was about to open up the zip when the security man stopped him.

'Sorry, sir,' he said, 'if you don't mind, I'll do it.'

'Don't you trust me?' Kelsey smiled.

'It's just airport policy,' the security man explained, 'we have to open the bags ourselves.'

Kelsey stepped back.

'Oh, well, don't want to get in the way of official policy.'

'Thank you, sir,' said the security man as he opened the zip and delved his hands inside and began slowly to unpack the bag. He pulled out a couple of shirts, some socks, underwear and a copy of *Time* magazine. He took out a small night bag and checked the contents: toothbrush, razor, nail file, tube of shampoo. He also pulled out a bright yellow peak-cap.

'Lakers fan, huh?' he asked.

'Yeah, just love them,' said Kelsey, his voice a little too loud, clearly nervous.

'Never been the same since Johnson left.' The security man shook his head and took out the last item, a sweat shirt which was wrapped around something heavy.

'That's a long time ago,' said Kelsey, trying to remain friendly. He swallowed hard, running his finger repeatedly over his moustache.

The security man carefully laid the sweat shirt on the table and began to slowly peel the folds apart, revealing two bottles of gold liquid.

'What's in the bottles?'

Kelsey pointed at the labels on them.

'Apple juice.'

The security man smiled and read the labels.

'Santa Louisa Apple Juice.'

'For my cousin back east,' Kelsey said, 'loves the stuff but can't get it out there.'

The security man was still looking at the label.

Santa Louisa Apple Juice – Produce of Northern California.

'I'm sorry, sir,' he said, 'I'll have to open it.'

Kelsey was about to say something but, glancing at the label of the bottle in the security man's hand, just smiled sweetly. 'Sure, go ahead.'

The security man covered the lid with his huge hand and with a single twist the cap popped open. Putting the bottle to his nose, he could smell the sour odour of apples.

'Smells good.'

'Tastes good too,' added Kelsey, almost tempting the security man to take a drink. But he just looked at Kelsey for a moment. He remembered that report on the news a few weeks back when some smart-ass reporter smuggled liquid explosives through the airport. It had made him and his colleagues look stupid. How could they test every bottle of liquid that went through the airport? It was just physically impossible.

He glanced at the queue of passengers which was lengthening by the second. They were understaffed as people had taken holidays after the Christmas rush. As he debated whether to detain Kelsey and run a quick test on the liquid, Kelsey reached out and took the bottle from the security man's hand.

'Shit, man,' he said, 'you're making me thirsty.'

Raising the bottle to his lips he took a long deep drink from it, draining about a quarter of the bottle.

The security man just watched him. Weird fucker, he thought. But at least it had proved one thing. The contents of the bottle were harmless.

'Have a good flight, sir,' the security man said finally, about to resume his station by the metal detector arch.

'I dunno . . .' said Kelsey.

The security man raised his eyebrow, wondering what he meant.

'. . . I always thought ol' Magic was kinda over-rated.' Kelsey smiled once more and walked off.

The security man shook his head. Yep, one weird fucker.

119th STREET, HAWTHORNE, SOUTH-WEST LOS ANGELES

Jones pulled up behind another car parked by the kerb. The street was quiet, no one around, just some people walking down at the intersection. An LAPD chopper floated somewhere high overhead.

'That's the place,' he said, pointing to a small apartment block across the street, an old twenties-style building. Ron could see some movement by the front door behind the railings that edged the steps leading up to the entrance. He could just make out some men in black flak jackets and black caps crouched near the ground. One pulled out his standard-issue Glock sidearm and held it firmly in both hands. Ron recognised him as Agent Phillips.

One of the doors of the car in front opened and Nancy Kronziac stepped out. She wasn't wearing her usual dark pants suit but was dressed in faded denims and a large dark anorak with the letters FBI on the chest and the back. Her hair blew about her face as she walked towards them.

'See you made it here,' she said, getting into the passenger seat.

'Wouldn't miss it for the world,' Ron replied. 'You sure it's him?' he asked, glancing across the road at the apartment block.

Kronziac checked her watch and took out a small walkie-talkie from her jacket, a red light pulsing on it indicating an open channel.

'We got a match on his name with LAPD records,' she confirmed. 'Some woman, a neighbour, made a complaint against him.'

'What did he do to her?' asked Willard.

Ron interrupted before Kronziac could answer.

'I'm sorry, this is Grant Willard . . . one of my colleagues.'

Willard glanced at Ron. At last they seemed to be on the same side.

'How do you do, Mr Willard?' Kronziac nodded a cursory hello. 'He killed her cat,' she continued.

Her walkie-talkie buzzed and Phillips' voice came on, informing her that the assault team was in place. Kronziac looked at Jones, who took out his own gun. This made Willard distinctly uncomfortable and he squirmed in the back seat. Kronziac shrugged and pressed the transmit button on the walkie-talkie.

'Okay, Phillips, go get the fucker.'

Ron watched as Phillips, followed by five other agents, all in black bullet-proof jackets, guns raised, rushed the front door and disappeared inside.

'Let's go!' shouted Kronziac as she and Jones jumped out of the car and ran across the street to the apartment block.

Ron turned to Willard, whose dark skin was looking a little grey around the gills.

Tin Kickers

'Well, come on, let's go,' he cried, and hopped out too.

Willard shook his head and followed.

ALLIED 419, AT GATE 13, LOS ANGELES INTERNATIONAL

Kelsey made his way down the aisle of the jumbo. Most of the 560 seats were already full, a busy flight. He found row 25 and saw that his seat, 25A, was empty. A woman on the aisle seat 25C stood up and let him in past her. The middle seat was occupied by a small boy with a mop of blond hair who seemed quite excited by the prospect of the flight. He was looking out of the window, telling his mom to watch the other planes as they took off.

'He loves planes,' the woman said to Kelsey, who just smiled back.

'Yeah, I like them myself,' he said. 'Does he wanna sit here? He'd get a better view when we take off.'

The little boy turned to his mother.

'Can I, Mom?' he pleaded. 'I'd have a cool view.'

The woman smiled at Kelsey again.

'Thank you. Are you sure?'

He was already standing up.

'No problem. I'll take the outside seat, let you two sit together.'

119TH STREET, HAWTHORNE, SOUTH-WEST LOS ANGELES

Willard had expected to hear gunshots as he ran up the stairs after Ron; a struggle, a chase maybe, the clicking of handcuffs and the reading of rights. But there was no reaction as they entered the apartment on the first floor. The FBI agents wandered around the rooms wearing expressions of disappointment.

'Little shit's not here,' Kronziac moaned, stuffing her gun into her belt. 'Okay,' she shouted, 'let's turn the place over.'

The agents began methodically searching the apartment for anything to link Kelsey to the crash.

'Do we have a warrant for this?' asked Willard.

Nobody answered, so he decided to keep his mouth shut on the matter.

Agent Phillips sat down at a desk by the large window which overlooked a balcony and the garden below. On the desk stood a computer, with an external modem hooked up to the phone line. He turned it on and began looking through Kelsey's files.

On the walls there were posters from old musicals – featuring Gene Kelly, Ginger Rogers, and of course Astaire.

On the mantelpiece, wedged into the side of a mirror, was a musty old copy of the Bible. Ron picked it up and a photograph fell out, sepia-toned with age. Ron looked at it closely. He vaguely recognised the small elfin boy in the picture, a good ten years younger than in the one Skid had showed him of the Gold Wings class of '75. The kid had his arm around a man close beside him, dressed in air force uniform.

Hanging above the mirror, in a dark hazel-wood frame, ran the words in black gothic – *I Know My Redeemer Liveth*.

Someone shouted Ron's name.

He put the photo back in the Bible and placed the book he'd found it. One of Kronziac's agents came out of the bathroom. They had found something. Inside, a red light burned on the wall which had lines of shelving on it, stacked with brown bottles. Over the bath hung a clothesline, large black and white photographic prints pegged to it.

'Makeshift darkroom,' commented Kronziac as she pulled one of the prints off the line.

'He must have been following Marx,' she said, handing it to Ron.

The photograph showed the mechanic standing on a sidewalk under a street lamp. The image was grainy, fuzzy almost, taken at night. Marx was talking to a thin young black girl who towered over him in her white stilettos.

Ron was speechless. He handed it to Willard who shook his head in disbelief.

'What age was she?' he asked. 'She can't be much more than a kid.'

Kronziac was looking at the other photos on the line. Like a disjointed movie they showed a series of shots of Marx and the girl as they walked down the street, their figures black against the oncoming lights.

'Must have tried to use these to blackmail Marx,' Kronziac suggested, 'in the hope it would get him into The Club. I suppose Marx's buddies wouldn't have taken to him associating with . . .' She stopped herself, suddenly aware of Willard's presence.

'A negro?' he said, staring at her.

She felt like apologising – but for what? she thought.

'I was going to say African American,' Kronziac said. 'I didn't mean any offence.'

Willard put his hand up.

'None taken.'

Ron broke the awkwardness of the moment as he picked up a camera which was lying next to one of the basins.

'A Canon EOS 1,' he said, twirling it around in his hand. 'Complete with timer.' He pointed at the small LCD attached to the back.

Kronziac looked around the darkroom once more. Tacked to the walls was a line of time-lapse shots of some birds nesting in a tree. In the last frame a white cat was crawling away from the nest, in its mouth a young bird.

Phillips called them from outside. He had been searching through Kelsey's computer files and had called up the Internet web browser as Ron, Kronziac and Willard came out.

'He's been downloading a lot of different shit from the net,' he said excitedly, 'everything from porn to religion; from ultra right-wing militants to how to make your own explosives.'

Kronziac leant closer to the screen. 'Check his e-mail.'

As Phillips went through Kelsey's mail Ron noticed Jones at the other side of the room. He was looking at a large square goldfish tank which was filled with a thick blue liquid.

'What is it?' he asked, going over.

Jones shook his head, baffled.

'Don't know,' he said, staring blankly at the glass, 'but it smells like . . . well, like detergent.'

Ron leant over the tank.

'There's something at the bottom,' he said, and rolled up his sleeve.

'Fuck . . . be careful!' warned Jones as Ron slowly lowered his hand into the blue liquid and carefully pulled out the thin silver tube from the bottom.

Jones squinted at the object dripping in Ron's hand. 'What is it?'

'I think it's a pen,' said Ron.

Phillips suddenly shouted out. 'He got an e-mail just last night, from Allied Air.'

He clicked the 'READ MAIL' icon and the message jumped up on screen.

Tin Kickers

'It's a booking confirmation,' said Willard, reading it.

From: bookings<dept2@m-net.alliedair.com

To: r. kelsey@dragonet.com

Subject: confirmation of flight booking.

_____

Dear R. Kelsey.

Thank you for your booking.

Details as follows;

FLIGHT DEP NO.	STOP	ARRIVAL
======= ============	======================	============

01/05 ALD419 LAX 09.45A ORD 15.12P (DEP 15.45P) IAD 18.06P
01/07 ALD420 IAD 08.15A ORD 08.36A(DEP 09.05A) LAX 10.40A

• ** Your booking has been confirmed. BOOKING REF. STM/032430
• ** Please allow 1 hour for boarding

-------------------THANK YOU FOR FLYING ALLIED-------------------

'. . . departing LAX at 9.45 today,' said Ron, drying his arm with his sleeve.

'Yeah,' nodded Phillips, 'and arriving IAD just after 6. He's on the move.'

'Where's IAD?' asked Jones.

'Dulles International,' Willard replied. 'Washington DC.'

'Shit!' cried Kronziac, looking at her watch. 'We'd never get to LAX in time.'

Willard glanced at Ron. 'We gotta go back and try and get him in Washington.'

But Ron was still staring at the screen.

'It's stopping at O'Hare for thirty minutes.'

Kronziac pulled out her cell phone.

'I'll call our field office in Chicago.'

Ron grabbed Willard's arm, twisting it around so he could see his wrist watch: 9.41.

'We might make it to Chicago before him!'

'Christ! On what?' Willard cried. 'The space shuttle?'

FAA COMPOUND, LOS ANGELES INTERNATIONAL AIRPORT

'Would someone please tell me what's going on?' Al demanded to know as Ron pushed him up the steps of the LearJet.

'Is she refuelled?'

'Yes,' said Al, 'just filled her up.'

He looked behind him as Willard, Kronziac and Jones followed them inside the plane.

'Where are we going?' he asked again.

Ron rushed him towards the cockpit.

'O'Hare.'

Al stopped and wouldn't go any further.

'O'Hare? . . . *O'Hare, Chicago?*'

'Yes,' Ron shouted, 'now get in,' and pushed Al into the skipper's seat.

'But I haven't filed a flight plan,' he protested.

'Never mind. Willard's gonna pull a few more strings with his people at the DOT to get us priority clearance.'

Ron took up the co-pilot's seat, and strapped himself in.

'We have to be there in three hours,' he said, running a pre-flight check on the instruments. 'Kelsey's on an Allied flight bound for Washington, twenty minutes ahead of us.'

'Washington?' Al said, alarmed. 'What's he doing going there?'

Ron just shrugged. He didn't know and he didn't want to think about it.

ALLIED 419, 41,000 FEET, CORTEZ VOR-DME, 822NM OUT OF O'HARE

Kelsey unbuckled his seat belt, smiled at the woman next to him and reached up to open the overhead bin. Though he couldn't actually see it he felt around for his bag and, finding the zip, opened it. He ran his hands through the items of clothing until he felt the cool glass of the bottles under the sweat shirt. He slowly eased one out and carefully brought it down. Looking closely at the label he smiled to himself – it was the same bottle he'd drunk out of at the airport in front of the security man: *Santa Louisa Apple Juice – Produce of Northern California*. He also took out his copy of *Time* magazine and zipped up the bag again, securing it in the compartment so that it wouldn't roll around during the flight. Settling into his seat he checked his watch. Nearly two hours to go.

One of the Allied flight attendants passed by, smart in her cherry red uniform, her make-up immaculately applied.

'Excuse me, miss,' said Kelsey, raising his hand to get her attention.

'Yes, sir,' she said and walked back towards his seat. 'Can I help you?'

Kelsey held up his bottle of juice. 'May I have a glass?' he asked. 'Flying always makes me thirsty. I hope you don't mind me bringing my own juice?'

'Not at all, sir,' she replied and opened down the seat tray in front of him. 'I'll get you one right away.'

'Thank you miss, I appreciate it,' he smiled as he watched her walking down the aisle towards the forward galley. Putting down the bottle he opened the magazine and ran down the headlines page – *civil war in west Africa, Uproar in the Duma, Hollywood actors threaten strike, victory for Conservatism in the Illinois Governorship race.*

The smile slid off his face, his lips curling to a sneer.

FAA LEARJET, 9,000 FEET, BUTTS VOR-DME, 1,108 NM FROM O'HARE

Ron unstrapped himself and moved aft, leaving Al to fly the plane while still asking a load of questions.

Were they sure it was Kelsey? Maybe he was just going on holiday and wasn't off to bomb the White House or anything. Why couldn't they just ground his flight at Chicago and go in and get him?

Ron couldn't even begin to answer Al's questions. It was Kronziac's call. All he knew was that the man he believed to be responsible for the crash of ACL248 was just ahead of them and with a bit of luck and a following wind they could intercept him at O'Hare.

Kronziac and Jones were busy on their phones, arranging security at both Chicago and Washington. Kronziac was dragging on a cigarette, inhaling deeply between sentences.

'What time is it?' asked Ron, taking a seat next to Willard.

'12.17,' Willard replied, changing his watch to Chicago time.

Kronziac put down the phone. 'I've just been on to Phillips and Morris. They're talking with the Allied staff and Airport Security at LAX to see if they noticed anything about Kelsey or what he took on board.'

She noticed Ron observing her as she took another drag on her cigarette.

'I didn't know you smoked,' he said.

She held out the cigarette, looking at it with disdain.

'Been trying to give it up,' she said dolefully and was about to extinguish it. 'I suppose this is a non-smoking flight.'

Willard reached into his pocket and took out an almost empty box of Marlboro.

'This plane's exempt from some FAA regulations,' he said, reaching to take a light from Kronziac.

Ron glanced anxiously out of the window as they climbed above the clouds into the sun.

'What time is it?'

'Christ, Ron, relax,' said Willard, 'it's 12.18, one minute later than when you last asked.'

But he was shaking his head.

'I'm not sure we're gonna make it ahead of Kelsey. Al suggested we just keep the plane on the ground, storm the fucking thing if we have to.'

Both Willard and Kronziac looked at him with concern.

'We can't do anything to freak him out,' Kronziac warned, 'we have people waiting in Washington when it touches down.'

'And what about Chicago?' asked Willard.

Kronziac took another breathful of smoke, blowing it back out in a dull grey cloud.

'Jones is just on to our field office in Chicago,' she said, 'where they're going to set up a checkpoint for those passengers disembarking. We'll also try and get a couple of agents on board to keep an eye on Kelsey if he stays put.'

'Let's hope he does,' Willard prayed, taking a drag on his own cigarette, 'we could lose him if he gets off in Chicago.'

Ron's eyes narrowed with concentration, 'Unless . . .' he mumbled.

'Unless what?' asked Kronziac.

'O'Hare is the busiest airport in the world, right?'

Kronziac shrugged, not really knowing.

Willard nodded. 'A flight every 30 seconds, 180,000 passengers a day . . . So?'

'Well,' Ron began smiling broadly, 'there are bound to be delays here and there, nothing unusual, nothing to alarm anyone. It's simple,' he concluded.

'Nothing is ever simple,' said Kronziac doubtfully and reached for another cigarette.

ALLIED AIR TICKET DESK, TERMINAL 1, LOS ANGELES INTERNATIONAL

Agent Morris suggested that they go to the little office behind the ticket desk out of view of the public. The Allied ground attendant sat down at the computer terminal on one of the small desks.

'What's his name again?'

'Kelsey,' said Phillips. 'Robert Kelsey. He was on the 9.45 flight to Dulles.'

'He booked by e-mail,' added Morris.

She began tapping at the keyboard, trawling the airline's ticketing records.

'A booking reference would speed things up,' she remarked.

Phillips reached into his pocket and produced a small scrap of paper on which he had scribbled Kelsey's details from the computer at the apartment.

'Right, here we go.' She began reading out the details. 'Flight ALD419, departing LAX 9.45, arrive Washington 18.06.'

Morris leant closer.

'Okay,' he said eagerly, 'can you tell us anything about his luggage? How many bags?'

'Yeah, I can tell you he didn't have any.'

She pointed at a small box at the bottom corner of the screen labelled *Baggage Ref*. The box was empty.

'None?' said Phillips.

She shook her head.

'He must have only had carry-on,' she suggested, 'but we wouldn't have any details of that . . . sorry.'

Phillips stood back.

'What now?' he asked.

Morris was still looking at the screen, trying in vain to find something that might give them some idea what Kelsey was up to, if anything.

'No idea,' he mumbled.

'Maybe security might help,' the Allied ground stew suggested. 'He'd have to go through the checkpoint at the departures hall.'

ALLIED 419, WHITESIDE NDB, 138 NM FROM O'HARE

Kelsey had finished reading every word of his copy of *Time*, had a cold ham-and-salad lunch, had emptied the bottle of juice and spent an hour in fitful sleep. He never slept well when travelling, could never get his stomach to settle, constantly buzzing with nerves.

He looked at his watch.

2.48.

The intercom was switched on and one of the flight attendants began informing the passengers in a slow, friendly voice of their imminent descent into Chicago.

'Ladies and gentlemen, we will be shortly landing at O'Hare International Airport. For those passengers staying on board for the rest of the flight to Washington we expect to be on the ground for about thirty minutes for refuelling and to pick up connecting passengers. For those departing at Chicago we would like to thank you for flying with Allied Air and hope to see you soon. Thank you.'

Kelsey looked at his watch again. Should be about twenty minutes to landing, he calculated. Time to move.

He stood up and opened the overhead bin once more. He pulled down the hold-all, clutching it close to his chest. As the flight attendants were busy gathering up cups and trays from the passengers Kelsey headed for the mid-aft washroom.

He closed the door behind him and snapped the latch, locking himself in. Looking at his watch once more, he could feel a tightening in his eardrums as the 747 descended slowly over Lake Michigan towards the vast grey sprawl of Chicago.

Kelsey knelt down and unzipped the bag. He picked out the various items of clothing one by one. Lastly he lifted up the sweat shirt which was still wrapped around the second bottle of apple juice. Carefully cradling it in his arms, he laid it on the floor.

He slowly unwound the shirt and stared at the bottle lying on its side, a large oblong bubble of air floating in the middle like a spirit level. After checking the label, just to make sure, he lifted up the bottle and held it against the light. The golden liquid swirled slowly inside like twining flumes of oil.

The bottle sighed as he twisted open the cap, releasing a slight hiss of gas.

There was a knock on the door.

Kelsey swung his head around, instinctively looking at the clasp to see that it was locked.

'Excuse me,' one of the flight attendants said through the door, 'but we'll be landing very soon so please resume your seat as soon as possible.'

'Okay!' Kelsey answered, glad it was the only word he had to utter as his whole body shook with nerves.

CHICAGO TERMINAL RADAR APPROACH CONTROL (TRACON), ELGIN, ILLINOIS

He put down the phone and stood up quickly from his chair. Pulling out the top drawer of the filing cabinet he ran his fingers over the files until he came to a folder marked *Federal Directives – Special Ops*.

He retrieved the folder and slammed the drawer back in place. Riffling through the twenty or so sheets of paper he found the DOT, FAA and Air Force code clearances.

ILK-030270

Codename: *Fencer*

'Goddamn' Feds,' he cursed and closed the folder.

Jim Bryce was an experienced controller who had survived the Reagan pogrom of '81 when nearly 11,000 of his colleagues were fired because of their industrial action. He always received a phone call from Washington with mixed feelings of dread and annoyance.

Bryce ran over to the operations wing of the 110,000 square foot facility and opened the door into the large control room. He looked about at the twenty or so men and women controlling the thousands of aircraft in the sky above the Great

Lakes area. He grabbed one of the men, who stood clutching a plastic cup of steaming coffee near a supervisor's station.

'Hey, Paul! Who's on West Arrival?'

Paul Iverson, taken aback by his boss's urgency, swallowed a mouthful of hot coffee.

'That's Frank,' he answered. 'What's up, Jim?'

'Federal Special Directive,' said Bryce, making his way down the control room, 'some Fed from the DOT requested a delay on an inbound bird.'

'Fuck!' Iverson gasped. This was a rare occurrence. 'You sure it's kosher?'

'Yeah, he gave the code number and verified the codename, and he checked out in DC,' Bryce shouted back as he reached the other end of the room.

He waited as Frank Pelsche finished handing off an inbound NorthWest Airbus to the O'Hare tower for landing. He put his hand on Pelsche's shoulder.

'Sorry, Frank,' he said, quietly interrupting.

'What's up, chief?' Pelsche turned around from his radar screen.

'You got an Allied seven-forty-seven inbound, western sector?'

'Yep.' Pelsche turned to his screen and changed the radar site selector to extend the sweeping eye of the ASR-9 radar. He moved the slew ball over a data block marked ALD419 – 280, moving slowly through a swarm of other little dots. 'There she is, coming into range, descending from 28,000.'

'Put her on a go-around when she reaches finals!' Bryce told him.

Pelsche turned around again, eyes searching Bryce's face for some indication that this was a joke. But he knew Bryce only too well. He knew there could be no joke.

Kelsey stood up and took out the silver pen from his jacket pocket. It felt heavy in his palm as if made of a precious metal. He pressed the button on the top part and the LCD changed to a five digit read-out, counting down like a stopwatch: ... 1.29:59 ... 1.29:58 ... 1.29:57. He held it next to his wrist watch, struggling to keep his hands steady as he synchronised the stopwatch facility on his watch with that on the pen.

He knelt down once again and slowly lowered the pen into the blue water of the toilet bowl. Pressing the flush button, he watched the bowl gush, the water bubbling and splashing in a white maelstrom, washing down into the waste collection tank beneath the floor. Standing up, he looked again at his watch. 1.29:41 ... 1.29:40.

Finally he picked up the bottle from the floor and opened the refuse bin. He carefully placed it among the rubbish, hiding it under a thick fold of toilet paper, and closed the top of the bin again. Taking up his bag once more, he opened the latch of the door and, catching his reflection in the mirror stroked his fake moustache and smiled to himself.

As Kelsey resumed his seat the intercom came on

once again, this time the Captain's voice called for the passengers' attention.

'Ladies and gentlemen, there will be a slight delay before we land at O'Hare due to traffic ahead. We've been put in a holding pattern but we don't expect to be held up for too long and we'll have you down as soon as possible. Thank you for your attention.'

The little boy was pointing out of the window at a boat below, a white speck slicing through the turgid waters of Lake Michigan. The plane banked to circle the city.

Kelsey held his bag tight.

FAA LEARJET, OVER THRESHOLD, RUNWAY 14L, O'HARE INTERNATIONAL

Given priority clearance Willard had managed to get them a landing slot sandwiched between a British Airways 747 from Heathrow and a US Air MD-11 up from Miami. The LearJet seemed like a gnat compared to the two giant silver birds as it swooped in over the airfield, bumping on to the asphalt and turning off halfway down the runway.

In the cabin Willard hung up the phone from the TRACON, smiling with satisfaction.

'Did we beat it?' Ron wondered anxiously.

'Just about,' confirmed Willard. 'She's stacked on a holding pattern.'

Kronziac was smiling. The first smile Ron had seen her give all morning.

A signal-man, in white overalls and earplugs, waved his paddles for Al to stop the plane by a maintenance hangar on the northern perimeter of the airport. Cold and grey – a typical winter's day in Chicago – the airport spread its 8,000 acres of grass and concrete out under the low ceiling of cloud. The four massive terminals looked like cruise liners stranded in fog, clusters of aircraft docked to their sides, disgorging their human cargoes. Other planes, everything from Boeing 777s to little Piper Cherokees, stood lined up on the aprons, like birds waiting for their turn to take to the air as others swept in, touching down on the runways. The air pounded with the screams and roars of hundreds of jet engines. It reeked of the gritty acrid odour of burning jet fuel.

Kronziac had to decide what they were going to do as she rode up front in the airport security van that was rushing them to Terminal 3.

'What if he does get off?' Ron wondered aloud.

'Then we'll pick him up,' she snapped curtly.

'And . . .' Willard was almost afraid to ask '. . . what if he stays on the plane.'

Kronziac turned to Jones.

'Agent Jones will be going on board and will keep in touch with us from the air.'

'Just one agent?' remarked Ron.

'No,' Kronziac replied, 'we'll probably send another agent with him.'

'Another FBI agent?' asked Willard.

Kronziac looked around her, frowning with disbelief.

'Jesus, guys, what is this?' she said. 'Of course another FBI agent. This is after all officially Bureau business, not NTSB, FAA or Department of Transportation.'

But Ron wasn't going to give in without a fight. He had come too far. He wanted Kelsey too much.

'One of us should be there,' he asserted, looking her in the eye.

Kronziac smiled expectantly.

'Let me guess . . . *you?*'

'Why not?'

Kronziac shook her head. 'No way, Carter. He surely knows who you are . . . don't you think he's been following the investigation?'

'She's probably right,' conceded Willard, 'your profile's too high.'

'You're too famous,' Al chimed in, affording himself a brief grin.

'Okay,' Ron relented, 'maybe not me, but someone from the NTSB should be on board that plane to nail that fuck. You put one of your agents who doesn't know anything about Kelsey on the case and we could blow the whole thing.'

Kronziac pondered for a moment.

'What do you think?' she asked Jones.

Jones glanced out of the window for a second as the van drew up near the terminal building.

'He may be right,' he said, turning back, 'and it may be a good idea to have someone with a knowledge of aircraft on board . . . just in case.'

Jones had articulated a fear that none of them had really confronted so far: the possibility that Kelsey might be trying to sabotage Allied 419.

'He's hardly gonna do anything stupid while he himself is still on board,' Willard asserted.

'Wouldn't put anything past that nut,' said Kronziac. 'I'm just wondering what the hell he's up to going to Washington.'

As the van stopped outside a security entrance to Terminal 3 they were about to get out when Kronziac stopped.

'So who's it going to be?' she asked, looking at Willard and Al. Willard looked back with an ironic smile. He pointed at his own face, indicating the obvious.

'I'm a black man, remember?' he reminded them. 'I don't think I should be anywhere near that racist whacko.'

Kronziac turned to Al, who had remained conspicuously quiet. 'Goddamn,' he cursed, 'where's Bob when I need him?'

SECURITY OPS. BOOTH, TERMINAL 1, LOS ANGELES INTERNATIONAL

'Shit, guys, who's it this time? NBC? CBS? Don't tell me . . . CNN.'

Morris and Phillips looked at each other. Phillips reached into his back pocket and flipped open his ID wallet for the security supervisor.

'FBI,' he said, allowing himself a little smile.

The security chief's expression changed from annoyed suspicion to one of extreme embarrassment.

'Jeez, sorry, guys . . . I thought you were from one of the networks trying to do another exposé on our setup here. You know, it's not easy to police all these people.' He waved over the concourse which buzzed with throngs of passengers and airport staff.

'We know. Thank you, Mr . . .' Morris looked at the man's name badge, '. . . McConell. But we're in a bit of a rush here.'

'Okay. What can I do for you?' asked McConell.

'We need to ask your people some questions.'

'What about?'

'Well,' Phillips began, 'we're wondering if your guys remember a man who would have passed through this morning for a 9.45 flight to DC.'

'This morning, you say?' McConell glanced at his

watch. 'Well, you're in luck, they're still on duty . . . come on.'

McConell led them through the crowds in the main concourse and up to the security checkpoint before the departure gates. They passed the queue of people lined up at the X-ray machine waiting to put their hand luggage through.

McConell raised his arm and beckoned one of the security men at the detector door to come over and join them behind the X-ray machine operator's station.

'Hi, Mike,' McConell greeted the big security man as he approached.

'Hello, Mr McConell, everything okay?' he replied and glanced at Morris and Phillips.

McConell smiled genially. 'Yeah, everything's fine. These gentlemen are from the FBI. This is Mike LeVell, watch officer.'

'Hi, Mike . . . I'm Special Agent Phillips and this is Special Agent Morris.'

The security man nodded a cautious hello.

'We're looking for a male passenger,' said Phillips, 'in his forties, five-seven, five-eight, 150 pounds. Woulda come through here about 9, 9.30.'

LeVell shook his head, laughing lightly.

'Hell, that covers a lot of guys.'

'Well, like we said, it would have been around 9,' Morris persisted. 'Anybody like that stand out?'

LeVell narrowed his eyes in concentration.

'We had some guy who kept putting off the alarm,

turns out he had his dick pierced with a huge metal stud, but he was about twenty, twenty-five maybe. Then had someone with about 50 pounds of dirt in his baggage, wanted to start a vineyard back east.'

LeVell began scratching his head, trying hard to remember.

'We caught a couple college kids with some coke . . . and some guy we suspected of carrying a large quantity of narcotics but he was clean, though it gave the guys in the office a bit of a fright. Turns out he is actually a *she* . . . we get all sorts,' he chuckled. 'Oh, yeah, then there was the Lakers fan.'

G – RAMP, TERMINAL 3,
O'HARE INTERNATIONAL

After a smooth landing Allied 419 had edged itself to a stop near gate 19 on the tip of Concourse G which stretched out like a huge glass and concrete limb from the main Terminal 3 building.

At the gate a beleaguered Allied representative had to deal with two very disgruntled passengers. Overbooked, he explained, and would make sure they got to Washington on the next available flight. What he didn't tell them was that their seats were being taken by an FBI agent and an NTSB investigator who were going on board to find a crazed bomber. The Allied rep herded the two passengers away from the boarding desk. Keep them out of sight, no scenes, an FBI agent told him.

The Bureau's Chicago office, with the co-operation of the O'Hare airport police, had set up a temporary security checkpoint just outside gate 19 with FBI agents disguised as airport security. If Kelsey were to get off, this was where they would get him.

Jones was checking his gun as Kronziac gave him and Al a few last instructions.

'If you do see him, just sit tight and keep an eye on him. The airline said he was in row 25, window seat A.'

She handed them each a small communications unit.

'You'll be in contact with us at all times.'

Al was beginning to feel more nervous than he'd thought he would. 'Should we take some hand luggage or something?'

Jones placed his hand on Al's shoulder.

'We'll be fine as we are,' he reassured him, 'just relax.'

An airport security official came over to escort the two men down to the plane. The other passengers had already boarded and the departure gate would be closing soon.

'Remember,' Kronziac warned, 'no heroics.'

Al smiled nervously.

'No worries there.'

Ron felt a little guilty that he couldn't go himself.

'You sure about this, Al?' he asked. 'You don't have to. It's just . . .'

Al put up his hand to stop Ron going any further.

'It's okay.' He grinned. 'I need the air miles . . . might get a free holiday or something outa all this.'

'Ready to go, gentlemen?' the security official asked.

They nodded and followed him to an elevator near the departure gate.

'See you in Washington!' Willard shouted after them.

'Yeah,' Al replied, 'see you later, fellas.'

*   *   *

As the elevator opened on the ground floor, Al and Jones found themselves in the baggage handling area. They would now be able to walk out on the apron and directly on to the plane.

'You guys VIPs as well?' the official shouted, as the engine noise of the waiting jumbo made it difficult to be heard.

Al glanced at Jones for a moment, not sure what to say.

'Nah,' he shouted, 'just routine security.'

As the security official had obviously not been fully informed of the exact nature of the operation Jones felt it better not to tell him now.

'Oh, you're with that guy.' The official smiled, pointing at a long black limousine which had pulled up outside the VIP lounge – an area reserved for dignitaries and premier-class passengers. Al glanced over at the limo. A large man in a dark suit was opening one of the doors for an older man to get out. Al wasn't sure if he recognised him or not.

The petrol tanker pulled away from the 747, the aircraft's fuel tanks topped up. Al and Jones were the last to board. Remembering Kronziac's instructions they glanced around carefully at the other passengers, hoping they might catch a glimpse of someone who just might be Robert Kelsey.

'How many were supposed to get off?' Willard

asked as they watched the last of the passengers file through the checkpoint.

'They're not sure,' Kronziac replied, a shade of annoyance in her voice. 'Twenty, maybe twenty-one.'

Willard was appalled, his sense of correct procedure affronted by the carelessness of the airline.

'They don't know for sure?' he cried.

'Said they had problems with their computer system,' explained Kronziac.

'Says a lot about security,' Willard uttered, triggering a few unfriendly looks from the airport officials in the room.

Ron watched the screen closely, counting the passengers going through the security check. The last of them, two very annoyed old ladies, were having their bags searched.

'They're all through,' he said, 'and no sign of anyone remotely like him.'

'Well, he must have stayed on board,' Kronziac concluded with relief.

The door of the room opened and a young agent hurried up to Kronziac, whispering something in her ear.

'What is it?' Ron asked.

'The senior stew on the flight just got on to dispatch,' she said.

'And?'

'She reported seat 25A is occupied.'

*　　*　　*

Al looked around him as the doors of the aircraft were being pushed shut. The pilot welcomed the passengers aboard and assured them that they would be taking off soon. By the looks of things Al thought the plane was almost fully booked, with every seat occupied. He squinted his eyes at the row numbers up the aisle, looking for 25 but he couldn't see it. It was too far up the front of the plane. He moved towards the tail of the aircraft to take up his own seat. He passed Jones who had settled on an aisle seat on row 41.

'That's it,' Kronziac stated, 'they're the last ones through. He's still in his seat.'

The two old ladies were walking away from the checkpoint, still glancing back at the disguised customs officials, mouthing complaints.

Kronziac was about to order her agents to stand down when Ron grabbed her by the arm.

'Hold it!'

She looked back at him but he was still staring at the screen. Walking towards the security check was a man with a moustache. A little below average height, he was wearing a brown jacket and dark jeans. His face was thin, very pale, almost ashen, his hair lank and thinning, dirty blond, a darker shade than his moustache. He was carrying a dark green hold-all.

Kelsey hardly saw the small desk set up by the customs officials as he sauntered through the concourse. It was strangely quiet, he thought, peaceful.

He looked at his watch and exhaled with relief. He was off the plane.

. . . 0.49:50 . . . 0.49:49 . . . 0.49:48.

'Excuse me, sir,' a young woman's voice interrupted him, 'can you please place your bag on the table?'

Kelsey shook his head.

'It was checked at the other end,' he complained as he walked over to the table.

'I'm sorry, sir, this is just a routine security check.'

Kelsey looked at her. She was very pretty, not too tall, nice smooth pale skin. He glanced at the gun in her holster.

A Glock 9mm.

'Oh, well,' he smiled, 'I suppose it's the price we pay for our own safety.'

He placed the bag on the table and stood back.

'Can you open it, please, sir?' she asked, smiling courteously.

Kelsey blinked in surprise. 'You want *me* to open it?'

The customs officer nodded. 'Yes, thank you, sir.'

He glanced around him. There were several customs people standing around, as well as some airport policemen.

'Okay.' He smiled awkwardly and pulled the zip open.

In the surveillance room they watched him closely.

'You think it might be him?' Willard whispered, but Ron and Kronziac just watched the monitor as the man took out some shirts from the hold-all, then a few pairs of socks and a small wash bag. The customs official was carefully looking through Kelsey's things, unravelling the socks, peering inside the overnight bag, taking out the razor, the little plastic tube of shampoo.

Kelsey still had his hand in the bag, he seemed to be hesitating.

'Doesn't have too much stuff, whoever he is,' remarked Willard.

Then Kelsey took out another item and placed it on the table. A bright yellow peak-cap.

Al leant back in his seat and smiled as the aircraft hurtled, bumping and shaking down the runway, the four Rolls-Royce RB211 turbofans pushing nearly 360 tonnes of metal, 50,000 gallons of fuel and 560 humans into the sky. As the plane rotated, reaching Vee-1 lift velocity, Al was almost giggling. He loved the 747, best plane ever made, its fuselage longer than Orville Wright's first flight. The rattling stopped as the plane lifted from the ground and drifted into the lightness of the air.

Kronziac whispered into her walkie-talkie to the agents at the security point.

'Don't make any sudden moves,' she told them, 'just keep him calm till we get there.'

'You sure it's him?' Willard interrogated Ron, concerned that the only evidence was a hat.

But Ron was nodding firmly.

'That must be him. He had the Lakers hat the day we tailed him with Marx.'

Kronziac came off the walkie-talkie. 'Well, what are we waiting for?' she said to Ron and Willard, making for the door.

'. . . And the rest please, sir,' the young FBI agent told Kelsey, noticing his hand was still in the bag. There was one item he had not taken out. He was keenly aware of all the security men watching him closely. He had noticed one of them whispering something on his radio unit.

The FBI agent was beginning to get edgy as Kelsey's hand still lingered in the bag. She moved forward, her expression changing from polite persuasion to direct confrontation.

'*Please*, sir, empty the bag.'

She rested her left hand on the butt of her gun.

Kelsey's eyes darted around, creating for himself a mental map of where all the other guards were. Then he looked directly at the young woman.

He smiled.

'Do you like apple juice?'

She had moved forward to see what was in the bag when Kelsey drew his arm up in a swift arc. In his hand he held an empty bottle which he swung into her chin, instantly smashing it on her jaw and breaking the bottle into a circle with jagged glass edges which dragged across her face, slashing her nose and cutting her eye lids. She screamed in agony and threw her hands up to her streaming face. Kelsey shot his other hand down to her holster and snatched out the gun. As the other agents drew he had already pushed up the firing pin safety catch and blasted one of them in the leg. Without stopping he swung his other hand out and grabbed the young woman by the neck, dragging her over the table and jamming the gun up to her temple.

All the other agents just stopped themselves in time from spraying him with bullets as he held the girl in front of him, her face barely recognisable with blood flooding her features.

Like a cornered animal, he turned his gun in all directions to ward off the other agents who now surrounded him.

'Get the fuck back!' he shouted, squeezing his hysterical hostage close against his chest as he began retreating.

'Get the fuck back!' he screamed again. 'Or I'll put this bitch out of her agony.'

'Oh, sweet Jesus!' Kronziac cursed as they ran up to the scene. She took out her gun.

'Okay, everyone be calm!' she shouted. 'Let's all just take it easy!'

The other agents and police officers relaxed their weapons a little and stopped moving forward against

Kelsey but Kronziac knew they were just itching to get off a shot at him.

'That's it,' she shouted again, 'let's not be stupid here.'

The whole area which was now fully closed off became strangely quiet but for the agonised sobbing of the young agent whose face was a red mess of slashed skin. She was shaking convulsively with shock in Kelsey's grasp as he gripped her tight around the neck with his arm.

He turned to Kronziac.

'Who the fuck are you?' he screeched.

Kronziac took a moment before answering. She had to win control of the situation.

'Special Agent Nancy Kronziac.'

Kelsey nodded, his face contorted with hatred.

'A goddamn' Fed . . . a goddamn' shit-sucking Fed!' he cried. 'Just like this little bitch . . . I knew it.' He tightened his strangle-hold on the young woman and dug the barrel of the gun further into the side of her head.

'No!' Kronziac shouted, 'she's with airport security.'

Kelsey sneered back.

'Like fuck!' he spat. 'Airport dicks don't pack these babies.' He rattled the Glock in the air before twisting it again to the young agent's head. She shook with pain, her ripped eye lids flickering as she began to lose consciousness.

One of the airport policemen had hidden behind

a pillar and was the nearest to Kelsey. He gripped his .38 tightly, ready to take a clean shot if he got the chance.

But Kronziac saw him out of the corner of her eye.

'All right, let's continue to take it easy,' she said, '*everyone* take it nice and easy.'

Ron and Willard stayed well back but watched Kelsey closely. He seemed like a miserable mouse of a man, his pale milky skin blotched with red spots, eyes narrow, red-rimmed with anger and fear.

He began moving slowly backwards, dragging the girl with him. His eyes darted around the place as he searched for some way of escape.

Suddenly the policeman behind the pillar made his move, jumping out to take a shot at Kelsey, but as he did so Kelsey swung around, shielding himself with his hostage. The policeman's shot glanced off the young woman's shoulder, shattering her shoulder blade. The policeman, so shocked by what he had done, froze for a moment on the spot, staring at the girl who hung limply in front of Kelsey, barely alive.

Kelsey raised his gun and shot the man in the chest, knocking him against the pillar, blasting a red hole in his shirt. Kelsey swiftly pulled the girl around again, shielding himself from a possible hail of bullets from the other agents.

But Kronziac screamed at the top of her voice: 'Stop! Everyone just fucking stop!'

An uneasy peace descended as the dead policeman slid to the floor, a small stream of blood dripping from his mouth, his chest motionless, eyes fixed in a frozen deathly stare.

'You better listen to her, boys and girls,' Kelsey laughed, enjoying his position of control. His face was smeared with the young woman's blood which continued to gush from her face.

'Nothing gives me more pleasure than blowing away some government flatfoot,' he laughed again.

Kronziac tried to think quickly. There were too many guns, someone else was bound to get hurt.

Kelsey began moving backwards again, very slowly, dragging his hostage with him. He spotted an elevator about twenty feet away.

'Where are you gonna go, Kelsey!' Ron shouted out suddenly.

He stopped and glanced about at the faces behind the guns. 'Who the fuck said that?' he shouted.

'Or should I call you Jimenez?' Ron cried.

Kronziac threw Ron an incredulous look.

'Are you trying to get everyone killed?' she uttered, trying to muffle her voice so Kelsey wouldn't hear.

'Who the hell are you?' he asked, seeing Ron in the background. He noticed Ron had no gun and didn't have the same clean-cut look as the rest of the agents.

'I said, who the fuck are you?' he shouted again at him.

Ron glanced at Kronziac who nodded back, urging him to answer quickly.

'Ron Carter.'

Kelsey began smiling.

'Yeah, that's right,' he said, recognising Ron. 'I read about you, saw your picture in the paper . . . you're the fucking tin kicker sniffing after the 248 crash. Got yourself a real interesting job there, man.'

Ron remained silent, not knowing what to say.

'Jesus,' Kronziac whispered, 'say something . . . anything.'

Ron moved a little closer towards Kelsey. He could see the young agent, collapsed against Kelsey's chest, her face covered with blood.

'Yeah, a very interesting case,' he said, keenly aware of the absurdity of the conversation.

But Kelsey was still smiling, genuinely wanting to talk to the crash investigator.

'You know,' he began, 'I think you're a bunch of morbid fucks, spending all your time kickin' over bits of dead people and wreckage.'

'Well, someone's gotta do it.'

'And you just love it, don't ya?'

Ron nodded, his smile gone.

'I guess I do.'

'Well,' Kelsey looked at his watch, 'stick around, 'cos in thirty-three minutes you've got yourself a new case.'

He punched the elevator call button.

Ron turned to Kronziac. 'He's left something on the plane,' he whispered in desperation.

Willard also made his way closer, keeping an eye on Kelsey from a distance.

'You've got to make sure your people don't do anything stupid,' Ron warned Kronziac, 'we need him alive. If he's planted something on the plane, we might get it out of him.'

Willard nodded in agreement.

Kronziac looked at the girl, hanging by the throat, her uniform soaked to maroon red.

'What can we do about it? Just let the bastard walk out of here?' she said, desperately trying to find a way to resolve the situation. Her agents and the policemen were getting restless, knowing that Kelsey could get away when the elevator came.

'We've got to stall him,' said Willard.

'And how exactly do you propose we do that?'

Willard moved forward through the agents and police, raising his hands.

'She's no good to you!' he shouted defiantly.

Kelsey, who was waiting for the elevator door to open, swung around, snarling with annoyance.

'Look at her,' Willard continued, moving slowly to within ten feet of Kelsey, 'she's nearly dead, you won't get far with her.'

Kelsey squeezed his hostage tighter, almost choking the life, or what was left of it, out of her. He snapped his gun at Willard, pointing it menacingly at his head.

'I should have known,' he said, leering at Willard. 'I should have known there'd be a damn' nigger around here somewhere, stinkin' things up.'

'Let her go,' Willard pleaded, 'while you've got the chance. The minute she dies, which isn't far off by the looks of things, these people are gonna . . .' He paused, looking around. 'Well, they're not gonna stop to read you your rights. You'll be dead before the last gun's even stopped shooting.'

Kelsey glanced nervously at all the guns pointing straight at him, the agents and police officers almost smiling, at last feeling they were turning the tables on him. He looked at his hostage. She was near unconscious, moaning incoherently, blood dripping from her hair.

'Okay then!' he shouted. 'Get the fuck over here, boy, you just volunteered for duty.'

'Don't do it,' Kronziac warned Willard, 'he'll kill you.'

'I'll go!' Ron insisted.

But Kelsey had his mind made up.

'Nobody else!' he shouted. 'I want the nigger.'

He pointed his gun at Willard.

'Where are you from, boy?'

Willard felt powerless. He wanted to pick up a gun himself and kill Kelsey there and then, end the whole thing with one bullet.

'Louisiana,' he said quietly.

Kelsey hooted in celebration.

'Well, well . . . a good ol' Southern boy.' He snickered. 'Then you'll know what it's all about, you know you shouldn't be in this country.' He waved his gun at all the agents. 'Except for traitors like these you'd be hunted down and shot like a dog . . . now get the hell over here!' he screamed.

Willard walked slowly towards him, his arms raised.

'That's the boy.' Kelsey smiled.

He unwound his arm from the girl's neck and as she flopped to the floor, limp as a rag doll, reached out and grabbed Willard by the throat and quickly drew him in front of him. Willard was shocked by the smaller man's strength. He pinned the gun against Willard's head, making him gasp with pain and fear.

A bell above the elevator sounded and the doors slid open. All the agents moved forward, their guns still trained on Kelsey, but he held his ground.

'Stay back!' he shouted. 'Or I'll take this damn' nigger to hell.'

Kronziac put up her hand to prevent her people from taking a shot. Kelsey laughed as he dragged Willard into the elevator and prodded the button for the doors to close.

Ron ran up to the elevator.

'Goddamn!' he shouted, watching Willard's face as the doors closed shut, the gun jammed against his head, his eyes wide with terror.

Two of the agents ran to their young comrade lying on the ground. As some airport paramedics rushed on to the concourse Ron and Kronziac looked frantically for another elevator to chase after Kelsey.

'That's the only one!' Kronziac cursed, and began shouting for everyone to look for the stairs.

Ron watched as the light over the doors of the elevator flashed.

'He's locked it on hold!' he shouted. 'The son of a bitch has stalled the elevator.'

He grabbed one of the O'Hare policemen while Kronziac shouted down her walkie-talkie for the airport exits to be sealed off.

'Where does the elevator go?' he asked frantically.

'To the baggage area,' the policeman answered. 'Downstairs. It leads out on to the ramp.'

'Shit, we could lose him!' Ron realised. 'What's the quickest way down?'

The policeman tried to think quickly.

'Come on! Come on!' Ron roared.

But the policeman was shaking his head.

'The elevator is the only way down from here,' he said. 'You'd have to go back to the main hall and take the escalators to the lower levels.'

Ron looked around him.

'There must be a quicker way,' he said out loud, and ran over to the windows which looked out over the ramp. Dozens of aircraft were lined up below. Extending from the concourse he could see several jetways – the moveable bridges used to take passengers directly out to the aircraft from the departure gates.

He grabbed Kronziac, who was still running around shouting out orders on her walkie-talkie.

'Where the hell are we going?' she yelled as Ron

dragged her up past the desk at one of the departure gates.

'This is the quickest way,' he insisted as they ran down the narrow corridor which led on to the nearest jetway.

ALLIED 419, CLIMBING TO 41,000 FEET, GIPPER VOR-DME, 465NM OUT OF DULLES

The 'Fasten Safety Belt' sign had been extinguished a good five minutes and the flight attendants were beginning to hand out drinks and peanuts to the passengers. Jones felt it was safe enough to leave his seat and check out if Kelsey was in 25A.

He was sitting in row 41 so he had a good idea of when he would be passing row 25. He caught a glimpse of Al down near the back, around row 58. Unbuckling his seat belt he headed forward, noting the seat numbers as he went by . . . 39C . . . 38C.

As he neared row 25 he slowed down . . . 30C . . . 29C . . . 28C. Glancing over casually, he pretended to look out of the window as he passed . . . 27C . . . 26C . . . Row 25.

Sitting in the window seat was a ten-year-old kid with a thick thatch of blond hair, scribbling in a colouring book. Next to him was a woman, his mother probably. She looked up and smiled at Jones as he walked by.

He nodded politely back and continued walking.
Shit.

The aisle seat, 25C, was empty, a copy of *Time* magazine lying on it.

PASSENGER JETWAY, DEPARTURE GATE 19, O'HARE INTERNATIONAL

The floor shook beneath them as they hurried down the gangway. 'Are you nuts?' Kronziac shouted, as she saw it was closed off at the end. Usually there would be the open door of an aircraft there, waiting to take passengers on board.

When they reached the end of the gangway Ron banged his fists on the solid plastic door that sealed them off from the outside.

'What now?' Kronziac asked, out of breath and still clutching her walkie-talkie.

'There has to be a control panel somewhere,' cried Ron, searching the wall. 'There!' he shouted and slammed down a small lever next to the door which began to move, racking up into a fold like an accordion.

'Oh my God!' Kronziac exclaimed as she looked out of the door. They were about twenty feet off the hard concrete. A mild wind was blowing and they could feel the heat of an engine exhaust as a DC-8 crept past them, its passengers looking out, pointing, wondering what they were up to.

'Okay, I'll go first,' Ron said as he lowered himself over the side to hang by his hands. His feet dangled in the air for a few moments before he let himself fall.

'It's too high!' Kronziac screamed, trying to make herself heard over the noise of another jet which was taxiing by.

Ron let himself go and landed unhurt on the tarmac.

'Come on, Kronziac, jump!' he shouted up at her. 'He's getting away.'

She was looking down at the ground apprehensively. In her training she had got through a great many difficult physical tasks but that was out on an obstacle course, on grass. The ground below was black and oily, dark patches of water on the surface.

'Come on, for Christ's sake!' Ron was calling again.

She took a deep breath, stuffed her walkie-talkie into her belt and lowered herself on to the edge, knuckles whitening with the strain.

'Bend your knees when you hit!' Ron advised her.

'Okay . . . okay, just shut up,' she snapped back as an L-1011 taxied by, its three engines whining at a deafening pitch.

She let herself go and hit the ground in a crumpled heap, sprawling into Ron's arms as he caught her by the waist.

'You okay?' he asked, holding on to her.

She didn't say anything at first, waiting for one of her ankles or her knees to scream with pain.

'I'm okay,' she confirmed with relief.

Ron turned in all directions to see if he could catch any glimpse of Kelsey and Willard. He spotted a red oil truck speeding across the grass between the runways.

'There!' he shouted. 'It must be them.'

On the slip roads around the airport they could see a fleet of police units, their roof strobes flashing, their sirens wailing. Kronziac immediately pulled out her walkie-talkie to tell the airport police not to fire at the truck. They needed Kelsey alive.

She turned around to Ron, but there was no sign of him. A bright white stair-truck screeched out of the baggage handling bay, one of the handlers running after it, shouting. It screamed to a stop next to Kronziac and the passenger door swung out.

'Get in!' Ron shouted to her, his hands gripping the steering wheel while he revved the engine impatiently.

Kronziac just shook her head and didn't ask any questions.

Before she had even closed the door he swerved the truck around, its tyres painting two crescents of black rubber on the concrete as it sped off towards the airfield.

They could see the red oil tanker in the distance, speeding across one of the outer runways, narrowly missing a landing 727.

'He's heading for the northern perimeter,' Ron shouted.

Kronziac's walkie-talkie bleeped. She raised it to her ear, holding it tight as the truck jolted over grass. The line was bad, a steady wave of interference making it difficult for her to hear who it was.

'Hello?' she said, covering her other ear with her hand. The line got a little better and she could just make out Phillips' voice. He was calling from LAX.

'Hello . . . Kronziac?'

'Yeah, Phillips, go ahead. I can just hear you.'

'I talked to the security people here . . . and one of them thinks he remembers a guy who might have been Kelsey . . . boarding an Allied flight this morning.'

'Yeah, we're following him right now,' she shouted as Ron swerved the truck once more to avoid a row of landing lights, the tyres shooting up a spray of mud and grass behind.

'Well, he carried on board a small hold-all which was searched . . . he had no other luggage according to the airline's ground staff.'

'Yeah, we've seen his bag,' Kronziac answered a little impatiently, and was about to tell Phillips to get off the line when Ron turned to her.

'Ask him why they searched his hand luggage?'

Not everyone has their bag searched, the security people must have had their suspicions.

Kronziac put the question to Phillips.

'They saw two bottles in his bag when it went through the X-ray scanner.'

'Say again?' Kronziac asked as she wasn't sure she'd heard him properly.

'*He had two bottles of liquid in his bag,*' Phillips repeated. '*Turned out to be apple juice or something . . . I don't know . . .*'

Kronziac turned to Ron who had also realised the significance of this.

'He came off with just the one bottle, didn't he?' he asked.

Kronziac nodded. 'I think so.'

She pressed the transmit button once more.

'Okay, Phillips, good work.'

Ron jumped on the brakes and the truck skidded across the grass, coming to a halt at the edge of a runway.

Kronziac sat speechless, just staring out of the windshield with an expression of absolute terror frozen on her face. A huge Airbus screamed past, its wing tips no more than twenty feet from them, the heat from its engines blasting in the windows, rocking the truck from side to side as if hit by a small hurricane.

Ron snatched the walkie-talkie out of her hand. She was unable to resist, in fact she was unable to do anything for a few seconds as the plane roared off down the runway and lifted into the air.

'What channel is Jones on?' Ron asked, looking to left and right down the runway as if about to cross a busy intersection. There was a Lufthansa 747 building up speed near the end of the runway. It was a few seconds away so Ron pumped the gas pedal and the truck screamed across the hot, rubber-scarred asphalt.

'What channel is Jones on?' Ron roared at Kronziac again.

ALLIED 419, 41,000 FEET, ANGOLA NDB, 410NM OUT OF DULLES

Al had followed Jones to the forward galley where they were asking the flight attendants some vague questions about a male passenger – not very tall, a south-western accent, travelling under the name Kelsey. So far they had drawn a blank.

'He must have gotten off.' Al smiled, relieved.

'Guess so.' Jones nodded. 'We've missed all the fun,' he added with a half-disappointed smile. His walkie-talkie bleeped with an incoming call. He pulled it out of his jacket pocket.

'Jones here.'

'Jones! It's Carter.'

'Go ahead, Ron,' Jones replied, and glanced at Al who stopped talking with the senior steward to listen.

'Listen, Jones, Kelsey got off at O'Hare . . .'

Jones nodded at Al. They were right, he wasn't on the plane.

'Yeah,' said Jones, 'we guessed.'

The signal suddenly broke down, a wash of static wiping out the line.

'Hello, Ron! . . . Ron! . . . I'm losing you!' Jones shouted and tried to tweak the tuning on the handset.

Ron's voice faded in again.

'. . . bottles of juice . . . apple juice . . .'

Jones frowned, unable to make sense of what Ron was saying. 'What? Say again,' he shouted into the handset. 'Repeat.'

Ron's voice crackled on the line again.

I think Kelsey may have left something on board . . . it may be a long shot but he could have left liquid explosives in a bottle of apple juice somewhere on the plane.

Jone' face slackened with horror. Al shook his head. For a split second he pictured a crash site – 500 burning bodies, one of them his.

'A bottle of apple juice?' he said, hardly believing the absurdity of it.

I know it sounds crazy but . . .

Jones nodded firmly, finishing Ron's sentence.

'. . . but Kelsey *is* crazy. Okay, we'll get on it right away.'

He put the walkie-talkie back in his pocket and turned to the senior steward, who had suddenly grown pale, having overheard the conversation.

'We've got to ask your crew some more questions.'

The senior steward nodded, his face rigid with fear.

'I'll assemble everyone now,' he said and walked off to get the rest of the cabin crew together.

Al peered out the galley at the passengers, peacefully enjoying their flight.

RUNWAY 22 RIGHT, O'HARE INTERNATIONAL

Ron threw Kronziac her walkie-talkie as they scudded across another runway. They could see another jet coming in, its landing lights like eyes bearing down on them.

As they reached the safety of the grass Kronziac pointed ahead. Near the perimeter fence the red oil tanker was standing still, both its front doors open, its engine still idling.

'He's stopped!'

'Yeah, but where are they?' Ron wondered, looking around the field, as they neared the abandoned truck.

Kronziac was looking upward, into the sky.

'Oh, God.'

By the runway was a small white building with red markings. Rising out of it was a tall radio mast that was topped by a narrow gantry which jutted out at right angles about fifty feet above the ground. It was one of the glideslope transmitter towers for the airport's instrument landing system, sending out radio waves to shepherd the aircraft in on a smooth descent path.

Halfway up the tower, a criss-cross mesh of bars and guy ropes, Kronziac could see the struggling figure of Willard as he was being pushed at gun point by Kelsey towards the gantry at the top. Ron pinned the stair-truck to a halt, skidding on the damp grass under the tower.

'What the hell is he doing up there?' asked Kronziac as they got out of the truck.

Willard had reached the top of the tower and Kelsey immediately swung his arm around his neck and pushed him out on to the gantry. Kelsey looked down. He could see several units of airport police arriving on the scene, converging on the tower.

'Don't come any closer!' he shouted as a plane swept in overhead, the wheels of its undercarriage less than fifty feet above.

The police officers got out of their cars and, taking cover behind the doors, pointed their guns up at Kelsey.

'*EVERYONE GET THE FUCK BACK!*' he roared.

The heavy silver fuselage of an American Airlines DC-10 floated above them, flaps extended, engines rumbling, drowning out all other sound.

Kelsey shot his gun into the belly of the giant aircraft.

'Holy shit!' cried Ron. 'He's shooting at the god-damn' planes.'

He and Kronziac ran to the bottom of the tower.

'We may have to make a decision here,' she said ominously, spotting a Chicago Police Department SWAT team arriving outside the perimeter fence.

'If he's gonna be a threat to the aircraft we might have to take him out,' she warned.

Tin Kickers

'Just give me a chance to talk to him,' Ron pleaded as he began climbing the tower.

Kronziac said nothing, promised nothing, just took out her gun and followed him up the steel ladder.

One of the young stews led Jones and Al to row 25.

'He asked me for a glass,' the stewardess told Al. 'He had his own bottle of juice with him.'

'How come he was sitting in the aisle seat?' Al wondered. 'He was assigned 25A, the window seat.'

The woman looked up, hearing what they were talking about. 'Excuse me, sir,' she said, 'but is there something wrong?'

'No.' Al smiled, trying not to alarm her. 'We're just looking for something a passenger may have left behind.'

'Yes, there was a man here,' she said. 'He kindly gave my son his seat so he could have a good view out of the window.'

Jones and the stewardess began searching around the seats. Al looked in the overhead bin, but they found nothing.

'Excuse me, ma'am.' Jones leant closer to the woman, keeping his voice low. 'Did the man go to any other part of the plane while he was on board, anywhere at all?'

'Well, I wasn't taking that much notice, but I do

recall him going back down that way, I presume to the rest room.'

Al turned to the stewardess.

'Without making it too obvious, get the rest of the stews to search all the rest rooms.'

RUNWAY 22 RIGHT, O'HARE INTERNATIONAL

As Ron and Kronziac reached the top of the tower they could see Kelsey and Willard out on the edge of the gantry which jutted precariously from the tower. Willard's eyes were bulging as he strained under the pressure of Kelsey's stranglehold.

'Get back!' Kelsey shouted again.

'Okay, Kelsey, take it easy.' Kronziac tried to calm him but her words were drowned out as another jet slid in just above. Ron and Kronziac instinctively ducked their heads, fearing they could be hit by the plane's huge landing wheels.

Kelsey looked down at the police units, the officers hunched behind the car doors, their guns trained directly at him. Outside the fence the SWAT team had two sharpshooters lying on the roof of their van, focusing the cross hairs of their Remington high-velocity rifles on his head.

He turned towards Kronziac and Ron, keeping Willard as close as possible to deter them all from taking a shot.

'Come any closer and the nigger gets it in the head,' he cried.

He jammed the gun even harder against Willard's skull and looked at the stopwatch as he pulled his other hand tight around Willard's neck.

. . . 0.07:03 . . . 0.07:02 . . . 0.07:01.

He stared at the digits, praying for them to go faster. A shot rang out as one of the SWAT team snipers fired a round at Kelsey from the top of the van. The bullet ricocheted off one of the struts on the gantry, producing a loud pinging noise.

Kelsey swivelled around and shot three bullets in rapid succession at the SWAT van, shattering the windows and scattering the sharpshooters off the roof.

Kronziac reached for her walkie-talkie to issue a general order for everyone to hold their fire.

Kelsey turned to her, pointing the gun and screaming: 'You can't control them, can you? . . . You stupid bitch!'

He pulled the trigger and blasted a shot at them. Ron dived, driving his chest against the hard metal tower.

Another jet screamed overhead, a jumbo, its giant fuselage and wings darkening the sky over them, engines shattering the air.

Ron picked himself up and put his hands up, maintaining eye contact with Kelsey all the time.

'All right . . . take it easy . . . no one's gonna try anything again.'

But Kelsey moved backwards, pulling Willard towards the edge of the gantry.

Ron still kept his gaze firmly on Kelsey, didn't want to turn his back on him for one second.

'Kronziac . . . Kronziac . . .' he whispered, his voice rasping. But she didn't answer.

'Kronziac!'

Still no answer.

As he turned around, Kronziac was lying face down on the metal plating of the walkway. She was moving her hand up to her shoulder.

'Jesus!' Ron cried. 'You okay?'

Kronziac slowly raised her head, her face screwed up with pain as she pulled her jacket off over her right shoulder. A dark wet patch of blood was seeping through her shirt, just above her armpit.

'Fuck . . . fuck!' she cursed, grimacing with pain.

Ron leant down over her, unsure what to do.

'I'll call the paramedics,' he said, and took the walkie-talkie from her.

'Hold it, Ron,' she stopped him, 'we're running out of time.'

He glanced around at Kelsey. He had Willard right at the edge of the gantry. Willard's whole body was trembling, hands shaking helplessly by his sides, face shiny with sweat.

'You'd help me a lot more by nailing the bastard,' Kronziac said, her breath laboured as she took out her gun and slid it along the walkway.

'Put an end to it, Ron.'

ALLIED 419, 41,000 FEET, MARATHON NDB, 359NM FROM DULLES

Al followed one of the Allied stews from row 25, where he had been asking the woman more questions about the passenger in the aisle seat. The stewardess led him to the mid-aft port washroom. Jones was already in there, standing over the refuse bin.

Al leant down to see.

Lying in a swaddling of toilet paper in the bin was a bottle, its glass sparkling in the light.

He read the label.

Santa Louisa Apple Juice – Produce of Southern California.

RUNWAY 22 RIGHT, O'HARE INTERNATIONAL

Ron had taken his jacket off and wrapped it around Kronziac's shoulder to try and staunch the bleeding.

'I'll be okay,' she assured him, her face pale with shock.

He picked up the gun and stood up.

'Don't you go an' do anything stupid!' Kelsey shouted to him as he saw the gun in Ron's hand. 'Or your friend here's going for a little dive – not that that's gonna matter with a bullet hole in his head.'

'You holding up?' Ron shouted to Willard.

But he could barely speak.

'Sorry, Ron.' He managed a slight smile. 'I forgot to tell you I was afraid of heights.'

Kelsey gripped Willard even tighter and waved his gun back and forth between Willard and Ron, threatening them both.

'Shut the fuck up!' he shouted. 'Both of you.'

'Come on, Kelsey, there's no place left to go,' Ron tried to reason with him, inching forward on the gantry.

Kelsey smiled, his nostrils flaring, his red-rimmed eyes widening.

'No place but down,' he answered, glancing over his shoulder at the ground below.

'You're not a bird, Kelsey,' said Ron, 'you can't fly.'

'What the fuck do you know about me?' he yelled.

Ron continued to inch forward, very slowly, almost imperceptibly.

'Oh, I know a lot about you,' he said in a calm voice which provoked Kelsey even further as he glanced at his watch.

. . . 0.02:14 . . . 0.02:13 . . .

'You know shit,' he jeered. 'You know shit.'

'I know what you did to Juarez' plane. My hat's off . . . it was a really neat job. Just three little firecrackers and Juarez was gonna take all the blame. And for what? They still wouldn't let you in The Club, would they? Too crazy even for them.'

Kelsey's face bristled with rage. He dug the gun against Willard's head, puncturing the skin.

'Shut the fuck up!' he howled.

But Ron continued.

'Marx said you were crazy . . . is that why you killed him?'

Kelsey shook his head, the ends of his hair wet with perspiration.

'I never killed Marx!' he cried. '*They* did it . . . keep him from talking . . . then those bastards came after me.'

'Who are they?' Ron asked, his voice low, almost sympathetic.

Kelsey began smiling again, a wide grin of yellow teeth. He ripped off his fake moustache, leaving a thin line of blood above his mouth.

'Who are they?' Ron shouted, moving forward closer to Kelsey, 'Who's trying to kill you? . . . Who's Mr Grey? . . . Did he give the order?'

Kelsey was teetering on the edge of the gantry, still clinging to Willard who by now was almost choking, a tiny trickle of blood dribbling down the side of his head from the pressure of the gun barrel.

Ron shouted again.

'Who is Mr Grey?'

Kelsey grinned.

'I've turned the tables on that motherfucker.'

He loosened his hold on Willard slightly to look at the stopwatch. . . . 0.01:01 . . . 0.01:00 . . . 0.00:59 . . .

'Looks like we're under starter's orders,' he sniggered.

The walkie-talkie Ron had taken off Kronziac crackled. He pressed it against his ear. At first nothing, then a voice. It was Al, very faint, the line buzzing with static.

'Ron . . . Ron . . . Is that you?'

'Yeah, it's me, go ahead, Al.'

'We found the bottle! . . . We found the bottle!'

Ron felt his heart pound, almost leaping out of his chest.

Al shouted down the line: *'Ron . . . Ron . . . Can you hear me? . . . Can you hear me?'*

Kelsey was also shouting at Ron.

'Come on, tin kicker, time waits for no man.'

Ron squeezed the handset excitedly.

'Yes . . . yes . . . I hear you!' he cried. 'Take out the fuse! . . . Take out the fuse!' he instructed Al. 'It should look like a small silver tube.'

But Al didn't answer, the line crackling vacantly. Ron was about to shout out the instructions again when Al's voice returned, wavering with the bad signal.

'I can't . . . I can't . . . There's nothing in the bottle! . . . The bottle is empty!'

Seeing Ron's expression of horror, Kelsey began laughing.

'Come on, tin kicker, haven't you figured it out?' he hooted, and started counting down the seconds out loud.

'0.00:31 . . . 0.00:30 . . . 0.00:29 . . .'

Al was still on the line, shouting at Ron.

'What'll we do? . . . We've searched everywhere!'

Ron closed his eyes tight, fighting desperately to think.

'Time's runnin' out, Ron,' Kelsey laughed, 'and you were so close, almost sitting on it.'

Ron's eyes blinked open.

Maybe, just maybe.

He remembered the thick blue liquid in Kelsey's apartment and the smell of detergent from it.

He squeezed the transmit button on the hand-set.

'Al! . . . Al! . . . it's the john . . . he's flushed it down the john!'

The smile was swept off Kelsey's face. In its wake

a blaze of anger shook his whole body as he gripped Willard tighter and counted down the time, willing the seconds to go faster.

. . . 0.00:28 . . . 0.00:27 . . . 0.00:26 . . .

ALLIED 419, 41,000 FEET, MANSFIELD
VOR-DME, 321NM FROM DULLES

Al held the walkie-talkie closer to his ear. Ron's voice was screaming at the other end.

'. . . He's flushed it down the john! Release the waste! . . . Release the water! . . . For pity's sake, Al, just do it! . . . Do it now! . . .'

He threw the handset to Jones.

'I've got to pull the waste release,' he shouted and searched the floor for some sign of the waste-release panel.

'Shit . . . shit . . . where is it?' he cried.

One of the bemused flight attendants pointed casually to a clip, about one inch in length, sunk in the floor behind the toilet bowl.

'I think that's it,' she said, and stood around while Al scrambled across the floor of the toilet. He dug his index finger under the clip to flip it up but the stump of his bitten finger nail was useless against the hard metal.

'Jesus Christ!' he roared, 'Someone give me a knife, a key . . . anything. Come on, come on!'

Jones pulled out his car keys.

'Here, try these.'

Al dug one of the keys under the clip and pushed as hard as he could.

RUNWAY 22 RIGHT, O'HARE INTERNATIONAL

Kelsey's gun slid against the lather of sweat which glistened on Willard's temple.

'I think I'll pull the trigger just before we reach zero.'

He began to smile, feeling confident again as Ron shouted into the walkie-talkie for some response from Al on the plane.

But the line hummed with static.

Ron raised the gun at Kelsey, sorely tempted to take him out there and then. But Kelsey held Willard tightly, just in front of him, shielding himself from Ron and any attempts by the SWAT team shooters, who kept their sights firmly fixed on their target. Willard struggled to say something as his captor counted down the last few seconds

'. . . 0.00:15 . . . 0.00:14 . . . 0.00:13 . . .'

Willard knew he was going to die, soon.

'Ron . . . Ron . . .' he gasped, his voice dry and hoarse '. . . he's nothing but a snake.'

Kelsey wrenched his arm tighter around Willard's neck.

'Shut the fuck up!' he screamed.

But Willard persisted, his legs kicking like a horse in a trap.

'Ron!' he choked. 'He's gonna' kill me anyway . . . he's nothing but a snake . . . you hear, Ron?'

Kelsey roared again for him to shut up.

But Ron could see Willard's eyes burning, pleading, trying to say something.

He nodded and took aim.

'Yeah, you're right, Willard. YOUR RIGHT.'

'Shut up, the both of you!' Kelsey shouted, eyes fixed on the timer. . . . 0.00:08 . . . 0.00:07 . . .

He began counting down as the seconds fell away, his breath panting.

'Six . . . five . . . four . . .'

Ron shouted.

THREE!

Willard jerked his head to the side.

A single bullet opened a small neat red-black hole in the middle of Kelsey's forehead.

He staggered back, body convulsing, the last twitchings of a dying man – his face bone white, eyes blackening, a shocked look frozen there.

His eyes rolled back and the rest of him followed, off the gantry, falling clean as a diver.

ALLIED 419, 41,000 FEET, MANSFIELD
VOR-DME, 314NM FROM DULLES

Al's face was turning puce, every vessel bulging. The clip flicked open, popping up the cover of the waste-system control panel.

'Thank God,' Jones panted with relief.

Al saw the small release switch and immediately squashed it down with his thumb. They could hear a slight rumble beneath them as the release cock opened and forty gallons of human waste, detergent agents and a litre of liquid explosive were sucked out from beneath the belly of the plane. On meeting the freezing air the liquids solidified into a large chunk of blue ice that fell away from the plane like a stone.

There was a crack.

The plane shook as if rocked by a cross-wind.

Fifty metres below them the chunk of blue ice shattered with a pink-white flash into a million twinkling crystals that sprinkled like a shower of little stars over the clouds below.

RUNWAY 22 RIGHT, O'HARE INTERNATIONAL

'We're okay, Ron! . . . Everything's okay! . . .' Jones' voice crackled with excited relief over the walkie-talkie.

Willard picked himself up. He glanced below at Kelsey's body lying motionless on the ground, limbs spread, the bones of his shattered torso bursting through his chest.

Turning around to Ron, exhausted and drained, he smiled. 'Are all your investigations like this? Because if they are then I think I'll transfer myself back to the Railroad Office.'

But Ron wasn't listening.

He leant down over Kronziac as her eyes flickered open, like someone waking from the buried darkness of a deep sleep.

'Is it over?' she whispered wearily, her lips pale, quivering with pain and shock.

He laid the gun down gently on the walkway.

'It's done,' he said quietly, putting his arm carefully around her bleeding shoulder. 'It's done.'

SWANKY SCOUNDREL BAR, NORTH CAPITOL STREET, WASHINGTON DC

Al and Bob climbed wearily on to their stools at the bar.

'What'll you have?' asked Bob.

Exhausted, Al was barely able to speak. He had spent three hours at Dulles after they landed, briefing the police and authorities on what had happened.

'I'll just have some coffee.'

'Maybe you should go home, get some rest,' suggested Bob, concerned for his friend, who seemed to be on the verge of collapse.

'Nah, fuck it . . . I couldn't sleep anyway,' he snarled, cranky as a sore dog.

Bob glanced up at the TV over the bar, overhearing a piece from the news.

In the corner of the screen was a picture of an Allied jumbo. The anchorwoman was wrapping up the late-evening news.

'. . . newly elected Governor of Illinois Phillip Mayhew was delayed in collecting his seal of office from the President at the White House today when his flight from Chicago was involved in what was described by Allied Air officials as a minor incident . . .'

The anchorwoman's image disappeared as they showed footage of the new Governor walking with the President in the snowbound Rose Garden. In the background stood two men, one with a tight crop of silver hair, the other a tall man with thick glasses. They were smiling, waiting for their turn to shake hands with the President. The man in the glasses extended his left hand, a silver band glinting on his third finger, waiting for the President's embrace.

Al turned to Bob, a look of appalled disgust on his face.

'A minor incident? Holy shit, we almost got blown to smithereens up there . . . *a minor incident!* Well, fuck that.'

'I suppose they didn't want to panic anyone,' Bob rationalised. 'Besides people would find it all a little bit hard to believe.'

HIDALGO DEL PIERO AFB, SINALOA, MEXICO

Jerry ran into the office at the end of the hanger where Greg Mates was standing over the fax machine as it slowly squeezed out a message.

'Guess what?' Jerry said excitedly.

'Well, unless it's word that we can get the hell out of this damn' place, I'm not interested,' said Greg, worn out from the months of picking over the thousands of pieces of wreckage.

Jerry held up a thick bundle of electrical wires, from the electrics service bay.

'I found it at last,' he said triumphantly.

'Well, hold on there, Sherlock,' Greg said as he tore the fax from the back of the machine, 'looks like there's a slight change in the plan.'

Jerry put down the wire bundle on the desk and took off his plastic gloves.

'Who's it from?'

Greg handed him the single sheet. 'Vice Chairman of the Board, no less.'

NATIONAL TRANSPORTATION SAFETY BOARD

490 L'Enfant Plaza
20594
Washington DC

TO: NTSB site office Hidalgo Del Piero AFB, Mexico
ATTN: Jerry Wojowski

FROM: Richard Smyth
SUBJ: Wiring sample

URGENT---URGENT---URGENT---URGENT---URGENT

With ref to electrics service bay wiring sample please do not ship to FBI Forensics at Westwood Park.

Instead please ship to NTSB Materials Laboratory in Washington.

Previous directive by IIC now invalid.

Please confirm ASAP.

Richard Smith

Office of Vice Chairman Safety Board

Tel: 202–959–3009
FAX: 202–959–3018

NATIONAL SIGINT OPS CENTRE, FANX 5 BUILDING, FORT MEADE, MARYLAND

'You want a coffee?' Gayley asked, looking at his watch. It had been a whole hour since his last cup.

'No, thanks,' said Truchs, 'I'll make my own in a minute.'

In his two months at the NSA Dalton Truchs had become quite accomplished at his job of filing and collating the written security communications.

He scanned down the tower of trays, each neatly labelled with a group designate. In his left arm he held a stack of files, ready for dispatch into the trays for eventual retrieval by each group's courier service.

A-Group – Former Soviet Bloc

Empty. No files today.

B-Group – Asia

He looked at the file on top of the bundle. Blue – inactive. Satellite reconnaissance shots of Northern Iraq. Previously thought to have been chemical weapons facilities, but turned out to be meat processing plants.

C-Group – Policy and Resources

No file.

Tin Kickers

D-Group – Director
He placed a thick yellow admin file of collated recommendation reports from the regional NSA Directorates for the attention of the Director of Operations.

E-Group – Contract Support
Another admin file – tenders for Oversee and Maintenance contracts for UK NSA sub-station – NATO theatre ground segment node for high altitude intelligence satellites.

F-Group – No Designation
Empty.

G-Group – Operations
Encrypted correspondence from Chief, Central Security Service to SIGINT-OPCON Deputy Director.

H-Group – No Designation
Empty

I-Group – Info. Security (INFOSEC) Systems
Another yellow admin file, marked 'All Personnel' – recommended best practices for family security compiled by Info. Systems Security Directorate.

J-Group – Legislation
A Copy of White Paper on National Security –

Department of Defence document as used by Secretary of Defence in House Committee for National Defence.

K-Group – Operations Research
Classified research findings on cryptological methods as used by Middle Eastern terrorist factions. Red file – active. Classified 2 – sensitive.

L-Group – Logistics
New codes, dates and times and itineraries for Defense Courier Service. Classified 2 – sensitive.

M-Group – Administration
He smiled as he looked at a report by Airman Dalton Truchs on Servicemen Families Group outing to Mount Rushmore last weekend. He read his own words printed in the NSA newsletter.

'Should be classified most crappy,' he said out loud, embarrassed by his own clumsy writing style.
    'What?' Gayley said, sitting at his desk, sipping on his coffee, looking through some intercepted diplomatic communiques from Columbia and El Salvador.
    'Nothing,' Truchs replied and continued his filing.

N-Group – Programs
Another yellow file on work practices. Recommendations to alleviate stress on NSA employees.

O-Group – No Designation
Empty.

P-Group – Production
There were five files, all marked P-Group. All blue.
Incidental intelligence information for other agencies
such as the FBI, CIA and ATF as well as one file for
the Navy.

Truchs threw them all in.

Q-Group – Plans and Policy
No files today.

R-Group – Research and Engineering
There was a blue file containing a thick manual in
Russian, detailing new plans for a communications
satellite held up in construction.

He laid it carefully on the tray, glad to unburden
himself of it.

S-Group – Standards and Evaluation
Monthly computer efficiency figures from the Cryptological units.

T-Group – Telecommunications
Some ISS intercepts. Blue file – inactive. Class 2.

U-Group – General Counsel
Some legal documents pertaining to possible links with cancer and telemetry dishes. Red file – active. Class 2.

V-Group – Network Security
No files.

W-Group – Space
Test results from Jet Propulsion Lab on 'LapWing' space vehicle. Red file – active. Class 1 – highly sensitive.

X-Group – Special Access Systems
Red file – active. Project *WORM*. Unknown content. Class 1.

Y-Group – Unknown Designation
No files.

Z-Group – No Designation
Empty.

Truchs had one file left over. He examined it carefully.
A red file.
Active.

Class 1.

But no group designation.

'Hey, Marc!'

'Yeah?'

'I'm not sure about this one, no designation.'

'Open it up, take a look.'

'I can't, it's Class 1.'

Gayley looked up from his desk.

'Okay, bring it over.'

Truchs laid the file in front of his superior, who wiped the remnants of a muffin from his fingers and proceeded to open the security clips, spreading open the hard covers.

'Okay,' he said, 'we've got two documents.'

'Should I leave?' asked Truchs, aware he was not cleared for Class 1 material.

'No, you're okay,' Gayley laughed, 'I trust you.'

He examined a small strip of paper.

'We have an active Deep Sleeper, requesting a transfer.'

'Deep Sleeper?' Truchs repeated, intrigued by the term.

'Didn't you ever read your Graham Greene?' Gayley laughed. 'A sleeper's an undercover agent. A deep sleeper is, well . . .' he smirked again '. . . a *very* undercover agent, non-active, but this guy's awake.'

'CIA?' asked Truchs.

'No, he's NSA, rare breed of animal,' said Gayley. 'Looks like he's asking his Director to be transferred back into the bed.'

Truchs shook his head, amused.

'Bed?'

'Yeah, it's a term for the organisation he's been planted in, in this case it's the FAA.'

Gayley turned over to the only other page in the file.

'Well, well, what've we got here?'

He looked down the sheet.

'An FTD.'

'What's that?' asked Truchs leaning closer to have a look.

'Transcript,' Gayley nodded, 'of a tap on a federal building.'

'A government building?' said Truchs, a little shocked.

Gayley nodded.

SIGINT Channel exchange tap authorization FTD-897

Date: 1/6

Time: 14.03 (EST)

Trans-state relay call direct.

CALLER DETAILS		RECEIVER DETAILS	
NPA code	: 202 Washington Sub-exchange 002	NPA code	: 213 (local) El Segundo SCAL
Node	: 1B	Node	: 5A
CO code	: 959	CO code	: 950
Tel No.	: 959-3009	Tel No.	: 950–2105

Tin Kickers

Excerpt transcript:

FEMALE 1: . . . good morning . . . General AirFactors . . .

MALE 1: . . . good morning . . . Jacob Roseman's office, please

FEMALE 1: . . . yes, sir . . . putting you through . . .

Tone connect – internal PBX line switch

FEMALE 2: . . . good morning, Director of Operations office, Catherine Dickenson speaking . . .

MALE 1: . . . Can I speak with Mr Roseman please . . .

FEMALE 2: . . . may I ask who's calling, sir? . . .

MALE 1: . . . It's Mr Smyth . . . from Washington . . .

FEMALE 2: . . . just one moment, please . . .

Line hold
Transfer connect –
Internal PBX extension switch

MALE 2: . . . hello, Dick . . .

MALE 1: . . . morning, Jake . . .

MALE 2: . . . is this . . . wise? . . .

MALE 1: . . . what's up? . . . I've a secure line . . .

MALE 2: . . . okay . . . I dunno . . . things were gettin' a bit hot . . . someone rang up . . . a couple of days ago . . . said he was Mr Grey . . .

MALE 1: . . . was it one of the boys from Chicago? . . .

MALE 2: . . . I don't know . . . scared the shit out of me though . . . thought he was going to chew me out over Kelsey . . . you got some good news yet?

MALE 1: . . yeah, the Board's recommending pilot error . . .

MALE 2: . . . well, thank Jesus for that . . . good job . . . what about Carter?

MALE 1: . . . he's out of the picture . . . you guys don't have to worry about him . . .

MALE 2: . . . and McKenzie? . . .

MALE 1: . . . he'll be fine . . . he knows he's in too deep . . . what about Taylor?

MALE 2: . . . yeah, I think he's cool . . . after Marx's elimination I don't think his conscience will get in the way . . . we can count on his . . . continued allegiance . . .

MALE 1: . . . a'right . . .

MALE 2: . . . we're gonna close down the club in LA though for a while . . .

MALE 1: . . . yeah, probably a good idea . . .

best to cool things until this case is wrapped up . . .

MALE 2: . . . sure . . . I agree . . .

MALE 1: . . . besides we gotta start planning the new campaign . . .

MALE 2: . . . new campaign? . . . (laughs) . . . Jesus, we've only just taken Illinois . . .

MALE 1: . . . exactly . . . now we gotta start thinking about getting him to Washington . . . . . . it's never too early to start planning . . .

MALE 2: . . . Jeez, Dick . . . I don't think Mr Grey wants to go back to the Senate . . . he can do far more on the ground where he is now . . .

MALE 1: . . . I'm not talking about the Senate, Jake . . . I'm talking about the White House . . .

MALE 2: . . . (laughs) . . . sometimes you crack me up . . . you crazy son-of-a-bitch . . .

MALE 1: . . . (laughs) . . . I'm serious . . . who knows how far we can go now? . . .

MALE 2: . . . eh . . . The FBI? . . . The Government? . . . The people? . . . they'll have to elect him.

MALE 1: . . . fuck it, Jake . . . we are the government . . . and as for the people . . . well, they'll only thank us when they see our way is the only way . . .

MALE 2: . . . (laughs) . . . I gotta go Dick . . . I've got work to do . . . (laughs)

MALE 1: . . . okay Jake . . . but remember, it's only beginning . . .

MALE 2: . . . (laughs) . . . Goodbye, Dick . . .

Call terminates

Gayley closed the file and clipped it up. He handed it to Truchs.

'So, where'll I put it?'

'Y-Group,' was all Gayley would say.

'Y-Group?' Truchs exclaimed.

It was the first time he had ever handled a file for Y-Group.

'That's what I said,' snapped Gayley, his usual jokey manner gone.

'How do you know?' asked Truchs.

'I just know,' said Gayley, 'and no, I'm not going to tell you who or what they are or what they do.'

He grabbed the file and threw it into the tray marked Y Group. 'Sometimes you ask too many questions, son,' said Gayley as he sat down again to pore over his own paperwork.

Truchs glanced at the NSA insignia by the window.

Protect the Protector, Watch the Watchers.

Perhaps now he was beginning to understand what it meant.

GOLD WINGS FLYING SCHOOL, BARSTOW, CA

It was nearly evening as Ron brought the car gently to a halt on the soft sandy ground, stirring a gentle whirl of dust from the tyres.

'You should've let me drive,' Kronziac complained as she got out of the car slowly, still nursing her shoulder.

'You can't drive with one hand,'

'Wanna bet?' she dared him.

It had been less than a week since she was shot but her wound was healing fast. Kronziac looked about at the deserted airfield and the old planes, slowly withering under the sun.

'You brought me all the way out to this shit-hole?'

'You didn't have to come,' said Ron, taking out a folder from the back seat of the car.

Kronziac shrugged.

'Had nothing better do.'

They found Skid Mortensen in the hangar, draining some oil from the engine of an old crop duster.

'Hey, Skid!' Ron shouted.

'Hello, Mr Carter, what brings you back here?' Skid stood up, wiping his hands with an old rag.

Ron held out the folder with Juarez' files from his cadet days at the school.

'I promised I'd bring it back.'

Skid smiled broadly.

'Thank you very much . . . and who's this?' he asked, looking at Kronziac. 'This your wife, Mr Carter?'

'No,' Kronziac answered smartly, 'just a friend.' She offered her good hand and introduced herself. 'Nancy Kronziac.'

Skid bowed courteously, taken by her beauty.

'Very pleased to meet you, Miss Kronziac.'

'Watch it, Skid, she's a Fed,' Ron warned.

Kronziac smiled.

'Don't worry, I'm off duty, and will be for another couple of weeks.'

Ron was looking around the hangar, searching in the dark recesses. 'Hey, Skid, where's the old P-51?'

Skid's face lit up.

'Got it out back. She's all fixed up, as good as she ever was and raring to get into the air . . . if only someone was interested in taking her up,' he added suggestively. 'I'm afraid I'm a bit too beat up for the ol' gal. Why don't you two kids go out and I'll get us a coupla drinks.'

The sun was retreating west over the Mojave, surrendering the sky to the coolness of evening.

Ron ran his hand along the gleaming silver wing of the Mustang, the sunlight shining brilliantly off its polished glass canopy; blazing in a silver wave along the fuselage.

'You ever miss flying, Carter?' Kronziac asked.

'Sometimes,' he said. 'Maybe I should go back to it, get a seat with one of the small airlines, flying coconuts outa the Florida Keys or something like that. How about you, gonna miss the Bureau?'

Kronziac leant against the plane, gazing out over the desert.

'I'll only be out for a short while. Then it's back to the grindstone chasing the bad guys, if we can find them. What about the NTSB? Aren't you going back?'

'Not sure if I can,' he replied, 'Not sure if it's safe to.'

'How far up does it go?' she asked.

Ron shook his head.

'As far as the Board maybe. They knew what they were doing when they made me IIC.'

'Well you proved them wrong,' she assured him.

'Did I?' he wondered, 'Juarez is still going to get the blame. Kelsey and The Club never existed.'

Kronziac stood up straight.

'And you're gonna leave it at that? Let the fuckers get away with it?'

Ron remained silent, not meeting her eyes.

'Is that it, Ron? You gonna give up?'

He turned swiftly to her.

'Jesus Kronziac! What do you want from me?' he demanded.

'My credibility is shot to hell, I don't even know who to trust. Can I trust the FBI? Can I trust you?'

She closed her eyes and fell back against the plane again, her shoulder throbbing with pain once more.

He was right, they could never prove the connection between Kelsey, The Club and the sabotage of ACL248.

Ron began walking along the fuselage.

'Let's just hope the dogs will start barking,' he remarked, running his hand along the smooth metal with his palm as if stroking the flank of a thoroughbred.

Kronziac opened her eyes again and was about to ask him what he meant when Skid returned from the hangar, carrying a bottle of bourbon and three cups.

He poured them each half a cupful.

'Easy on there, Skid,' said Ron, picking up his cup. 'I know another guy down in Mexico who you'd get on with just fine,' he added, remembering the old trapper.

'I'm fine where I am,' said Skid. 'I've lived here for near fifty years, and I never get tired of looking at the desert. There's nothing out there but bush scrub and a few lizards, burning under the sun. It's probably the closest thing to hell on earth,' he smiled, 'but at night you can watch the storms out there, battling with the dark, flashing in the sky, rumbling in the distance yet never too far away . . .'

He took a long drink from his cup.

'You two should stay the night,' he suggested, 'get away from it all.'

Tin Kickers

Kronziac turned to Ron.

'It is kinda beautiful here,' she agreed.

But he was looking out at the desert, at the golden sands fading beneath a black-blue cloud that rose like a wing to gather the tired sun.

EDIT SUITE 3A, ANN STUDIOS, 13TH STREET AND NEW YORK AVENUE, WASHINGTON D.C.

Mary Shaw was assembling a rough edit of footage about a possible outbreak of Legionnaire's disease in a Baltimore hospital when there was a tap on the door.

'Come in.'

The door opened and the studio runner handed her a thick brown package.

'This just arrived for you, Miss Shaw.'

Shaw looked at it. There was no indication who it was from. She held it to her ear to see if it ticked. Seemed to be a load of paperwork by the feel of it. She looked at the stamps – it had a Los Angeles zip code.

'That'll be all, Cal,' she dismissed him and he closed the door behind him.

Using scissors she tore open the package and spilt out a folder of files and reports, and a DVD box. She opened it and held in her hand a bright disk labelled: ACL248 – FLIGHT ANIMATION – INVESTI-GATION COPY.

She looked more closely at the files. They were copies of all the reports pertaining to the Aero Centrale disaster. On a yellow post-it stuck to the front of a little notebook she read some scrawled words, written in a hurried hand.

'This will have to do instead of that interview you were looking for. But there are still many unanswered questions, STILL UNQUESTIONED ANSWERS.'

There was another knock on the door.

'Yes!' she bawled, annoyed at the intrusion.

It was Cal again.

'What is it?' she barked at him.

'Sorry, Miss Shaw, this just came in on the wire, the editor thought you'd like to see it.'

He handed her a brief press statement just released.

PRESS STATEMENT

NATIONAL TRANSPORTATION SAFETY BOARD
490 L'ENFANT PLAZA
WASHINGTON DC
20594

TO WHOM IT MAY CONCERN

It will be announced later today that the NTSB investigation report into the crash of flight ACL248 will attribute the accident to a combination of weather conditions and pilot error. The report will not be fully ratified pending further investigation procedures.

Personnel changes:

Bill Murphy

Mr Robert Tunamachier has been appointed as Investigator In Charge of the ACL248 case, replacing Mr Ron Carter.

Also Mr Grant Willard is no longer acting as media liaison officer with the NTSB Office of Aviation Safety but will be returning to his post as Department of Transportation liaison in the Federal Aviation Administration.

The vacancy at the NTSB is yet to be filled.

Please direct all enquiries to Mr William McKenzie's office at the Office of Aviation Safety.

Contact: Tel: 202–959–9832

Fax: 202–959–9814

WEST POTOMAC PARK, WASHINGTON DC

The morning peeked its head above the eastern suburbs and crept across the city, the splendid edifices of the Government buildings blooming in the copper-white light of the early sun. The dark shadows behind them dwindled, lightened and dissolved into the thin air like ghosts fleeing in the bright glare of the heavens.

Bill McKenzie sat down on a bench by the Tidal Basin and dug his hands deep into the pockets of his thick overcoat, clenching his whole body against the keen air. The park was empty, the grass and shrubs coated in a candy gloss of sparkling frost, the water of the pond smooth plates of ice, the cherry trees draped in crusted floes of snow. Along the river path a single hardy jogger in thick sweats puffed by, his feet tapping on the dry white concrete.

McKenzie inhaled and his chest felt as if it was filling with hard cold water. He felt dizzy again and pushed out a grey plume of breath. He yearned for the comforting hot smoke of a cigar to warm him.

A voice shattered the frigid air.

'Sorry to get you out here so early, Bill.'

McKenzie shielded his eyes as Richard Smyth walked out of the sun.

'Morning, Dick.'

Smyth sat next to McKenzie. He seemed invigorated by the icy air. While everyone else covered themselves, huddled and hidden, shielding their hot flesh from the pinching cold, Smyth seemed to relish the bitter temperature as he rubbed his hands with satisfaction.

'What a beautiful morning,' he declared, looking about the ice-gripped park, his face flushed with two rosy plums on each cheek. 'Makes you glad to be alive.'

But McKenzie wasn't in the mood for the Vice Chairman's little rhapsody.

'Jesus, Dick,' he groaned, 'what did you bring me out here for?'

Smyth reached into the breast pocket of his black crombie and, taking out a brown envelope, handed it to him.

'What's this?' McKenzie asked, reluctantly taking the envelope.

'Just open it,' Smyth instructed him.

McKenzie's fingers felt clumsy as he took out the single sheet of paper from the envelope. It was a prepared statement on flight ACL248 from the Safety Board Accident Report Review Committee.

He read through the few succinct lines quickly.

'So we're going with pilot error,' he said, unsurprised.

Smyth nodded.

'We'll need to arrange a press briefing today.'

McKenzie folded the paper and put it back in the envelope.

'Get Willard to do it.'

Smyth smiled, about to impart more bad news.

'Willard's gone. We already issued a statement on that.'

McKenzie turned quickly to Smyth, his voice ragged, almost trembling.

'What do you mean . . . gone?'

'He requested a transfer out of the NTSB and back to the FAA,' Smyth explained calmly, 'effective immediately. Guess the whole thing's kinda freaked him out.'

McKenzie closed his eyes, knowing he had to ask the question.

'And what about Carter's report?'

Smyth shrugged nonchalantly.

'Without the lab tests on the wiring his report remains an unproven theory. Nobody was going to buy it anyway.'

'What about the samples?' wondered McKenzie.

Smyth seemed unsure as to how he should phrase his answer.

'Well, you know, things can get mislaid, or indeed contaminated, making the results inconclusive.'

McKenzie shook his head in disgust and turned away.

'Ron nearly went the whole way,' he muttered.

'Nearly.' Smyth smiled nervously. 'But . . .' he hesitated '. . . when you had your heart trouble we had to think quickly and Carter seemed our best option . . . the youngest . . . the most inexperienced. The most easily controlled.'

McKenzie turned back, eyes widening with anger. 'I warned you against making him IIC,' he growled. 'I told you he was good. He'd only been with the Board a short while but he was a natural . . . I knew he'd be no push-over.'

'Okay, okay, I fucked up,' admitted Smyth. 'I thought we could handle him the easiest out of any of your guys but we didn't mess up completely.' He couldn't restrain himself from grinning again. 'That little leak to Shaw early on got everyone thinking pilot error.'

'He coulda nailed us all, for Christ's sake!' McKenzie raised his voice.

'Take it easy, Bill,' Smyth warned menacingly, 'we're dealing with the situation, we've appointed Bob to take over.'

But McKenzie seemed inconsolable, his anger subsiding to disbelief. He shook his head again. 'How could things go so wrong?'

'We had a bad apple,' Smyth calmly rationalised. 'Roseman and the west coast boys fucked up big time with that crazy bastard Kelsey. He nearly got Mr Grey but, thank the Lord, he's gone now and The Club can continue with its work quietly and effectively. With his success in Illinois we now have a chance of making some real reforms in the mid-west and soon we'll start making a difference here too.'

'Oh, Jesus!' McKenzie sighed with sickly remorse. 'A hundred and forty-eight people were killed, and Marx and the girl. I mean, Jesus, what are we doing here?'

Smyth thought he was going to have to shake McKenzie, even smack him in the face to keep him from losing it.

'Look, it's not our fault, Bill,' he insisted, 'it's nobody's fault.'

But McKenzie stared at him, unable to hide his revulsion. 'You're as crazy as Kelsey was,' he said with dull realisation.

Smyth took a deep breath and ignored it as one tries to ignore a petulant child.

'I know things have been hard for you, Bill, and we all appreciate your concerns. We do understand, believe me,' he added with rehearsed sincerity, 'how difficult it has been . . . I know Carter was like a son to you.'

'Nothing's going to happen to him, is it?' McKenzie asked, sitting up. There was something in Smyth's voice that scared him.

But the Vice Chairman stood up and replaced the envelope in his pocket. McKenzie's gaze followed him, still waiting for an answer.

'What's going to happen to him?' he pleaded again.

Smyth carefully buttoned the top of his coat and looked about the frozen park, his eyes squinting in the sunlight.

'Nothing,' he said simply, and suddenly turned to look down at McKenzie. 'If he keeps his mouth shut . . . nothing will happen to any of us if we just keep our mouths shut. Soon it will all go away. Like the snow . . . it'll just melt away.'

He stared at McKenzie for a moment, searching his eyes for any hint of defiance, wordlessly warning him to leave it alone.

Then just as quickly he smiled and turned to walk away.

'I'll see you later, Bill, maybe we'll do lunch.'